Mythv<

Part 2

SNAFU!

Written by Vas Constanti

ISBN: 978-1-326-58146-6

Copyright © 2016 Vas Constanti

All rights reserved, including the right to reproduce this book, or portions thereof in any form. No part of this text may be reproduced, transmitted, downloaded, decompiled, reverse engineered, or stored, in any form or introduced into any information storage and retrieval system, in any form or by any means, whether electronic or mechanical without the express written permission of the author.

This is a work of fiction. Names and characters are the product of the author's imagination and any resemblance to actual persons, living or dead, is entirely coincidental.

www.publishnation.co.uk

Dedicated to the innocents who have lost their lives as the result of needless conflicts between warring nations and to our fathers and mothers, guardians and mentors, whom without, we are nothing!

For Sullivan.

Vassos Constanti was born in London in 1967 where he still resides with his family. His childhood was greatly influenced by his aunt and uncle who worked for the RSC as costume and set designers respectively, and family holidays to Cyprus and his beloved Crete, where he fell in love with mythology. He went on to study at the internationally renowned Guilford School of Acting, graduating in 1990 with distinction. He has performed on the stage in the West End of London, as well as nationally and in Europe. He has also featured as an actor on television and film.

The ideas for Mythvolution came about in 1992 when Garston was born in a series of letters.

"With circumstance and fate you face the fear behind your eyes!"

Mythvolution:

Noun:

The doctrine that the true story of the creation of the known Universe is still not quite as recounted in the Bible, especially the first chapter of Genesis, but due to the probability that mythology may not be a myth after all and is still responsible for evolution!

Mythvolutionism:

Noun:

As Mythvolution but still with an ism!

Mythvolutionist:

Noun- adjective:

A believer in the doctrine of Mythvolutionism and still, undoubtedly a complete 'nut nut!'

GREAT MINDS

Expectations are a part of life. They can be a blessing, but are usually a trial placed upon us by others of a pious nature, who often callously, take an imperious view of those they believe to be an unworthy underling. When expectations are at their lowest ebb, we are more than delighted when they are surpassed, and we usually ride the wave of jubilant satisfaction that frequently follows. However, when they are not achieved, endless days of irritation and anxiety haunt a peaceful existence!

***

It was the morning after the pool house fire and the scent of burnt, smouldering timbers still filled the smoky, misty air. All of Arcadia's ladies were peppered around the ash sprinkled, luscious garden. None of them were looking, or feeling, a million dollars and all of them were a little dazed, tired and pretty confused! It was as if someone had been in their heads for a while and then had left suddenly, leaving them with the world's worst banging hangover and a sense of utter bewilderment.

Mr White walked out of the villa's glass doors accompanied by Clipboard Girl, who started a headcount!

"What time is it Clipboard Girl? Are they all here?

"Yes sir, I think so, and it's 6.30 am," she replied.

"OK then, well, I'll start.

Hello everyone and good morning." He said addressing the suspicious, sunglasses garnered crowd. "Now, before I begin, I would like to say thank you for all of your hard work in, enthusiastically putting out the fire yesterday." He paused in thought, before continuing. "I'm afraid today, for me anyway, is going to be a very, very sad day, as I have to say goodbye to you all." There was a murmur. "However, it's not all bad news." Silence. "You have each been given a substantial severance package of $4,000,000." There was another murmur! "This has been directly placed into your own personal bank accounts." Mr White paused briefly once again as a sadness filled him. "Your services have been so appreciated, as have your efforts, but it is time for you to once again make your own choices! If you would like to pack up your belongings, I will sail you all to the mainland where a fleet of taxis will be waiting to transport you to, well, anywhere you want to go, the airport, beach, Brazil, Europe, it's up to you, so please, off you go. We will be leaving in a couple of hours. I'm sure some of you want to get back to a world that you will eventually remember. I do hope that you all learn, in the future, to consider your time spent here as a wonderful experience, full of joy and adventure, as I often have." Mr White smiled and clapped his hands together in a 'that's it' gesture, and the group began to disperse. The ladies mooched around Arcadia for a while, picking up bits and packing as they went, all still a little bemused, their memories having been befuddled by lapses in history. Except for one of them, that is! Clipboard Girl was standing behind Mr White, watery eyed, trying to hold back a snivel.

"Are you alright?" Mr White asked with a degree of concern.

"Yes Sir, well, no Sir." Clipboard Girl raised her head reticently. "All I can say is that this is the best job I have ever had and however strange the demands, or goings-on here have been, I have loved every minute of it."

"Really, so what would you like to do?" he asked.

"Please Mr White, can I stay sir? I have no family to get back to and I have never had a long term boyfriend."

"Hold on, how old are you again and what have you been doing since you left university? Err, sorry, did you go to university?" Mr White asked.

"I'm 23 sir, and I was educated by nuns in Austria, which is also where I took my exams."

"What are you qualified to do again?" Mr White asked, as if playing a game he knew he was going to win.

"I'm a trained animal behavioural therapist," Clipboard Girl replied.

"Really, rather an obscure occupation isn't it? Have you had many clients, I imagine the pickings are slim?"

"I've had none sir, this was my first job."

"...And that's why it's the best job you ever had, huh?" replied

Mr White smiling.

"No sir, you've been like a big brother to me, really looked after me, I have enjoyed being your, err, messenger! You have often confided in me, but that is all, just confided. I'm not like Miss Ballet or any of the others, Miss Pilot or Miss Captain, I never had a skill you've required."

Mr White gave an instant retort.

"I didn't really require ballet skills, did I now? And your ardent organisational skills are second to none, remember that."

"Well, probably not and probably! What I'm trying to say is that I have never had the sort of relationship that you have had with the other ladies. I have never minded as I always felt as if I was your trusted friend."

Mr White looked a little confused.

"I have definitely not have had any 'kind of relationships,' as you put it, with any of the ladies."

Clipboard Girl looked at him quizzically as if she didn't believe him.

"Alright Faith, you can stay. Would you like the position of my Personal Assistant?"

"Sorry, sir, did you say your PA, and what did you call me?"

"Yes, PA, and your name is err, Faith right?" Mr White answered, dithering.

"Faith! It's been so long since someone called me by my name. I can't believe you remembered."

"Yes, I'm sorry about that!" he replied

"So, I can stay and work with you and all of your adorable animal friends?" Faith asked squeaking with delight.

"Yes you can," Mr White replied.

"Thank you sir, thank you." Faith ran up to him and pecked him on the cheek.

"Don't call me sir," he blushed, "Mr White is fine."

"OK, fantastic, what happens now then sir?" Faith asked.

"It's Mr White, and now you need to pack for us both, and make sure the jet is made ready and please get that insignia removed from the tail fin. We are going on a trip. I will pilot myself, so that should make your job a little easier"

"Where are we going sir, sorry, Mr White?"

"Home Faith, we are going home!"

"I don't understand. Arcadia is your home."

"It is now, but once upon a time it was not."

" Oh right! Can I ask you a small favour sir, sorry, Mr White?"

"Of course you can," Mr White nodded.

"Can I still be Clipboard Girl, I kind of like it?" Faith asked.

"Clipboard Girl you are," Mr White chuckled. "Now, before you start tenaciously packing, I need you to solve a problem for me." Mr White beckoned Clipboard Girl to him and whispered in her ear. "It is your task to find someone, with the right background knowledge, and bring them here to keep an eye on Yin and Yang and Freak, whilst we are away. Oh, and get the fire damage repaired, will you?"

"What about Spike and Escobar?" Clipboard Girl asked.

"They will rendezvous with us at our destination. We will need passports."

"Alright si…Mr White, leave it to Clipboard Girl, she'll get it done."

"I know she will," Mr White replied smiling.

Clipboard Girl tottered off, but then turned.

"Sorry, Mr White, but when do we leave?"

"As soon as you have completed your tasks and we drop everyone off on the mainland," he replied.

Clipboard Girl set off with a skip in her step and Mr White turned to Spike.

"Do you think she bought it?" he whispered.

Spike shrugged his shoulders, as much as a lizard could!

"I don't know, maybe, but why all the secrecy?" Spike asked.

"No idea, never been told, but I think she bought it!" Mr White replied.

He changed his tack and strolled over to where he had left Freak suspended, motionless in mid air, in the lounge, the previous evening.

"So, how are you today Freak? Are you a tad upset with me?"

"Well, I'm a little peckish, for…human blood, you scumbag. And was that Spike talking?" she replied.

"Maybe, so you're still a little tightly wound I see. Well, the sooner you calm down and get used to me being in charge, the faster you can get back to your palms and quench your thirst."

"Let me down now and I promise you that I will kill you without toying with you," Freak replied.

Mr White huffed in exasperation.

"Think on this Freak. I could have killed you, split you into a dozen arachnid pieces with the power of my mind, but, I chose to let you live," he paused. "The point is, I can do exactly that, at any time I wish. You are not at the head of the food chain, and you'd better come to terms with it, for your own sake. So, what do you say, do you want to comply or die?"

There was no reply, merely silence.

"I'll tell you what, in a fortnight someone will ask you the same question. That will give you a little time to mull things over," said Mr White.

"A couple of weeks, are you mad? I will be close to death, if not departed by then, starved!" Freak replied.

"Don't be so melodramatic, I could always put you in with Yin and Yang. I'm sure they'll get close enough at some point, if you're feeling that ravenous."

"Eat Yin and Yang. I would rather poke pins in all of my eyes. I would also wager they taste disgusting."

"On the contrary, in some far flung countries they are considered a delicacy. We will see how disgusting they taste after about ten days," said Mr White.

Yin and Yang piped up from their tank.

"You wouldn't eat us would you? We are *your friend's Freaky Deaky*, baby. We had a plan remember, we were to run the world and you were to be the most deadly hench, err, thingy on the planet! *Revered and feared."*

"I would rather chew off another claw then eat you two, boys," Freak replied reassuringly.

***

"And then, this prehistoric relic from the past, decided to park its crocodilian carcass on our bag of corn. Oh, you should have seen his face, loves! Hysterical, it was absolutely priceless. I wish you had all been there, darlings."

The occupants of the cottage were sitting around the table in the lounge listening to Albert impart the details of his and Garston's adventure to Alcatraz Island. Wide eyed, everyone sat and listened intently. Intermittently roaring and squeaking with laughter, more than not, at Garston's expense!

"Well, I congratulate both teams on their success and am, in honour of your audacious achievements, declaring today a holiday, a day where we shall all sit and play games and most importantly, buy ourselves a treat, shopping online. Yes, I thought that after the stressful past few weeks of strain, turmoil and suffering, the old human trait of purchasing a gift for oneself, when one feels the world is conspiring against one, should be strenuously adhered to." There was a cheer. "Let us begin. Maurice, get us on line."

"You got it, Seth."

Seth turned to Steve.

"What have you always wanted but never got round to owning Steve? What tickles your fancy? There is no budget to worry about, so go on, let yourself go," said Seth.

"That's a tough one buddy, but, what about a nice rib of beef?"

"I like it, understated and yet so indulgent," said Albert, excited about some retail therapy.

"Done! What about you Albert?" replied Steve.

"Ooh, that's easy. I would like a large detailed map of the world on the wall in my loft and a box of coloured pins, so I can mark all the wonderful places I have visited, and all of the glorious places I have yet to grace with my esteemed presence."

"Did you get that Maurice, a map of the world and pins?"

"Yez Seth, I did."

"I want a motorbike."

"You want a what, Hannibal?" asked Maurice taken aback.

"A motorbike like Vincent," Hannibal reiterated.

"That's a possibility," said Vincent nodding. "There are fantastic little miniature motorbikes out there, in fact, one of them is called a Monkey Bike, so leave that to me Maurice, I'll have Hannibal racing around level 5 before he can say, I dunno, 'Keep the motor running, head out on the highway,' said Vincent chuckling.

"What about you Seth?" he asked.

"I'm running out of lipstick, so I am going to check out the MAC makeup website."

"Ooh, you old so and so you. You're just so bad!" said Albert.

"What about you Maurice?"

"I would like an insect eco zystem. Wormz, antz, beetlez, in a glass box that is filled with zome rich zoil please, Seth, a living znacky, takeout!"

"Ooh Maurice, you slippery, gluttonous devil you," Albert was getting quite mushy!

Everyone then turned to Bandi.

"And what about you then Bandi?" asked Vincent.

She responded without hesitation.

"Caviar," she said in a heavenly yearning tone, "some tangy, dark, rich, savoury Caviar."

"Ooh, you are such a lush!" said Albert poking her with a wing.

Bandi smiled and let out a flirty giggle.

Err; excuse me, what about me?

"Oh Peuja, of course, I am so sorry," said Seth, "What would you desire?"

World of Warcraft, the Internet Computer Game please!

I shall destroy the realm of the Night Elves, and buy the Isle of Man and change its name to the isle of Peuja!

"Agreed," said Seth.

Now, don't forget Chief and the workers.

"Good idea Peuja, well reminded," said Seth. "What about the contents of an entire fruit and vegetable stall and a miniature rabbit supersized tool kit."

Excellent Smithers!

Vincent, What about you?

"Well, I need some socks and some boxer shorts!" he replied after a moments thought.

"We really need to get you out more," said Albert completely unimpressed.

The rest of the day seemed to fly by such was the celebratory atmosphere. Steve and Hannibal's dynamic improvised sock puppet show was a hoot, as was karaoke tea, but the highlight of the day was provided by Chief and his team, a little Rabbit bowling. Rabbit bowling is of course exactly as it sounds. Pick up a rabbit and bowl it underarm at some stationary rabbits and see if you can knock them over! The more rabbits sent tumbling, the higher the point score!

***

Jill Jenkins ran in from the rear of the shop, excitedly waving a piece of paper in her hand whilst John, her doting husband, was standing by the till.

"John, John, I don't believe it, look. We've won a holiday! And not just any holiday, a luxury villa holiday on an island in the Pacific Ocean!"

"But I never entered a holiday competition, did you?" John replied.

"Well, yes," said Jill. "You see, while I was on the Internet ordering some new terrapin pet food the other day, I received a pop up that said enter this competition for free, so I followed the links and entered and, well, we've won."

"Are you certain it's not just one of those Internet hoaxes?" John replied.

"I've checked already, we are flying on a British Airways flight tomorrow evening, first class, and all travel details after that have been taken care of too. I phoned the BA desk at the airport and they confirmed our reservations. I then rang the international number at the bottom of this email confirmation certificate, and spoke to the holiday company's representative, a nice lady called Faith and she also verified and confirmed everything. Apparently it's a competition endorsed by the government of Costa Rica to promote tourism and trade!"

"Costa Rica, tomorrow, but we can't do that. What about the shop? Who's going to look after all of the animals?"

"Well, I've had a word with the kids and Jane said she would come back from university and look after the place, she's jumping on the train this afternoon. She's run the shop before remember, when we were away in Las Vegas watching the Boxing, so I thought, why not hey! She said she could do with the money too, I said we would pay her a little."

"But what about her coursework?" John asked.

"She said they've not got much on at the moment."

John fell quiet and thought everything through.

"We can't really afford it darling. We've paid out an awful lot of money to restock the shop after that spider incident. I did tell you the man from the insurance company wouldn't believe us."

"Don't mention that beast, and that's why we need a break, and this holiday is all paid for." Jill's frustration grew. "It's a private villa on a private island, for heavens sake, with fresh food and drink, including alcohol, delivered to us daily. It's a once in a lifetime trip and it's for a whole two weeks, come on darling!" Jill was almost pleading.

"Two weeks, on a private island in a, what did you say?"

"Private villa! A luxury private villa!" Jill was getting irate.

"Oh, it sounds too good to be true Jill."

"Oh, can we go John please, please?"

"No money needed at all, you say?"

"Not a penny, they even give us Costa Rican Colon to the value of $5000 dollars to spend on duty free. Oh, please, John can we go, please?"

John looked around the shop and saw that everything seemed to be in the usual order. What could go wrong he thought to himself. He looked at his wife's hopeful expression?

"Jill, lock up and get the car, Costa Rica here we come!"

Jill shrieked with delight and threw her arms around her man.

"I love you darling and you're going to get so spoilt, really spoilt. And I mean in a naughty way," she said looking into his eyes.

"I love you too," he replied blushing.

***

"Good morning Freak, good morning boys and how are we on this fine sunny day? Quiet without the ladies isn't it."

The captives stayed silent.

"What no reply. Oh, come on gents you're not still sulking about your plan of world domination being scuppered and put on the back burner are you? You didn't really think that I would let you get away with destroying the human race and quite probably in the process, commit irredeemable harm to the planet?" asked Mr White rhetorically.

"*This planet that you speak of, so endearingly,* is being destroyed by its human inhabitants every second of every day for reasons of *greed and* avarice. Human life is dispens*able and the ramifications for letting humans live are worse than dire. It is for the greater* good, you numpty!"

"Not all human life, and what's a numpty?" Mr White replied delving.

"I'm going to kill you White."

Mr White turned to look at Freak still suspended in mid air where he had left her the night before.

"Ah Freak. No you're not, because I don't plan on ever seeing you again. You are to become someone else's responsibility."

"Then I will kill them first."

Mr White became agitated.

"Can't you just stop thinking about killing for a moment? What about Scrabble, it's a great pastime."

"I have a mind that can calculate the pros and cons of nuclear fusion and you want me to spell! I swear to you, on the lives of all of my previous unsuspecting victims, as soon as I am released from this tableau, I will kill you, White, and your little precious Clipboard Girl too."

Mr White raised his hand. Freak slowly turned in mid-air and floated towards him. He raised her to his eye level and spoke to her softly, in a chilling tone.

"Look into my eyes Freak, do you see fear? Do any of your senses, sense fear? Can you smell fear? The answer is no, is it not?" Mr White opened his palm, Freaks eight legs extended and stretched outward. "Can you feel the pain Freak, can you?" He asked.

A quivering, straining voice replied.

"Yes, yes I can."

"Stop this you monster, stop this at once. Spike, Escobar, help, help."

Escobar flew into the lounge closely followed by a scuttling Spike. They took one look at what was happening and then joined Mr White by his side, he continued.

"The pain of every death endured by your victims is nothing compared to the pain you will suffer upon your own demise. The sensitivity of your nervous system is so heightened, due to the fluid you know as SPAFF running through your veins, that the sensation of pain will be magnified a thousand times in comparison to any normal carbon based organism. It will completely engulf you. You are not indestructible Freak, and right now you are at my mercy. The only reason I continue to let you live is because your destiny is still unknown to me, as are the repercussions of your passing. However, do not push me Freak, I am human after all. Well, sort of!"

He allowed himself a chuckle and closed his fist. Freaks legs relaxed, however, she still remained suspended. She gasped with relief.

"Now boys, you are to be cared for by some guests for a while and Freak, well you will remain…" Mr White took a look around and placed Freak high on the wall as if she were a hunting trophy, "…there until, well just until. Spike, Escobar, will you please find me something to feed to Freak."

They both ran into the garden. Mr White talked on.

"Yes, Freak, I am going to feed you before I go, so there is no need for any undue concern. Now, you will be polite to our guests and treat them considerately. Clipboard Girl tells me they know a thing or two about the animal kingdom, so best behaviour please. Oh, and just in case you were thinking that the speech programme you embrace will still be able to be utilised, to perhaps, fool our guests into some kind of ineptitude. Well, in a word, no, you won't be able to. I have disabled the programme on all of our computers, and with you on the wall and the gents in the tank, err, no chance. I will also be leaving a note, on a Post-it, on the side of your tank, too!"

Spike ran back into the lounge with a couple of juicy earthworms hanging out of his mouth and Escobar fluttered in with a giant stick insect in his beak. They dropped them at Mr White's feet.

"That will do the trick, thank you," said Mr White.

Freak bitterly delivered another threat. "I will kill you White, I promise you this, I will grow stronger in mind and body and your hocus-pocus won't be able to hold me forever. And then I'll unleash pain and suffering like you have never imagined!"

"Maybe one day you will, and maybe one day you'll kill me too, but not today, because today, we begin a new adventure," Mr White replied happily.

THE LORDS OF PANGEA

How should you feel when you're somewhere in your sixth decade and you and your husband, who own a small pet shop in Manchester that has suffered a recent murderous disaster, like a bolt from the blue, win the holiday of your dreams to a tropical island in the Pacific? Well you feel ecstatic; you drop everything and go, don't you? You get one of the kids to look after the business, run around, double check you haven't left the iron or the gas on, cram your luggage with sun cream, corn plasters and tissues and take a taxi to the airport. But, when you get to your destination, what should you expect? Well, you would hope for the bee's knees wouldn't you, or the mutt's chestnuts!

***

Sweating and dishevelled from travel and craving blissful respite, John and Jill Jenkins wearily climbed the final few steps of the stairway that clung precariously to the cliffs of Alcatraz Island and made their way into the lush rear garden of Arcadia, where they were immediately struck by its glorious wonder! They stood for a moment breathless, washed by relief. Having travelled across the Atlantic on a jet and then sailed the short distance from the mainland on a yacht, they were now alone with their luggage, a set of keys and swollen feet!

"Look at that John; it looks like something out of a James Bond movie."

"It's breathtaking, amazing, you were so right to talk me into this Jill. Look at that pool, oh heavens! Shall we have a browse inside the main house, have a shower, see what there is to eat and then perhaps have a long cool beverage by the pool, darling?"

"Well, it would be rude not to, John! Perhaps a little skinny-dipping," Jill replied with a glint in her eye unaware of the fact that the pair were being listened to by a few critters in the lounge.

"Someone is here and approaching, they *are at present in the Kitchen. I can hear the refrigerator door, quickly; I need a plan, as*

do I. I must lie on my back, belly up and play dead, as must I, no I mustn't, you must flip I and *nuzzle I, it is I that shall play dead and lie in wait for the simple minded, yes, yes, but the* note? The note is nothing compared to the predictability of *human sympathy."* Yin and Yang giggled.

Jill entered the lounge and was immediately engaged by its splendour.

"John quick, quick you have to see this, it looks incredible." She said before suddenly letting out a rip-roaring scream.

With a mouth full of an exotically filled baguette, John ran to her aid from the kitchen. He chewed frantically, painfully swallowing an oversized mouthful before spluttering.

"What is it darling, have you been stung or something?" he said, spitting crumbs at his beloved wife with the corners of his mouth speckled with mayonnaise.

Jill said nothing; she just raised a shaking hand and pointed at the wall. John's eye line followed her arm and then, he too let out a scream. He instinctively grabbed hold of his wife and began to creep backwards. It was Freak, statuesque, still and motionless, hanging on the wall, that had chilled them both to the bone. Slowly and cautiously John mustered some bravado from somewhere, removed a flip-flop and threw it at Freak with the action of a six-year-old girl chasing butterflies. To his disbelief it struck home, a direct hit and yet, Freak didn't move.

"It didn't move," Jill said whispering.

"It might be dead, I think it's dead, is it dead?" said John.

"Go and have a look," Jill replied.

John gave Jill a glance that said, 'are out of your mind?' and then resigned himself to his fate and tiptoed, like a mongoose on hot coals, towards Freak's still body. He pulled up a little occasional table and placed it by the wall.

"Be careful," said Jill.

John waved an arm behind him and hushed his wife; he wiped his forehead with a hairy arm and stepped up onto the table, standing slowly until Freak was at eye level. Tentatively he raised a finger and gingerly touched one of Freak's eight legs. Freak didn't move. John tried again but this time poked a little harder. Jill squeaked, John jumped, but still Freak didn't move. Perspiring madly from every pore and holding his breath, John bravely touched the back of Freaks abdomen, still nothing! He let out a sigh and grabbed at his own chest.

"Oh, darling, it's dead, look. I think it's had an appointment with a taxidermist."

Hugely relieved he stepped off the diminutive table.

"Really? Thank goodness, now make me a double gin and tonic and see if you can find a mop. That was all a bit much for me," Jill replied.

"Oh, alright dear!" John replied.

"No ice, no slice and no tonic please!" Jill ordered.

***

"That was 19 seconds by the clock, Hannibal," said Steve.

Hannibal pulled up next to Sinatra who was surrounded by tools, small tyres, oil and everything else you would find with a mechanic in a pit lane.

"It's all very well riding around in here and taking on this course, but this Monkey Bike should be feeling the breeze through its spokes and teething gravel with its tyre tread. It's built for the great outdoors and not inside these walls."

"You'll get to ride it like that one day buddy, but I have to say, you're very good at it. You've not had it long and you've taken to it like a dog to a lamp post mate," said Steve.

Hannibal sighed, "Level 5's walls are so depressing Steve?"

"Yeah, they are a bit," Steve paused. "Here, I've got an idea, come with me, buddy. Sinatra, would you put the bike and bits away please?"

Sinatra, covered in oil and wearing a jaunty baseball cap fashioned by Albert, saluted them both and watched as they hopped back into the tunnel and disappeared from sight.

Seth and Vincent were sat in silence, staring at a monitor in the lounge. They were studying scanned images of the eight symbols and the sign of Ankh from Vincent's bequeathed notes. Steve and Hannibal jumped through the fireplace.

"Hi boys, I was thinking, would you mind us decorating level five?" Steve asked.

"No, not at all Steve," Seth replied still staring at the monitor.

"Great, would you mind us getting Maurice to order some paint and stuff online, you know stuff that we will need?"

"No, not at all Steve," replied Seth still viewing the monitor.

"Are you two alright? You just seem a bit preoccupied."

Hannibal had noticed that Vincent and Seth were not themselves.

"Yes, of course, Hannibal, we're just a bit stumped that's all. This lot has got us both a bit baffled."

Hannibal leapt up onto Vincent's shoulder.

"What lot?" he asked.

"The symbols and stuff from my father's notes," Vincent replied.

"Hannibal hasn't seen them," said Seth, "he was with Bandi in the lab, when you brought them back and placed them on the table."

Hannibal looked at the monitor.

"The Lords of Pangea," said Hannibal.

"Sorry, what did you say?" asked Seth.

"The Lords of Pangea, it's the face of a shield belonging to 'The Lords of Pangea'."

"How do you know that?" asked Vincent.

"I have no idea," Hannibal replied.

"Well, who or what are 'The Lords of Pangea'?" asked Seth.

"Well, Pangea was the Super Continent that broke up some 250 million years ago to form the 8 continents we have today."

"I know what Pangea is Hannibal, but there are only 7 continents."

"You forget the sub-continent of India, Vincent," Hannibal replied and, on a roll he continued, "The Lords of Pangea are, or rather were, 8 animal lords worshipped by mankind. They are, or were, selected from the worshipped animal Gods of the world, to watch over the lands, I think! None of them know, or knew, who the other chosen Lords are, or were, but all together, they hold a secret."

"Wow! Who selects, or selected them?" asked Vincent.

"How would I know?" replied Hannibal sighing.

"And what's the secret?" asked Seth.

"If I knew, it wouldn't be much of a secret would it!" replied Hannibal.

"How do you know all of this?" Vincent asked.

"Truly, I have no idea Vincent. I swear it." Hannibal was doing a pretty good impression of an open palmed politician.

"Well, I suppose that some of that was helpful," said Vincent cheerfully.

Seth jumped in and thoughtfully mused aloud, pacing like Jessica Fletcher on a few shots of the little green fairy!

"Therefore we can surmise that Bastet is one of the 8 lords and that each Lord represents a continent and that makes it pretty obvious that Bastet is the representative of the continent of Africa, because of the evident history concerning Bubastis Egypt. However, who are the other seven? And why is she here? And who chose them?" Seth was tormented by his own hypothesis.

"Perhaps I can be of some assistance Seth," said a voice from behind the troop.

A smartly and yet casually dressed athletic figure of a man was standing in the open doorway of the cottage with the evening behind him.

"Would you mind calling in the others Vincent, it will save some time in the long run?"

"Excuse me, who are you? Do I know you, and how did you open the door?" Vincent asked.

"Hannibal shall we tell him?" said the visitor.

Hannibal jumped down from Vincent's shoulders and gingerly walked up to the man.

"I'm sorry, do I know you?" he asked.

"You all do in one way or another," said the man.

At that point Bandi, Albert, Maurice and Garston entered the lounge.

"It's Mr White," said Garston dumbfounded.

Everyone jumped to their feet, paws or claws, nervous and unsure of what action to take. Bandi's eyes misted over as she immediately prepared to change to her fiery form, but before her metamorphosis could be realised, Mr White swiftly dropped to one knee and bowed his head.

"Lord Bastet, Bandi, please, I am not under the influence of Yin and Yang, in fact I never have been."

Mr White looked subserviently to the floor. Bandi, sensing no danger, allowed him to continue.

"Would you mind if I stayed a while and explained a few things. The real reasons for Project Commune and why, you are what you are, and why I can understand all of you, that sort of thing."

Nobody answered.

"Look, why don't you put the kettle on, Vincent, whilst I pop to the car, I'll be back in a moment."

Mr White turned and walked out of the open door and back down the garden path to where a familiar car and two men dressed in black suits were standing. Vincent popped to the kitchen, put on the kettle and started making tea.

The group turned to each other.

"Is anyone gonna say anything? Are we all gonna just sit hear with our mouths open staring at the door as if we were waiting for the Tooth Fairy to appear drinking a pint of Bishops Finger?" asked Steve.

Again, not a word from anyone.

"I guess not then," he said.

Mr White returned.

"Right, I've had the boys take my luggage to Vincent's old apartment in the big house, they'll return for me later. Oh, I am sorry, please excuse my manners, this is Faith my PA."

Faith was standing shyly behind her boss, her face partially hidden by her ever-ready clipboard. She was wearing a pair of jeans, a T-shirt and trainers, nothing special, but still, as Vincent returned from the kitchen, he was captivated by her sultry beauty and couldn't help but stare. Faith felt herself blush beneath his gaze. At that moment Escobar hopped in through the open front door with a sauntering Spike.

"Oh heavens, again forgive me, you guys probably all need to say hello to each other don't you," said Mr White.

"Hello, hombres have you missed us?" said Escobar flapping his wings and turning a spin.

"Streuth you guys, it's good to see ya blooming faces again," said Spike.

Everyone was a little dumbfounded.

"You can speak," said Seth.

"Of course they can, it's all been part of the ruse. We had to keep up the deception to fool Yin and Yang, but now, amongst friends, we can all be ourselves," said Mr White.

"You mean these two won't try and kill us?" asked Steve.

"No, of course not, they are your chums and always will be. So, I think it's time for a group hug, what do you say huh?"

Mr White stretched out his arms and waited for a response and then put them down by his side, slightly embarrassed by the group's lack of commitment!

"Why would you want to fool Yin and Yang and..."Seth was interrupted.

"...Escobar and Spike have been working with me since the precise moment you all slid down the Grid's waste disposal pipes. They have been familiar with the, err...strategic plan from the get go! They have never been under the control of Yin and Yang and all of their previous actions were made voluntarily and with my knowledge. You see there are only two species that Yin and Yang can control. They are humans and strangely enough, terrapins, possibly! Would their plan have worked and would they have produced psychotic terrapins? Well yes, however would SPAFF infected terrapins have followed the orders sent to them via the food dispensers? Only fate knows. They may just have gone to battle against one another!"

"Why did you let Yin and Yang take their wicked plan that far, and why can't they control apes and chimpanzees or even dolphins?" asked Vincent.

"Apes, chimps and dolphins, good question, and the answer is, because of the rate that they have evolved. It is not in their genes."

"But back at Ostonial beach, sir, the dolphins they..."

Mr White interrupted.

"Those dolphins are my highly trained friends, Faith, they used to live in the manor you know! They were never controlled by Yin and Yang, and why did I let Yin and Yang get as far as they did with their plans? Because I needed you guys to put the pieces of the jigsaw together, work as a team and realise your true potential. Carry out a test run, if you like, of things to come. Otherwise this would have all been for nothing. Isn't that right, Peuja?"

Yes, it is, darling.
Potential!
SPAFF and evolution are the difference. How have you been my sweet?

"Fine thanks, Peuja."

Mr White returned to addressing the stunned group.

"Do you mind if we take a seat?' he asked already taking a pew in the middle of the sofa. "I needed you all to think they could control the minds of any living creature. Their talents were stumbled upon. An accident that turned into a military and scientific community bunfight; to see whether successful human control was obtainable. And yes, as you can see, I know about the Grid and Peuja and everything else the Manor has to offer. I was, of course, the benefactor sanctioning and enabling all off the research."

"So when Yin and Yang spoke to us, without words, you…"

"Had already activated the little JR's in all of you, that are coupled to your microchips Garston," Mr White replied.

"We all have robotic ants in our ears! And talking to each other isn't because of SPAFF?" Garston asked.

"But Seth created JR, so how…?" asked Vincent.

Mr White cut Vincent off mid sentence.

"SPAFF does do its bit, after all it is in the microchip and Junior. The JR design programme was already dotted around Seth's microchip memory. He just had to piece together the components, and build one for Vincent."

"So you are the reason that all of us and others of our species have been subjected to different forms of analysis and torture, not the military?" Seth asked sternly.

Mr White bowed his head.

"Seth I am, sadly, fighting a war, and to win it, I have to make sacrifices. Unfortunately, yes, they have been of the creature kind and you are incorrect to conclude that the military are not involved, too. Remember, they also have their financiers. The only way to resurrect The Lords of Pangea was and is, to play a numbers game, trial and error!"

"The Lords of Pangea, who are…? I am a little lost," asked Steve.

"Bandi is a Lord, Steve, a Lord of Africa and Pangea." Mr White answered.

"Are any more of us Lords?" said a still very confused Steve.

"That's not for me to say!" Mr White replied.

"Not for you to say, why? And what about Yin and Yang?" Hannibal asked.

"Well, they are another story, but as far as I can gather, because obviously there are two of them, err no! And why? Well, because, I don't know! But what I do know is that death has to become you! It has to be accepted before rebirth by each Lord and each needs a specific concoction of the elements to aid that event."

"What about Freak? What does she have to do with all of this? And where is she?" asked a very suspicious Garston.

"So, where's that tea then, it should be soundly brewed and any chance of a biscuit?" Mr White asked with a charismatic smile, avoiding the question as best he could.

"Sorry. How very rude of me. Would you like a cup of tea, Faith?" Vincent asked coyly.

Faith said nothing, but nodded a flirty yes. Vincent jumped up from his chair and went to fetch the well brewed tea.

"Sorry, please make yourselves comfortable. Take a seat." Vincent said politely, on his way to the kitchen.

"OK, so where shall I start from then?" asked Mr White.

The group gathered around the settee and stared at him expectantly. Vincent walked in with a tray of tea and biscuits and some saucers and milk.

"The beginning would be good," said Vincent offering Mr White some sugar.

"Alright then, pull up a chair, will you. This might take a while," Mr White replied.

Vincent obliged, and sat down.

"The beginning, you may find to be in several places!"

"What do you mean?" asked Vincent.

"Well, there is my beginning, earth's beginning, your beginning, well, I could go on but, let me start with your beginning. As you know, you hail from a line of great men, really great men, men that have changed the face of mankind in one way or another."

"Yes, Vincent's lineage is exceptional," said Seth.

"Oh, truly extraordinary, Seth, and soon you will understand just how unique!"

"Well go on then the excitement is killing me, actually, hold that thought, I need a pee," said Steve.

"Why doesn't everyone have a pee, come on all of you, outside," said Faith unable to stop herself from organising.

The animal menagerie weaved their way outside and sniffed

around the garden, Vincent walked out after them. "Not you, Vincent, you can use the inside lavatory."

"Oh yes, of course." Vincent said pulling up his fly.

"He may need a little finessing, Faith," said Mr White turning with a whisper.

"It's Clipboard Girl to you, sir, and don't you forget it!" she replied softly, with a smile.

A girl after my own microchip!

***

John Jenkins was sat relaxing in the lounge at Arcadia sipping Long Island iced tea and pondering the state of the universe, as the twilight of a golden South American evening crept through the wide open glass bi-fold doors. Jill was mooching around, having just got out of the shower.

"Look at that terrapin John, do you think it's dead? It's been on its back for quite some time and the other one keeps stroking it with a flipper. Look it's so sad. Do you think they're like swans and mate for life or something?"

"Mate, mate! I's his brother you voluminous trollop!

Keep it up, the sorry excuse of a mammalian female is falling for it!"

"I don't know darling, but there's that note that says we should not touch them under any circumstances," John replied.

"But it might need help, or simply flipping back onto its front. I would hate to be responsible for its death, if we could have saved it!"

"But they're white, Jill! Have you ever seen white terrapins before? Maybe they're some kind of poisonous breed. Surely you haven't forgotten what that tarantula on the wall did!"

"That's not the same spider. Believe me, the one that gave us a visit back in Manchester was much smaller than that. And the coincidence would just be ridiculous!" Jill replied.

"Oh is it? Look at it darling, look at the metal claw!" said John rising from his slouch.

"Oh my god no," Jill began to nervously stutter, "that, that's just beyond comprehension. What's happening here?

MYSTERY HISTORY

"I knew your father and your grandfather, and his father you know?" said Mr White. "I'll start that again. Judging by the look on all of your faces, this is going to be tougher than I thought."

"How could you know his great-grandfather, sir, that would make you, well, very old?" asked Faith.

"Yes, it would Faith, sorry, Clipboard Girl. Now be patient and bear with me. Right let's see. Your family Vincent, err… have been entrusted with taking care of a great secret for many years. There that was easy," said Mr White very pleased with himself.

"Exactly, how many years is many and what's the secret?" Vincent replied.

Everyone was sat in front of Mr White, hooked on his every word.

"I'll get to that in a minute, but first a brief history lesson, alright?"

Everyone duly nodded.

"Right then, well, between the years of 1536 and 1550 AD, the monasteries of England were dissolved and their lands and buildings seized by the Crown. All of these incredible institutions housed great treasures, historical documents and artefacts of great value. Now, under the guise of spreading wealth for better social living and turning the buildings into scholastic seats of learning, King Henry VIII set about discrediting the monastic lifestyle and other religious orders by creating evil whispers concerning corruption and their uncommon activities."

"Err, hold on, what are we doing starting this story in the 1500's mate?" Steve asked.

"Quiet Steve," said Hannibal, "you'll put him off. Please continue, sir!" Mr White gave Hannibal a thankful nod.

"The truth is that Henry VIII was not a well man. He had a nasty disease, very nasty! I don't really want to expand on that, so you guys can just look it up! However, all the power of a kingdom couldn't cure its brain poisoning, maddening effects."

"Sounds gruesome, I'll Goggle it!" said Steve.

"It's Google darling," Albert replied.

"What, even if you're just having a look at it? Steve asked.

Mr White cut in by raising his voice!

"He was a scholarly chap, he used the plundering of the monasteries as a catalyst to develop his own religion, the one we now know as the Church of England, but, it was the legends of Glastonbury Abbey that particularly fascinated him. The raiding of the other religious buildings in Britain and the development of the Church of England were merely, 'red herrings' that disguised his true objective."

"Red Fish!"

"A ruse or great pretence, Steve," said Seth.

"Gotcha," Steve replied. "Please carry on, sir."

Mr White continued.

"The King knew that if he took Glastonbury alone, the Abbey said to be most prominent in all the land, he would be lambasted by his nobles and probably ignite a revolution, thus, the fabricated stories of sinister monks and their illicit behaviour came about as an excuse for his deeds. However, it wasn't until Henry's son, Edward VI, also a sickly king, took to the thrown and perpetuated his father's exploits, that Glastonbury was finally savaged. You see in reality, this whole calamitous period of religious and English history was due to something very different. The Nanteus Cup!"

Steve's ears pricked up.

"Before you ask Steve, would anyone like to jump in and explain what the Nanteus Cup is?"

"It's the Holy Grail."

Everyone turned to look at Hannibal who had responded in a dreamy tone; he was staring toward the heavens, seemingly his thoughts miles away. He suddenly broke off from his hypnotic state and repeated himself.

"The Nanteus Cup is the Holy Grail."

"Well done, Hannibal, you said it is the Holy Grail and not, it is believed to be the Holy Grail," said Mr White, beaming.

"So the Grail exists?" Vincent asked in astonishment.

"Oh yes, but it's not quite as you expect it to be. It's not a chalice crafted in the fires of heaven from precious metals, no, it's just a little wooden cup simply made from a hardwood, probably Olive."

Albert, who had been relatively quiet until this point, spoke up. "I have just searched 'Holy Grail' on the net and there are several listings, love. One says it's the cup that Jesus Christ used at the last supper, another says it's the cup that collected his blood as it dripped from his wounds whilst he was being crucified, and the other says that it is the bloodline of Christ, his genetic make up, his cipher! So, forgive me, when I ask Mr White, which one is it, babe?"

"It's all of them, Albert, and more."

"More." Albert replied.

"The Nanteus Cup is probably one of the oldest surviving relics of time."

"So what gave the cup its great power? Was it the blood of Christ then, darling?" Albert asked.

Mr White looked at the group in a way that said, 'I'm 'darling' now am I?' and then continued.

"I was right the first time. This is going to be much more difficult than I first imagined," he said taking a sip of tea and then, rather surprisingly, he spoke softly and reflectively as if he were leaping in thought.

"The Earth is alive you know! She is alive."

No one said a word. They were too entranced.

"She is called Gaia, Mother Earth, and she was born from chaos by pathogenesis. She went on to couple with her equal, Ouranos, the starry black skies that cover us all, and together, they had a few demanding children."

"Her children were called…"

Hannibal interrupted. "…The Titans! They were giant beasts, a mix of reptile, fish, bird, insect and mammal and their number was twelve. Evolution was at its birth."

"What the fudge are you talking about now?" asked Steve.

"Give him a little time to finish please, Steve, be patient," said Mr White. Gesturing to Hannibal to continue.

"Now, as they grew, these titanic beasts fought amongst themselves, you see, they all suffered a smouldering torment, an inner turmoil. They did not know whether to love each other, as they were siblings, or kill each other, as they were rivals. Some were huge, I mean massive, the size of mountains, but some were not, however, all were formidable."

"That's right, Hannibal, please continue," said Mr White.

"Kronos was their leader, the leader of the Titans, and by all accounts not very nice. One of his children, the youngest was called Zeus and it was he that eventually took power by killing his father with the help of his mother, Rhea, who was also Kronos' sister, weird huh, anyway, you see Kronos was wary of his son's popularity and plotted to kill him, but Zeus got to him first."

"Kronos married his sister? And by the way, I've goggled it. That Henry kings disease was disgusting!"

Steve was astonished that his little mate Hannibal seemed to be as much of an oracle as the Internet.

"Yes, Steve, just keep listening," said Mr White.

"Now Zeus united his warring brothers and sisters and formed a group that he named, The Gods. They, guided by Zeus, fought the rest of the Titans and then Gaia's other offspring, the Giants, over the lands of Gaia and then, after victory, Zeus either banished the Titans or put them to work or killed them, or something, it all gets a little fuzzy from here."

"Good job Hannibal, well done," said Mr White.

"I hate to be a bore but that's all just mythology, Greek mythology at that, it's not the way it all really happened according to science and the study of evolution. What about the other stuff, you know, religion?" asked Seth.

"Well, Seth, the Romans adopted the Greek gods as their own and renamed them after the planets, remember? Jupiter is Zeus, Venus is Aphrodite etc!"

"Yes but…" Seth was interrupted.

"The Hindus also have myths which are very similar, as do the Norse, Buddhists, Muslims, the Celts; even the Mexicans once knew Mother Earth as an ancient being Tonantzin Tlalli. From the heights of the far east to the canyons of the western world, from the frozen southern tips to the vast northern wastelands, each civilisation has a similar story of, 'the beginning,' so open your mind Seth, science isn't always the way. Could all of these ancient cultures be wrong? Could all of their beliefs truly be myths and not historical tales that have suffered a plague of Chinese whispers? Not on your nelly, oh rabbit King!" Mr White was managing to be condescending without being smug.

"What's a nelly?"

"No idea Steve. Shut up!" Seth didn't like being put in his place.

"Sorry Seth," said Steve.

"OK, well, back to the question of how many years has your family been guarding the secret?" said Mr White. "The answer is somewhere in the region of 450 odd years Vincent."

"And what is the secret?" asked Steve, impatiently jumping up and down.

"The Nanteus Cup," Mr White replied. "Once a year it is filled with blessed holy water and has blotting cloths dipped into it, they are then, in turn, sent around the world to people who are in need of some sort of cure or salvation."

"I still don't get it."

"Steve, work it out," said Garston, "It's Vincent's family, the Russell family, that have been entrusted with keeping and protecting the Nanteus Cup, I mean you can't just let something like that sit in a museum, right, Mr White?"

BINGO! Sorry, a little over excited! This is so much fun, it's like a game of Cluedo!

"That's ok Peuja!" said Mr White. "But that's not entirely everything."

"I have no idea where the Nanteus Cup is," said Vincent, "I haven't got the foggiest, honest."

"I know that Vincent, because it's in the car, your Nan sent it me some time ago," said Mr White.

"Nan, from Australia?" Vincent replied.

"Err, yes Vincent," replied Mr White.

"Well, I'll be blown," said Vincent.

"Sorry, wait can we just go back a little please? Did you just say the Holy Grail is in the car?" asked Seth.

"Yes Seth," Mr White answered, looking at the disbelieving faces around him. "It will all become clearer very soon. Shall I carry on? Good, right well, the 'Cup,' is of far greater significance than you can imagine. Not because of Christ but because of someone called Prometheus! Hannibal would you like to…"

"…Certainly. Prometheus was the wisest Titan, second or third generation, who worked for Zeus in the forge of heaven."

"Well done again Hannibal. Full marks and a house point." Mr

White patted Hannibal on the helmet. "Carry on."

Hannibal duly obliged.

"Gaia, or Mother Earth, whatever you wish to call her, survived because of her position within the Galaxy and proximity to the Sun and as a result she flourished and grew lush vegetation. However, this, of course, needed to be tended to, and so, Zeus instructed Prometheus to forge all creatures, great and small from the elements to cultivate the planet and thus the food chain was born. But, Prometheus made a mistake; he created the most intelligent of beasts, Man, with few defences. Man had no fur, fangs or claws to protect himself, no real strength, speed, agility or wings for escape, no gills, well, I could go on but I won't and so, to cut a long story short, Prometheus took the secret of fire from the heavens and handed it to Man against Zeus's will, therefore making one species the most powerful on the planet. Of course, this made Zeus very angry and so he punished Prometheus. He had him chained to the side of a mountain in the Caucasus, to be precise, and every night he sent his giant pet eagle to gorge on Prometheus's liver, which, because of his titan blood, regenerated as fast as it was devoured. However Prometheus felt the pain, all of the pain."

"That's a terrible story Hannibal. You speak as if the poor man, sorry Titan still suffers," said Garston.

Mr White picked up where Hannibal had finished.

"He doesn't any more, he was freed by Herakles, or Hercules if you're Roman, some 1300 years later. Herakles also killed the eagle, not a clever thing to do, kill the pet of Zeus! Anyway, I'll continue. Now, the Titans and the Gods, who let's face it are also Titans by descent, although called by a different name, are immortals, well most of them anyway. They are begat from Gaia, Mother Earth, and as old as time. They are not visible to any normal living creature and so, like any of the Titans or Gods, Prometheus can only be observed by those with, 'The Sight,' 'The Sight of Heaven' and this, this gift, was only granted to, err, any takers, anyone got any ideas?"

Steve raised a paw.

"Yes Steve."

"The Lords of Pangea?"

"Well done Steve, well done, here, have a biscuit!" Mr White passed over a digestive, which Steve took delightedly.

"So now for the bombshell!" said Mr White.

"You mean the Holy Grail in the back of a car, parked outside a cottage in a country lane in Cheshire, isn't?" said Garston.

"No, there is a revelation even greater!" Mr White paused. "Prometheus still walks the Earth!"

Nobody said a word, until Seth broke the silence.

"And as Bandi is one of the Lords of Pangea, she can see him, because she has…"

"'The Sight,'" said Steve.

"Oh more than that, Steve, it means we can find him! You see to any normal beast Prometheus appears to be human, but to the Lords of Pangea he also appears as his true form," said Mr White.

"Zo what'z he got to do with thiz 'Cup' zen?" Maurice asked.

"Well Maurice, clinging to a shelf on the rock face, beneath where Prometheus was bound and chained, there was a small plant, a plant that fed upon his trickling blood. It grew nowhere else and was the only plant of its kind! Now, and this is where it gets really interesting, in the year of 724 BC a princess called Medea used an innocuous looking small wooden cup or bowl, whichever you prefer, to grind up the young buds from this plant and make a strengthening potion to save a prince. He would end up her liberator and husband. However, later, she went completely nuts and chopped up her brother and killed her children in a jealous rage."

Everyone gasped with horror.

"But that's another story. Anyway, the prince was about to face three impossible tasks and each would have certainly caused his demise but, Medea prepared this brew, in the, 'cup,' and it gave him the power of seven men and he was saved. Sorry, the prince is Jason, of Jason and the Argonauts fame and his story is, well, found in the tales of Homer and in the plays of Euripides."

"Wow, this iz heavy dude," said Maurice completely enthralled. Mr White continued.

"Now, the little innocuous wooden cup, or bowl, was just thrown into a sack, with whatever else Medea could grab, and taken back to the ancient Greek kingdom of Thessaly with she and Jason, as they fled. This included something, an artefact called the Golden Fleece, a magical object that she was no stranger to. She had spent many of her formative years around this sacred article, because she was not only a princess but also the priestess of Hecate. Hecate was, sorry is, the female three-headed Titan entrusted by Zeus with all witchcraft. She had a special place in Zeus's heart. Called herself the Queen of Darkness, you know? Anyway, the Golden Fleece was kept under her vigilance upon the Earth and, as Medea was Hecate's priestess, well she knew how best to steal it. So she helped Jason, the prince from a land faraway, do, just that! Shall I move on, is everyone keeping up?"

Everyone was sitting open mouthed and looking a little dazed.

"What's the Golden Fleece?" asked Steve, his head tilted to one side.

"It's the fleece of a golden ram. A ram sent, by order of Zeus, to help rescue some children from being murdered by their wicked stepmother. It's a wonderful story; you ought to look it up sometime. The Fleece was very powerful, magical even. Those who possessed it were always healthy, wealthy and…" Mr White was cut short.

"…Do you mind if we take another pee break, please Mr White?" asked Steve wagging his tail.

"Not at all, you guys carry on, I need one myself," Mr White replied.

"I'm having the toilet, I'm a lady," said Clipboard Girl jumping to her feet, "the rest of you can go outside and water the garden."

Vincent and Mr White looked at each other and ventured out into the front soon followed by an animal procession in single file. Everyone stood together in front of a flowerbed and had a pee to a unilateral wiggle and shake! No one said a word, they all just stared straight ahead, all except Steve that is, who whistled the theme tune from the film Armageddon before going back inside, and assuming his previous position.

"Now where was I? Ah yes, Prometheus and the Nanteus Cup. Well, by no accident, the 'Cup' ended up at the last supper and then in the hands of someone called Joseph of Arimathea. He was the uncle of Jesus Christ and he used it to collect the blood of his nephew at the crucifixion."

"Sorry sir, but while we are on the subject of Jesus I need to clear a few things up."

"OK Hannibal, shoot."

"So God, as we know him, the father of Jesus, is actually…?"

"Zeus, Hannibal. You see, Christ, and the other religious icons from all the other religions were delivered by Zeus, and virtually all, on different continents. I know it's hard to believe. I'm not trying to be controversial, just keep an open mind. Here, I'll give you an example of Zeus's power."

There was a shuffling of bottoms.

"Once upon a time there was a maiden called, Europa. She had a beauty that was mesmerising and unquestionable. Her eyes were as bright as the moon and her skin was as pale as milk. One glorious day, completely by chance, Zeus discovered her and was immediately taken by her splendour. He decided that he would woo her and, so, to do so, he transformed himself into a huge magnificent white bull!"

"Odd choice!" Albert whispered to Garston.

"With the sun on his back, blinding the maiden's vision, he strode towards her, across a beach where she was taking a walk, through beams of sunlight. At first, she was frightened but, after a while, she tentatively approached the magnificent beast and then to her delight something incredible happened. The massive, powerful beast cowered and knelt at her feet. She felt overwhelmed with a feeling of encompassing peace and so, gently, she reached out and stroked the bull's silky muzzle and then, with little coaxing, climbed onto it's sturdy back. As soon as she was safely seated, the great bull, Zeus in disguise, jumped up and ran for the Mediterranean Sea. It carried her across the buffeting waves to the Island of Crete, the place of Zeus's birth, and there, it took her, if you get my drift!"

"Took her where?" asked Steve.

"Just 'took' her Steve! You know like bunnies," said Albert.

"Oh, sorry," Steve replied.

"She bore Zeus three sons, one a great king, one a great man and one a great beast. Europa was crowned the first queen of Crete and legends were born. There you go, the power of Zeus!" Mr White finished the story and clapped his hands together proudly.

"Wow, that's a great story,"

"I'm glad you like it Albert."

"So Mary the mother of Christ and…"

"…Was touched and handed a child by the elements that surrounded her and the light that was Lord Zeus, Hannibal. Christ was sent to try and heal us all, as at times, were the divine ones of every other religion. You see, when one species becomes too dominant and begins to threaten its own kind and the fine balance of Gaia's ecosystem is threatened, that's when Zeus steps in and attempts to fix everything. However, if he can't, which is mainly due to the belligerence of the species, then the great Titan Atlas is told to re-adjust the axis of the earth and Gaia then transforms into an ice cloaked orb. This permits life's magnificent forces to be reborn once more. The last of these great adjustments, together with a well-placed Hail Mary, purged the world of dinosaurs! However, the last time that Zeus interfered with human existence was when he brought about the end of the Roman Empire."

"Hail Mary? That was a meteor," said Vincent.

"No, it was Christianity!"

"No, I meant the dinosaurs!" Vincent replied.

Mr White's penny dropped.

"Oh, yes it was. A meteor thrown by Lord Zeus from the heavens, but still, he needed to hit the right target!"

"Sorry Mr White, but this is all just a little bonkers," said Vincent.

"You're sitting next to a talking rabbit Vincent, you need to re-evaluate the term bonkers!" Mr White replied.

"Sorry to butt in, however the both of you are talking absolute nonsense," said Seth. "The eruption of the Siberian Traps brought about the extinction of the dinosaurs! The massive release of sulphur dioxide gasses initially caused the Earth to drastically heat, but then, once the gasses had surrounded the planet and formed choking, suffocating, clouds, which blocked the sun's rays from penetrating the atmosphere, it dramatically cooled. The great freeze was the result, and it all ended a little messily. Thus, it wasn't some Titan moving the planet around the Galaxy coffee table, or even Zeus launching a shot putt rock from a far corner of his dining room."

"Seth, the Siberian Trap theory, well that's just conjecture. A myth created by non-believers." Mr White replied.

Seth burst into laughter.

"Mr White, bless you for believing whatever it is that you regard as reality or falsehood, but unless you have actually had a conversation with your Lord Zeus and have had him furnish you with the 'Great Golden Everlasting Carrot,' I am going to, not so reluctantly, stick with the evidence handed to us by science. The facts state that the Traps erupted at the end of the Permian era and as a result, for millions of years, the Earth's crust splintered. Yes you heard me right! For millions of years, the Earth spewed out lava, in a flood basalt eruption, over an area as large as all of Western Europe. It wiped out ninety five percent of all the life on Earth by either poisoning, boiling or freezing it. So, please don't take this the wrong way or anything but, whoever taught you the geological and paleontological history of the Earth, either lied to you, or is an idiot!"

Mr White was a little thrown, he liked the universally accepted meteor hypothesis, and the Siberian Traps theory had always been one of his personal bugbears.

Bandi stepped in to ease the tension.

"Excuse me sir, can we therefore surmise that you have done all that you have done so that I, or any of the other Lords of Pangea, can just help you find Prometheus, and Project Ankh came about to try and resurrect any of the Lords?" asked Seth.

"Yes, that's right Bandi, I discovered, along with the help of many generations of the Russell family, that Prometheus is possibly the key to solving an age old predicament!"

"So, Project Commune was just used to fool the military?" asked Vincent.

"No, it was also used to nurture your incredible gifts, Vincent and to of course utilise the power of SPAFF," Mr White replied assuredly. He then mused openly before the group.

"I was trapped, like a man tortured by the beguiling soul of an unobtainable love. All I could do was sit and watch things play out from afar. If I had revealed myself, then centuries of hard work would have been wasted. All I could do was hope that fate would take command. It was all terribly frustrating.

"Beautifully romantic of you, sir," Albert gushed.

"Thank you Albert. By the way, I have seen more love than you could possibly imagine, but for now, let us deal with what is in hand and leave those stories for another day."

"I'll look forward to it, some quiet chats and a bit of gossip, super! I'll get some special cocoa in," Albert replied.

"That would be lovely, Albert, just you and me on the balcony, watching sunsets, philosophising and recounting tales from the past."

Albert let out a satisfying groan. Seth stepped in and interrupted the love in!

"So," he said throwing Albert a glare, "Peuja lied to us all and has known everything all along?"

"No, it was actually very difficult keeping everything that needed to be kept secret from her. She is a self-learning thinker after all. Therefore, she is absolved of any blame, ok?"

I'm a self-learning thinking lady!

"Sorry, yes, lady!" said Mr White, correcting himself so as not to offend Peuja.

"You see, when you were all overexposed to the liquid you call SPAFF, it was a staged accident. The Internet mind stuff, well, that was your doing not mine, a stroke of genius on your part, Vincent."

Vincent's expression couldn't hide his surprise at his actions being called a stroke of genius. He thought they were more like an act of desperation! Mr White continued.

"Project Bastet was already prepared for initiation, but I didn't know how to resurrect our Egyptian friend, without losing her and decades of arduous effort. It was Freak that accidentally gilded the lily and set the process in motion. Then, thankfully, the amazing intelligence of Seth, paired with Hannibal's great courage did the rest and made it as you see it. You all becoming as advanced as you are, simply helps us all. My first initiative, of creating a way to control the minds of humans, I thought would be enough, but I didn't expect my tools i.e. Yin and Yang to have such a vengeful, misanthropic, psychotic nature."

"Ah, now I see why they were chosen!"

"Yes Seth, they were my plan A, or was it plan B! I thought they could aid me in getting the human race to rally round and save the planet form environmental doom and stuff, but how wrong can one be?"

Maurice called all the creatures together; there was some muttering from the huddle and then they all dispersed and faced Mr White.

"I am very zorry but, we have zome queztions," said Maurice.

Mr White gesticulated to Maurice to continue.

"What haz the Nanteus Cup got to do with anything at all? It seems superfluouz to the quest?"

"This may be difficult to understand but Vincent's Great, Great, Great, there may be another Great and maybe a few more, I'm not sure, Grandfather was weaned from the 'cup,' as were all the Russell sons after that. As a young child he was given milk to drink from the 'cup' itself, and therefore, like all of you, generations later, Vincent is special, as was his father before him and his father's father and so on, right, back to when the Abbey of Glastonbury was ransacked."

There was another huddle.

Maurice re-emerged at the front of the group.

"OK, so Vincent'z Great etc, Granddad and hiz male descendantz uzed to drink milk from an old cup. Human children will put anything in their mouthz! What'z the point?"

"The point is this. Right then, all of you, open mind remember. I have to take you back in history again in order to move forward, is that alright with everyone? Is everyone keeping up?"

The group all nodded.

"Now then, Joseph of Arimathea was a wealthy merchant. He sailed to England in search of trade and eventually discovered just that, with the fruits of Cornwall and Somerset's tin industry. However, imagine this. As he and his men rowed into the garden of England on that typically bitter morn surrounded by a thick blanketing fog, they came upon an island, made of clay and sandstone boulders, that rose from the water like the back of a huge stone whale. Joseph climbed to its peak but found nothing except a thorn bush, nothing else. He surveyed his breathtaking surroundings and found himself unexplainably filled with peace, and so, he took out the cup that he'd brought with him, the one that he had used to collect the blood of his nephew, Jesus, and ventured deep, through a maze of caves, into the island's heart, to where he eventually came upon two streams. One was white in colour and one was red. He followed them to their point of origin, a beautiful, mysterious pool that shone like daylight, and there he placed and left the cup. After that he went on to build the first Christian church of St Mary's on the top of the great hill, to mark the land above where the path to the cup lay. The Island was called Avalon, but over hundreds of years the waters withdrew and the island became consumed by the countryside. Moss and grass now shroud the Tor, Tor being the geological name of the natural anomaly, and it has come to be known as Glastonbury Tor. Hundreds of years later Glastonbury Abbey was built near the location of the church, and it survived until the King plundered it for the Cup and its incredible powers."

There was another huddle until Maurice emerged once more.

"But the Cup wazn't at the Abbey, it waz beneath the Tor."

"Ah yes Maurice, but a series of clues were said to be littered around the Abbey delivering the position of the cup and the route through the labyrinth."

"And how did ze Nanteus Cup ezcape the plunder?"

"Well, Maurice, on hearing that the King's men were on their way to the Abbey, 35 monks were sent into the caves of the Tor to try and retrieve it. 31 never came out, three returned gibbering madmen and one, the one who succeeded in finding the cup, carried it to a trusted friend, the Lord of Nanteus Manor and swore him and his family to secrecy. It eventually came to be bequeathed to a gardener whose family, the Russell family, have had it in their safe keeping for many years."

There was another huddle, but this time everyone crossed his or her arms whilst Maurice faced Mr White and asked the question.

"How do you come to know all of this, who are you, and what do you mean, Vincent has a power?"

"As I have said, I have been a friend to Vincent's family for centuries, indeed, he walks this world because of my actions." There was a beat as everyone considered Mr White's statement. "It was I that dragged his mother from the wreckage of the burning family car and cut him from her belly."

Vincent bowed his head.

There was an awkward silence.

"Please don't look at me as if I'm a monster. Vincent's mother felt no pain, she had already passed away, as had his father, and Vincent truly does have a power. How do you think you made that leap from your balcony into the canal Vincent? Any normal human would have fallen to their death, broken on the cobblestones below."

"How do you know about that?" Vincent replied.

Mr White raised an eyebrow at Vincent and continued.

"You are fit without exercise, lean without caring for your diet, intelligent beyond the depth and understanding of others, courageous without the scars of battle and to top it all off…"

At that point Mr White raised his hand and, as he did, Maurice rose from the floor and hovered, turning this way and that, a metre or so in mid-air.

"…You have this gift Vincent, the ability to manipulate the liquid of life, the liquid you know as SPAFF, wherever it may be!"

"Err, floating toad, floating toad everyone!" Steve said laughing.

"This feelz intereztingly disturbing," said Maurice, none too impressed. "But anszwer the question, who are you and how do you have thiz power?" Mr White put Maurice down.

"You will all know soon enough," Mr White replied. "Now you try, Vincent, just concentrate on one of the guys and try and lift them."

Vincent looked at Steve and raised his hand; Steve cocked his head to one side, broke wind and began to giggle.

"Stop it, that tickles, stop it," he said.

"Well, it looks as if you're going to need a little practice, but hey, you have years ahead of you!" said Mr White.

***

In the magnificent lounge belonging to Arcadia, the relaxed atmosphere was interrupted by an unfamiliar sound, a crackling that was halfway between the rustling of an autumn leaf and the crushing of a snail underfoot. This was followed by a thud and an odd tapping sound. Jill and John were sat on the sofa watching a subtitled Costa Rican soap opera having a cuddle and thought little of it. They had grown accustomed to the many strange and unusual noises coming from their beautiful surroundings. A scampering gecko, a crane swooping in the wind, a screaming gull, a buzzing grasshopper grinding its back legs, all of these sensual sounds of nature added to the splendour that was Arcadia, but then John suddenly realised that he was listening to something he found to be a little disconcerting!

"Jill, can you hear anything?"

"No love, not a thing, peaceful isn't it?" she replied.

"Exactly darling, I can't hear a thing, nothing, just the ocean; its deadly quiet out there, something's not right."

They both turned slowly and looked out towards the garden

where the glass doors were wide open to the romance of the evening. It was truly serene, beautiful in fact, but then something peculiar happened. A tiny steel claw came through the open doorway and scratched the marble floor. Freak then entered slowly, damp and shimmering pink, covered from head to claw in the blood of some very recent slaughters. She walked straight towards the wincing, petrified, pair and leapt over them both, landing on top of the computer.

'Hello again friends,' appeared on the monitor. 'Please excuse my appearance I hadn't eaten for a while and I had a date with a sea spider to keep, which in-turn resulted in some building work in the garden and then a rat distracted me for a while, but not for too long, quick little Roger rodent, anyway down to business. I need you to do exactly as I say, or you will die! Do you understand me? Please, don't run, you don't have anywhere to go.'

Jill and John were frozen to the spot.

'The first thing I require you to do, lady, is stand up and walk over to the Terrapin aquarium and reach in and remove both specimens.'

Jill turned to look at the wall where Freak was once displayed, but all that remained in her place was the crispy, sticky, shed skin shell. Jill looked nervously at her husband, who returned her a supportive look.

'He will not help you. You will do as I say.'

Freak crouched and then leapt at John. He pushed his arms forward in a vain attempt to shove her back, however skilfully avoiding his parry, she turned in the air and, in a singular motion, sliced off the tip of his little finger on his left hand. It fell to the floor as she landed by his side. John screamed with pain as blood poured from the wound onto the white marble tiles.

"No, stop, I'll do whatever you say, please don't hurt him any more."

Jill was crying, shaking, mumbling and sweating all at once, never taking her eyes off Freak; she stepped towards Yin and Yang.

"She's reaching for I's, she's reaching, what a soft, weak *willed example of her species she really is. She, and her mate, will be I's weapons of destructi*on, and mine! No more Mr Nice Terrorpin. White will die and we shall rule this planet *on I's own terms. She has*

37

I, nice work I'm out, I's out, and they're out of their minds and we're in. Hahaha!"

John walked over to his wife and calmly slapped her around the face; she stared at him for a second and slapped him back. They both inquisitively looked at each other and then rubbed their cheeks, a quick glance at Freak followed and then, like automatons, they strolled back to the sofa and took a seat, attentively.

"*We have them,* now let's find White, put I before a computer that I may hack and sort legalities with these two. I also need to know, as do I, where that *jet landed and take it from there. Are you with I Freak, and I?"*

"After I let him watch the torture of his beloved friends, I am going to suck the fluid from his eyeballs," she replied.

"*Nice I like it, not too subtle but, I's get the picture, so I's can safely assume you're with I and I! Now that human is bleeding all over the floor."*

John stood up and walked over to the kitchen; he turned on the hot plate and waited a while. With his eyes dead of expression he placed his sliced finger down wound first, it sizzled. A smell of burning flesh filled the kitchen, but John didn't flinch, he merely returned to the lounge and opened a bottle of vodka from the bar, walked out into the garden and poured it over his hand, sterilising the wound. He said nothing through the entire process. He walked back to the sofa and sat beside his wife, he held up his finger, Jill wrapped it in a tissue from a nearby box sat on a side table and kissed it better. They faced front.

"Yin, you old romantic you. Hahaha! I's will give them a little room in their minds as I's progress!"

***

"Sorry Mr White, so what is Prometheus the key to?" asked Steve.

"Saving us all, saving us all," he replied.

"What do you mean by, saving us all?"

Mr White turned solemnly to Albert.

"Exactly as it sounds and you imagine Albert, exactly that! At midday on the 21st of December 2025 a light, as blinding as the surface of the sun, will burn a channel through the skies and a doorway to a new era will be opened."

"What, why, how?" asked Seth.

"Well Seth, when the wars of Gaia were over, it was decreed by Lord Zeus that Gaia shall remain devoid of destruction until a certain date, and life would be able to evolve and become self sustaining. But if humans had not advanced to a sufficient level, meaning in spirit, well being, technology and everything else, in order to serve Gaia, then the reset button would be pressed and the Titans would be authorized a sabbatical on the, frozen wastes!"

"How on Earth do you know that?" asked Bandi.

"It is known because of an object called the Mayan Calendar. It depicts the various ages of man. That is how we come to know the date of judgement day, the 21st of December 2025. It is believed that the world as we know it is to end on that day."

"No it is not. It was supposed to be the 21st of December 2012 anyway, and yes, it was well documented and if you require the constant medical services of a Witch Doctor and chase fairies around on Hogswollop's Eve, then you must have been a believer!" replied Seth infuriatingly disgruntled.

"Seth, everyone, forgets to add 13 years on to the 2012 date, 13 years for the 13 ages of man. Believe me on this day in the year of 2025 the Titans will return together with the big freeze, unless we intercede."

"Well documented, huh! Let me get this right Nostradamus, or is it Methuselah. Giant beings that are invisible to any normal eye, wearing earmuffs and mittens, are gonna try and kill us all on that day!" said a sarcastic Garston.

"Not exactly Garston. After Atlas, alters the axis of the planet, and it becomes an icy grave for nearly all of its inhabitants, the rest of the Titans will arrive and toy, persecute and systematically hunt for sport and maybe the odd edible tasty treat, the few species that still linger, which includes humans! Gaia's axis, in its realigned position, will then allow evolution to begin again; however, the direction it will take is, of course, a mystery."

"Oh well, that's alright then!" said Garston dryly. "So this Atlas bloke, who is obviously also invisible, really floats in space with the Earth on his shoulders then?"

Mr White allowed himself a chuckle.

"No Garston, it's a metaphor that man has adopted from a myth. The weight of the planet does indeed rest upon his shoulders, but Atlas is responsible for the axis of the planet from wherever he is in the universe, that's what that means. Since Zeus's army defeated the Titans long ago, the Titans have been banished, imprisoned or, put to work, remember. Only Zeus knows where they are. However you must know this, most are beyond taming! Now, back in the day, the Titans were few but now their number is unknown. I'm waffling, can I get back to it all?"

Everyone was quiet.

"Good! You see right now, humans, the most advanced race on the planet are behaving like a cancer that is spreading indiscriminately. We are slowly cloaking the planet, draining her of fossil fuels and oxygen, melting her ice caps and murdering her ozone layer. Humans are incapacitating and destroying her. This needs to be addressed, especially as she has given us alternative clean fuels in plentiful supply. The air we breathe, the water that covers 70 per cent of her surface and, of course, solar energy, could easily replace all forms of power. Sorry, I got a bit frustrated there, but I feel very passionately about it all. Anyway, back to business. What all of that means is, humans have not evolved sufficiently enough to stop the end game; in fact they are making it a certainty."

"What? How do we know that the calendar is right?" Garston asked, mystified.

Mr White turned to Garston with a look that said 'this is about to get even more complicated,'

"The Mayans also left us a mysterious artefact, one of a few dotted about by the way, but the Mayan example is exceptional, a Crystal Skull"

Everyone looked at each other and then back at Mr White.

"That's a bit random," said Garston.

"Now bear with me," Mr White replied. "The Mayan Crystal Skull, like all the other crystal skulls, is made from an unusual type of silicon quartz, very similar to that of a silicon microchip, it is beautifully crafted, but as yet, the information that it holds cannot be read by human technology. Now, there is absolutely no way that the Mayans could have crafted such an object with the tools and technology in their possession, nor anyone else at the time, for that matter, be they Incan, Minoan, Egyptian, Hun, Mandarin, Phoenician or Atlantean, no-one had that kind of knowledge. Therefore, we can surmise, that the Skulls are not of this world and we can come to the conclusion that they are of Godly origin and thus all the myths could be true."

"What about aliens?" Steve asked.

"It's Zeus' universe Steve, we just live in it. There may be other planets out there that contain life in other galaxies, but as yet close encounters of the third kind are purely television fiction."

"What about Area 51 and Roswell?" Seth asked.

"A complete fabrication by the American Government to hide something they don't understand."

"What is it?"

"Well, Vincent, I'm glad you ask. There are places around the world, one on each continent, that harbour points of great significance. Roswell hides one, as does Avalon."

"A pool that shines like daylight by any chance?" Garston interrupted.

"Yes, that's it Garston, a 'Pool of Light.' Humans have discovered the one that belongs to North America."

"Are they testing it?" asked Seth.

"They have tried, but all of the pools have exceptional defences. Only those permitted may enter. If you haven't guessed yet; from the pools, life flows. Every living thing on the planet comes from them, evolution pours from them and they are the birthplaces of existence. They are where Prometheus placed all the gifts of his heavenly toil."

There was silence; no one said a word, everyone just pondered Mr White's bold statement.

Albert, not one for a quiet room, was first to speak.

"That's really flaming incredible," he said.

Mr White replied.

"If we were having this chat around, oh, I don't know let me say, err, the year 1810 and I said that within 200 or so years man would reach the stars, land on the moon, be able to watch a box of moving pictures from a sofa and fly around the planet in a matter of hours from country to country in a steel wardrobe, and on top of that, I could prove that the entire planet used to be just one singular land mass, I bet you would have laughed at me or had me committed to an asylum for the insane. So, when the Mayans build a Calendar that has been damn well pretty accurate until now, and then provide us with a real artefact from the Gods, we should listen."

"And so this leads to what?" asked Seth.

"Avalon, Seth. We are all going to Avalon to return among some bits, the Nanteus Cup. And to visit an old friend, my tutor who, I dearly hope, can aid us in our noble quest and point us in the right direction. No one must ever be given access to the 'Cup's' power ever again."

"Why not just burn it?" asked Hannibal.

Mr White collapsed into raucous laughter.

"Oh Hannibal, you think that fire could destroy it? Bless you. No, trust me this is the better way."

"Why is it necessary we all go?" asked Seth.

"Because we are a team and I just thought that you might want to see the, 'Pool of Light'. It will prove that every morsel of information I have imparted is true."

There was a universal nodding of approval.

"So we hope this bloke Promotheosos, will help us?" asked Steve.

That's Bingo Ringo, and it's Prometheus luvvy!

"Or, as I have already said. I would have wasted an awful lot of time and money," Mr White said wryly.

"Crystal Skulls, Giant Eskimos, this is all just too weird, sir. I'm just a girl from Austria brought up by Roman Catholic nuns. I need to go and have a lie down!"

"You can use my bed if you need to," Vincent stopped mid-sentence, suddenly realising the unkemptness of his sleeping hole.

"Just give me a couple of minutes to tidy, dear!" Albert shot off and returned almost instantly. "It's sorted darling," he said, "I've put those magazines in my loft!"

"It's fine, Vincent; it was a figure of speech," said Faith giggling.

"But you're not just any chicatita from Austricaca pretty lady! You…"

"That's enough Escobar," Mr White interrupted, "I think it's time we all had some rest. Be ready to travel first thing in the morning, Vincent, and not by motorbike. Come to the Manor by 7am. It's fine, no-one apart from us, will be there. The building was cleared a little while ago," said Mr White, rising from the sofa and preparing to leave.

"You know about the Commando?" said Vincent.

"Why shouldn't I?" Mr White replied, "after all, the technology that infests its frame comes from the Manor's research, my Manor!"

"I knew something odd was going on at the house, Chief pointed it out to me last week." Seth gave Mr White a down the nose stare. "Mr White can I ask you a question?"

"Absolutely, Seth, anything!"

"Who then, selects the Lords of Pangea?" Seth asked.

"Lord Zeus," Mr White replied without hesitation.

"And the secret they all hold?" Hannibal asked.

"How would I know?" Mr White replied.

He then turned and walked out of the front door and down the path to the car to where his black suited and gloved drivers stood waiting. Spike and Escobar soon followed, Faith however, lingered a moment, gave Vincent a beguiling smile goodbye, and then joined her boss. The car pulled out of the drive and moved away like the menacing, sturdy, power assisted limpet it was. Albert shot out of the door and flew high into the sky. He watched the car purr its way through the countryside and eventually park up in front of the Manor house. He flew back down into the cottage via the chimney.

"Well, loves, it all seems to be real for now. Has anybody got anything to say, dears?"

"Yeah, Albert, make sure everyone does a little bit of research on the subject of Glastonbury, and turn the lights off when you're done, it looks like we've got an early start. I'm off to bed." Vincent scratched his head and had a satisfying yawn before venturing up the stairs to his bedroom to settle in for the night.

"Right everyone, teeth, a bit of swatting up and then bed, tomorrow is the first day of the rest of our lives," Albert ordered.

"It's all such a considered convoluted chasm of contemplation, a complex conundrum creatively conceived like a crooked caper by a cautious cad!" said Seth pondering.

"Seth, you're such an old philosophising show off!" said Bandi slinking up onto the sofa.

ECONOMICAL WITH THE TRUTH

The once stark rooms of Vincent's old apartment were no longer bare and it now encompassed the entire top floor of the Manor. Walls had been knocked through and the whole living space had been given a facelift to create a magnificent, lavish penthouse. Where once, bold Swedish lighting gave a modern feel to the barren decorative mantle, chandeliers, expensive works of art and opulence had become the name of day! Standing elegantly in the recess of the front bay window and resting on an exotic, deep pile, Persian rug was a glossy, black, Steinway grand piano. A walnut, Rennei Mackintosh, dining table accompanied by long-back, tactile suede upholstered chairs, glistened elegantly in the far corner, and the lustre of beautiful hardwood flooring ran seamlessly through all of the rooms. In the kitchen, made for a king, light reflected from dark, mineral enriched, speckled granite surfaces and five sumptuous bedrooms enhanced and entranced, all the nooks!

The two men dressed in black suits carried the bags in, whilst Spike and Escobar made themselves comfortable in front of a large fireplace that ignited at the touch of a button.

"Don't get too close Escobar," said Mr White taking a seat.

Clipboard Girl sat down at the table and dreamily stared at her surroundings. Her tummy rumbled, loud enough for everyone to hear. Mr White turned to the slighter of his two companions.

"Jonas, can you get into the kitchen and rustle us up something saucy? Bedivere, give him a hand, would you?" Mr White and the burly bearded man burst into laughter. "Never fails to amuse me that one," said Mr White.

Clipboard Girl did a double take; she had never heard Mr White call the two men by their names before. The small man tipped and took off his Trilby to reveal a scarred, balding, shaven head whilst the larger man turned to Mr White and spoke to him with the articulation and tone of a country gentleman.

"After we dine sir, should we leave you to err, explain?"

"Yes, that would be good of you, Bedivere."

Mr White turned to Clipboard Girl who was sat agog.

"Don't look so surprised, my dear, sitting there with your mouth open really doesn't suit you. There is still much for you to discover."

"Discover, I think I've discovered rather a lot this last week or so, sir," she replied.

Mr White thought some explaining was is order.

"Jonas is, of course, the slighter of the two men. He's a fantastic cook, amazing really. If he had his own restaurant it would have Michelin Stars plastered all over its front door. He doesn't speak much, not at all in fact, hasn't done for as long as I can remember. Bedivere is the muscle, they are both loyal friends and very special to me."

"Have they been around for as long as you have, sir, I mean are they as old as you are?"

"Faith, no, and yes, and no they are not, ish! We have all been exposed to the elixir of life and this is our calling."

Faith was a little confused by the answer, but had something a little more pressing she wanted to clear up.

"One more thing, sir."

"Yes Faith."

"Why is it that I can hear the animals talking?"

Mr White didn't stir at the question but answered it politely.

"It's the computer programmes that have been all around us, in the cottage, in the car, even back at Arcadia, that's all."

"But I could hear them on the beach."

Spike and Escobar perked up to the conversation but Mr White didn't stutter.

"It's just your mind playing tricks on you, that's all Faith. Now the third room on the left is yours, it has an ensuite, you can freshen up before we eat if you like."

"Yeah, you're probably right, I'll go get ready for supper, oh, and it's still Clipboard Girl to you, sir!" said Faith whilst grabbing a wheelie case and leaving the room smiling.

There was a momentary silence.

"That was a close shave Baroni."

"Don't I know it Escobar, I started to sweat, and you can stop laughing, Spike. It wasn't funny!"

***

"So they don't know I and I are in London, and there is no way of them finding out?"

"No Mr Yang," said Jill. "The magnetic pulse that you asked John to zap you with has disengaged the shore to shore locator that we found hidden deep within your microchip circuitry. The compass within is really not very well, sirs."

"I'm Mr Yin, that's Mr Yang idiot and you think I's don't know that, you biped freak!"

"Hey, watch it boys, these claws could slice through your shells as if you were soft Italian tomatoes. Anyway, I think they do a fabulous job for humans. In fact, when this is all over I think we ought to let them both live," said Freak.

"What, why?"

"Because we are going to need humans to transport us, feed you and generally deal with all things human, you can call it red tape if you like. I may just also have a little soft spot for them."

"My, my, the arachnid has a heart. Well, for your information *I's are not as merciless as you expect. I and I have already made plans, rather large plans, actually. These two servants of amphibian patronage have become very wealthy, very wealthy indeed. They are worth millions, and their new home is being built as we speak. Well, our home* is being built as we speak! Arcadia *is no longer the haven it once was and so, now on a secret island, between the land and the sea, a cliff face is being excavated that will be accessed from* the water. I's have also named our new abode but I's are keeping it all a surprise. Its magnificence will make Arcadia look like a garden shed; nonsuch has ever been built! Hahahaha! *The offspring of these two morons have too been informed of the tragic death of their parents and also have been left a substantial financial cushion."*

"But they are not dead!" Freak replied.

"You think I's don't know that! You are looking at John and Jill Tittytuft. I's have arranged their new identities and artistically recreated their ancestry, they are retired botanists who came into some *money, err, about 200 million dollars! You can thank the Russian underworld for their paperwork and some innovative thinking."*

"Good job boys thank you, thank you very much that was really decent of you, I shall put my claws away. So, what is going to happen to Arcadia and the White Mistress?"

"*I and I have followed the example of implausible sacrifices taken by man during the* conquests of man, specifically those of *the Emperor Nero."*

"Err, right so where is this Island?" Freak asked.

"*It wouldn't be much of a secret if you* were told of its position would *it? A surprise is something a little unexpected a bit like this Claridges hotel. The restaurant is supposed to have once been run by that television chef* gentleman with the exciting vocabulary, and thus it is acclaimed as a *glorious eatery. I and I thought our two ten toed skivvies could have a treat* whilst I's hack into the shore locator programme. The others *must have a computer mainframe* somewhere to run all of their business. *I's will use this to track and find them and eventually get them out of the way, so I's may rule the world. Hahha!"*

"Oh dear, the laughing is really back," said Freak dryly.

***

Bedivere walked into the lounge where Mr White was sitting quietly by the fire reading a glossy with Spike and Escobar.

"My Lord, sorry, Mr White, I was just having a look at the website greenslimestuff.com, just to make certain Yin and Yang were not up to anything, and well, I think you ought to have a look at this."

Bedivere handed Mr White a laptop.

The website had been replaced by a looping recorded feed. Mr White stared at the screen in silence.

"I'm sorry sir; I know you loved them both."

"It was only a matter of time until they became casualties of war, Bedivere," said Mr White speaking calmly in contrast to Bedivere's anguished tone. "This means they could be close. Confirm there were no casualties and," Mr White looked to both Spike and Escobar with love in his eyes, "make sure the boys get exactly what they want for dinner."

"Yes sir, I will."

Bedivere turned to the duo who were both a little excited by the news.

"What would you two like then? We have some nice fresh coriander, Spike, and a couple of slowworms if you fancy them, Escobar?"

"Oh, I haven't had coriander since forever, dude," Spike replied in a longing tone.

"Slow-worms would be a nice morsel. I hate snakes even though they are worms, or even small legless lizards, sorry Spike, but, they look like snakes and I really hate snakes. Disembowelling and eating them would be a delight, just make sure you leave the decapitating to me, my friend. Bring them on," said Escobar excitedly.

"Bedivere we will need the special cutlery and we will be departing in two hours! Time is of the essence. We have to travel tonight. We need a head start. If they've escaped and are tracking our movements we could be in trouble."

"Yes sir, dinner will be in 20 or so minutes."

"And Bedivere, I imagine the others will arrive as soon as we are done, so be prepared for anything." Bedivere left the room.

Mr White placed the laptop down on a side table and walked towards the drinks cabinet. He poured himself a glass of Johnny Walker Blue label and downed it, neat, in a single swallow. He quickly poured himself another and took a sip. Spike and Escobar were watching him closely. They had never seen him this apprehensive before. Faith walked into the lounge from her bedroom. She was in a pair of blue jeans, Ugg boots and a clean black shirt, she had put a little make up on and washed her hair, she looked beautiful. Her eyes caught the laptop's footage.

"What's that sir?"

She gasped and brought her hands to her face with the reality of what she was watching.

"It's Arcadia and the White Mistress they are…"

Mr White interrupted her.

"…Burning, Faith. To the ground and to the sea! It's a barbaric, draconian gesture on the part of Yin and Yang, but this is a war and their actions are exactly the same as mine would have been."

"But what about Mr and Mrs Jenkins," she asked.

"We don't know about them yet, Bedivere is trying to find out if there are any survivors at all. I'm, I'm very sorry."

Faith felt the horror of grief run through her, she bowed her head.

"This is terrible sir, I feel responsible. I dragged them into this," she said.

"Random events often create circumstances that are beyond our control, if it was not them then, it could have been anyone. It's the universe playing with us all. Ah, Jonas, that looks lovely."

Jonas walked through the lounge to the dining area with a large, crammed tray and placed the small feast, some of it still moving, on the table. He smiled and gestured at the food, expressing himself like a wonderful mime artist in a Parisian Street Market. He kissed his fingers and rubbed his stomach, noticeably delighted and proud at the result of his efforts. Mr White returned to the conversation he was having with Faith.

"You must not think the worst until the worst has happened Faith. Please, sit down and eat. We are leaving tonight and it may be a while before our next meal."

"Tonight sir, why are we leaving tonight? Do the others know?"

"Not yet, but they will and they will join us I'm sure, now sit, please," Mr White asked kindly.

"Spike, Escobar come join us. Jonas, please don't stand there on ceremony."

Escobar was looking at the laptop computer screen. "It was a beautiful garden Baroni," he said softly, "I have so many wonderful memories of our time in its splendour."

"There will be other Arcadia's and one day you will find the one that belongs to you. Come Escobar, Spike, sit either side of me. I will deal with Alcatraz personally when I get a spare moment. Come on everyone, this is a celebration. We are about to save the world!"

Bedivere returned.

"Sir, no bodies were found, but the Mistress was sunk out at sea. The news says they are presumed lost."

"Hmmm, clever, that means they may have our holiday winners," Mr White said thoughtfully. "How is the night?"

"Clear and the moon is full sir," replied Bedivere.

"Good, let's eat," Mr White said.

Everyone took a seat. Faith reached across the table and tucked into the sumptuous spread. Tearing bread, she shoved a wedge of cheese into her mouth, forgetting all of her convent manners. Mr

White tapped his glass with a spoon, coughed, and bowed his head. Faith stopped eating, plainly embarrassed. She surreptitiously spat an olive pip into a napkin and bowed her head, shamefully. Jonas stood at his chair and led a silent prayer. He closed his eyes for a minute or so and then clapped his hands, looked up with a bright smile and pointed to the food. He grabbed himself a knife slice of terrine and supper began.

The meal seemed to last forever with everyone just eating and daydreaming in their own little worlds. The table was void of conversation, a silent feast, people and creatures around a table eating, nothing more and nothing else, until Mr White broke the peace.

"Could you pass me the, special wine, please, Jonas?"

Jonas nodded and rose from the table, without question. He reached into his suit and pulled out a weighty gold chain from beneath his shirt that was laden with 24 gold keys. He walked to a nearby cupboard, which had a dozen heavy-duty locks and, as if he was running through a very well rehearsed routine, methodically, passed the keys through his fingers. Silently, he counted to himself, pausing every now and then to place a key in a specific lock and then turn it. The final lock released the door, it popped and hissed open with the sound of a collapsing vacuum. Using both hands, he tugged at the handle as hard as he could. Surprised by the fact that the door was made of solid steel, several inches thick, Faith watched him closely. Inside, stood a small dented, globe shaped glass and tin bottle with a red wax sealed top, it glowed suspiciously. Jonas, transfixed, lifted it cautiously and handed it to Mr White.

"Thank you Jonas. Bedivere, would you mind?"

"Not at all sir," he answered quietly.

Without finishing his meal or even taking another mouthful, Bedivere stood up and walked over to a painting on the wall and gently lifted it from its fastening, exposing a wall safe with several dials. Faith again watched inquisitively.

"Is that what I think it is?" she said pointing at the painting.

"A Monet, yes," answered Mr White.

Bedivere worked carefully, but within minutes had unlocked the safe. He looked inside and then gently pulled out a black velvet bundle. The cloth was obviously wrapped around something very important; it was 16 inches or so long, very slim and by the way it was being handled, extremely valuable and possibly alive!

"It's time for us all to go outside and salute the moon, with this," Mr White paused; his face told a story of wonder, "extraordinary little bottle of antiquated wine!"

He got up from the table and walked over to the bay, opened the large French doors to the world and stepped out onto the Manor's great balcony.

"Come join me, Jonas a broom and gloves please," he said.

Faith, Spike and Escobar stopped eating and joined Mr White. Jonas, meantime, opened another cupboard, this one, however, was tall and slim and without the puzzle of a dozen locks. It housed a dustpan and brush, a mop and bucket, a broom, an ironing board and some old gardening gloves.

"That will do," said Mr White handing Jonas the battered bottle, putting on the gloves and taking the broom.

"Bedivere would you pass that to me and could you and Jonas do the honours with the wine, oh, and bring a dish for the guys and the lead thimble shot glasses."

Bedivere handed him the bundle and walked out into another part of the apartment. Mr White discarded the broom's brush end and, with his expression a picture of concentration, gently placed the end of the broomstick into one end of the bundle, feeling his way like a photographer not wanting to overexpose a piece of film. The sudden sound of crunching, splitting wood raised an eyebrow and he drew his hand back sharply. Bedivere and Jonas soon returned to Mr White's side. Bedivere was holding a tray of four, tiny, ornately decorated and carved thimbles and Jonas a matching dish and the bottle of wax sealed wine.

"Faith, stand back a little would you? Pour then boys, we haven't got all night."

Jonas and Bedivere held their breath; they both appeared to be very apprehensive and a little concerned. Bedivere, hair draped over his face, blew at the oily strands and then, delicately, cut away the wax seal with a sharp pocketknife. Jonas then carefully poured the gloopy, ruby red wine into the four thimbles and a little in the accompanying dish. With great relief and a big puff, Bedivere re-corked the bottle, whilst Jonas took a red candle and cigar lighter from a pocket and proceeded to melt its wax to form a new seal before placing the bottle away in a larger pocket!

"Good lads, now do as I do," said Mr White, "but first Escobar, Spike, I need you to know that I love you both very much." Mr White placed the dish on the floor.

If a Kite and an Iguana could look a little bewildered, they did!

"Drink boys," he said, urging them on and looking skyward. "Take a look at the moon, Faith. It's beautiful isn't it? Zeus's golf ball hidden in the bunkers of the universe! To the moon," he said. "We salute you."

Mr White took a thimble and raised it to the luminescent ball of meteor-scarred rock looking down upon the world.

Jonas, Bedivere and Faith followed suit.

"To the moon!" they said toasting in unison.

Faith raised her thimble and went to take a drink, but before she could put the thimble to her lips, Bedivere grabbed her arm. She looked at him quizzically.

"Do as Mr White does, remember," he said, staring intently into her eyes.

Escobar and Spike had already taken a drink; they peered up from the dish.

Mr White let the black velvet cloth fall away from the broomstick he was holding. It revealed a rudimentary spearhead as dark as pitch, not forged from iron or carved from stone, but crafted from something else, something indefinable. It was clamped tightly around the end of the broom handle, grasping it with self-fixing teeth.

Mr White tossed his thimble over the balcony and looked towards Bedivere, Jonas and Faith, who did the same. Jonas then bent down and carefully picked up the metal dish and also threw it over the balustrade, taking due care and attention not to get any liquid on his hands. The dish bounced and rolled on the hard gravel surface until it came to a stop in the centre of a square that the four free rolling thimbles had magically formed.

"Why did we do that and what are those thimbles doing and what's that sir?" Faith asked.

"Oh this, well, this is the Lance of Longinus," Mr White answered reflectively.

"Sorry sir, I'm still none the wiser," Faith replied.

"It is the head of the lance that speared the side of Jesus Christ during the crucifixion."

"What! Really? Why did you have to do all of that nonsense with it covered up like that?"

"Well, with the addition of a staff, like a broomstick, it becomes a spear, well not just any spear, because it's an instrument that carries a curse, a curse that can blind you as well as kill you!"

"How do you know all of this stuff, sir?"

"I had a good teacher," he replied, much to Faith's dissatisfaction. "This lance head gave us all a new beginning; you may know it as, 'The Spear of Destiny.' It is the definitive taker of life, named after the centurion Longinus who performed the deed. As a reward for ending the suffering of Christ he was cured of Ophthalmia when Christ's blood dripped upon him."

Faith looked at him blankly, he explained further.

"Ophthalmia is a horrible eye swelling condition caused by a number of different kinds of trauma, it now lives within the lance!"

"Oh right, but why do you have the lance head, sir? Isn't it precious, what's it made from, shouldn't it be in a museum or something?"

"Or something, yes." Mr White replied, holding it aloft, casting a contemplative eye over its elementary form. "It's made from the black bones of the Gorgon Medusa, by her sisters Stheno and Euryale the daughters of the sea gods, Phorcys and Ceto."

"Medusa! Snake haired Medusa! Clash of the Titans, the story of Perseus chopping her head off, with one look I'll turn you into stone, Medusa?" Faith asked disbelievingly.

"Yes Faith, all of the above."

Faith was blown away, she didn't know whether to believe or laugh at Mr White's statement. "You may know this but, then again, you may not. You see Medusa was the only one of the three sisters that was mortal. She was cursed by Athena, Zeus's daughter, goddess of wisdom and valour, for well, now how do I put this, doing something very naughty with a certain Lord of the Sea in Athena's temple."

"Poseidon, Zeus's brother?"

"Yes Faith. Now this you definitely won't know! On hearing of their sister's death, Euryale bellowed a deafening cry whilst Stheno, taken by madness when the body of her sister was returned, ferociously tore the decapitated torso's remains apart with her deadly bronze claws, tusks, fangs and hair of serpents. She then took her sister's bones and had her hair of serpents, inject and infect them with their deadly venom. Then, together, the two sisters fashioned this, this magnificent, murderous lance head, so that one day, it would enact a dreadful revenge upon the family of Zeus."

"Could that little story be anymore gruesome?" Faith asked rhetorically and a little squeamishly.

"Probably not Faith!" Mr White answered smiling.

Bedivere gave a chuckle, Faith quickly flipped him a stare that shut him up!

"So, Poseidon and Medusa making bunnies?" said Faith.

"Oh yes," replied Mr White.

"Wow! And how come you have the lance?"

"Years and years of searching!" Mr White answered.

At that moment Jonas noticed the dish and four thimbles on the ground below begin to glow. He knocked his knuckles on the balustrade and gained everyone's attention. A deep rumbling began to fill the air and the Manor started to creak and groan and then it, and the earth all around, started to shudder. Faith grabbed hold of the stone balcony.

"What's happening now? What's going on?" she shouted.

***

Vincent ran down the cottage stairs, doing up the belt on his jeans and slipping on a t-shirt.

"What the fiddle is that? Is anyone else feeling that? Seth, Maurice!" he shouted.

Garston came through the fireplace entrance with Bandi.

"It seems to be an earthquake," said Garston

"An earthquake, this is Cheshire, for pity's sake, and they're only supposed to last a few seconds when they hit, this isn't the, 'Ring of Fire!'"

Steve and Hannibal also joined them through the fireplace.

"Where are Seth and Maurice? Where are they?" Vincent asked

anxiously.

Nobody answered, Vincent decided to take charge and ran to the front door, struggling to stay on his feet as the cottage shook around him.

"Everyone outside now, and stay away from any tall trees, get out into the open," he shouted above the din.

Hannibal ran back towards the fireplace, "I'm going for my bike," he said.

"Peuja, I need answers now. Where are Seth and Maurice? What? Hannibal don't you dare." Vincent called.

Too late, Hannibal was gone.

Seth is in the tunnels, Vincent. Trying to get the rabbits out in the event of a collapse. Maurice is...

She paused.

The epicentre seems to be the Manor House. Vincent something's happening over there.

"Send Albert up to have a look, quickly," Vincent replied.

He's already in the skies.

"Will you be alright?" he asked.

Just dig me out if anything happens. Now get going, get out!

Vincent ran out into the open and headed for the Manor.

Albert was flying around in circles; his self-guiding system had been affected by the incident, it was as if there had been some sort of shift in the earth's magnetic core.

"OK, ok, I'm getting dizzy, need to stop, stop, stop! Now, luv!" he called out.

***

Mr White turned to his entourage.

"Do not panic," he said, "just stay calm, it will all be over very shortly."

Then, in one sweeping movement, he turned and thrust the lance deep into Spike's side, piercing his shiny, leathery reptilian skin with ease. Spike slumped to the floor. Mr White recoiled, and without taking a beat, plunged the lance forward into Escobar's chest. His brilliant white-feathered plumage began to flow red with his own blood. He looked at Mr White with an expression filled with incomprehension, and then, collapsed to the floor beside Spike, who was lying motionless in a pool of his own blood. Jonas and Bedivere bent down and lifted them both gently. As the anger rose up inside of her, Faith, overcome with horror, hurled herself at Mr White. He calmly raised a hand and she became a living statue, rooted to the spot, held static by an invisible force.

"What have you done? They are your friends, let go of me, you're all pigs, let me go, let me go!" she screamed.

Mr White lowered his hand slowly and Faith fell to her knees, sobbing uncontrollably.

The winds all around began to wail and lightning filled the sky. Mr White looked to the heavens as all at once a torrent fell and a tumultuous tempest howled. He fought the buffeting and clambered up onto the stone balustrade.

"Are you ready, lads?" he shouted.

Bedivere nodded; in his hands he held Spike limp and lifeless, whilst Jonas, teary eyed, carried Escobar close to his chest. They climbed up and stood either side of Mr White.

"With me then," he said. "Time to take a leap of faith and let faith lead us to the future. To the moon!"

And with that call the three men took an almighty leap from the balcony into the thimble square some 20 to 30 or so feet below. As they landed, crouched safely, Mr White drove the lance through the centre of the metal dish and deep into the ground beneath.

"Time to run boys. Run!" he shouted above the din.

Jonas and Bedivere placed Escobar and Spike down upon the dirt gently and ran beyond the borders of the thimble-cornered square.

"Stay there, Faith and don't look directly at the light, stay back," Mr White called.

Faith, shivering with the wet and the cold, struggled to her feet as the ground below within the square of thimbles, twisted and buckled, broke and burst with a light that engulfed the shaft of the Lance. She squinted and shaded her eyes with an arm, as incredibly, Escobar began to rise ethereally into the air. With his head slumped to one side and his wings spread open to reveal their full, beautiful, extended glory a sphere of white pulsating electrical strands fizzed, crackled and encircled him before erupting into a blue ball of flame.

"Well done Escobar. Now come on Spike," Mr White said

hopefully. "Come on, don't let me down, boy, I know you can do it."

***

Project Ankh active, subject Karura stable.

As the Christmas tree lights illuminating Camelot unnervingly flickered and dimmed, Maurice hopped as fast as he could through the tunnels to level 5 and Sinatra, dodging dirt and crashing, falling tiles and a few terrified bunnies scampering for the surface!

"Zinatra, Zinatra are you there?" He called, upon reaching level 5's hole in the wall entrance.

'Help I need somebody, help not just anybody,' the words of the iconic Beatles song filled the void. With his blue eyes flashing madly, Sinatra zoomed to beneath the hole in the wall, skidding to a screeching halt.

"Zinatra ride up my tongue."

Maurice flicked out his tongue, widening it as much as he could and with a slimy resounding slap, it stuck fast to level 5's floor some 10 feet below. Sinatra steadied himself, popped out a pair of arms, like a tightrope walker would for balance, and then buzzed right up, landing unceremoniously face down beside Maurice in the tunnel.

"Don't move Maurice," said a familiar voice.

Hannibal then flew past Maurice and Sinatra on his Monkey Bike like a stunt rider jumping London buses.

"Thanks Maurice, see you on the surface. I hope we can all fit through that fireplace!" he called, turning his head and waving as he shot into the distance.

Maurice's tongue darted back into his mouth. "Fluwblub, blim! I thesd folowglow dim! zorry, it takes a while to get the tongue back to normal! I said, follow him!"

Three tiny wheels popped out of Sinatra's body, two from the end of a couple of extended arms and the third from his cone shaped head.

"Nice," said Maurice, "any chance of a ride?"

Maurice jumped onto Sinatra's back or was it his front, well it could have been his side, and held on tight with his sucker feet for dear life. Sinatra turned on the Radio, 'I want to break free, I want to break freeee' and 'whoosh,' he and his toad jockey sped through

Camelot.

***

"*Tittytuft male; I and I need a limousine, something* that won't get stopped for any ridiculous reason by any overanxious constabularies due to the fact that you are *driving 3 miles per hour above* a stupid speed limit at silly o'clock. Something with a bit of *zip to it, you know comfortable, plush,* use your own judgement, oh, and it must be able to hold and hide *Freak, in* all of her spaniel sized glory, from the gaze of speculative, prying eyes! You will also need some *weapons*! *We'll stop at something called the Motorway Services as we exit London and pick up a couple of shotguns and a veritable goliath load of* ammunition from our Russian friends! I may shoot ourselves a rabbit! H*aha*ha. *You will* be driving *us all back to where this began. It seems* that the area *surrounding the Manor* house is still the home of Seth and his friends, *and if they are there,* then White is there."

"How did you manage to find that out?"

"*Well, creepy Freaky, I and I* hacked into a computer that is still *functioning at the house* and had a look at the shore to shore locators."

"Do they know I am here, in England?"

"*Your locator has been* disabled, I and I like the element of surpr*ise to be in I's favour. So, Tittytuft male, get out there and buy our Limousine. Oh, and how was your meal, did* you choke at all? Hah*a*ha. Is that craggy, wretched faced, cook's food *good enough to eat, or is it* akin to that last bit of *stagnated algae you get stuck in* your teeth for a couple of weeks after a turtle dinner party?"

"Sirs it's very late, I can't buy a car now, everywhere is closed. Can I do it first thing in the morning? And the food was very nice, thanks."

"*The food was very nice,* thanks" Yin and Yang mimicked sarcastically. "*You'll do it now, you s*ycophantic cretin! *Or you'll be swimming the Thames looking for the limbs of your spouse!*"

***

From the air, Albert could see his friends running across the rain sodden fields towards the Manor. They formed the shape of an arrow with Hannibal out in front zooming along on his Monkey Bike. He could also see the colourful, blinding, thunderous commotion happening on the Manor drive. He thought that, if he just stopped flapping and perhaps just dropped to the ground, he just may live, and then maybe he could just hop over! Then he thought perhaps a glided landing would probably be a better idea! Albert closed his eyes and suddenly felt his directional compass revive itself. From the stores of his memory he calculated his speed and trajectory against distance and altitude and then, like an aeroplane on a remote flight code, prayed that his sums were right. Needless to say he clattered to the ground and rolled to a stop in front of Mr White! He rose to his feet more than a little dazed.

"Oi! White," he said regaining his composure and pecking at an ankle, "what you up to? And who's on fire and…oh my lord you've killed Spike, his blood, it's seeping down those cracks, which means, that it must be Escobar on fire. If you and your two bullies are here and little darling Faith is up there, you absolute…"

"Now hold on Albert, sometimes you've just got to leave it all to the Gods!"

"Oh yeah, well you're not getting away with it, my old chestnut!" Albert replied once again, tapping at an ankle.

At that point Hannibal skidded to a halt and jumped off his bike.

"Hannibal," just in time," said Mr White. "What can you remember?" he asked.

"About what?" Hannibal replied.

"About Whiro, what am I missing? Look it's not working and there's only a little time left."

Hannibal looked at him blankly and then turned to Albert.

"If you know something that can help Hannibal, say it, or do it, before I really loose my temper and become malicious vermin!" Albert shouted angrily.

"Albert's right Hannibal, now is the time," Mr White reiterated.

Hannibal turned and looked at the thimble square and considered his next move carefully. Within its boundary, steam and electrical charges were dancing and exploding from the cracks in the earth. He took a deep breath, gave Mr White and Albert a salute, and then, he ran in and jumped into the middle of the mayhem.

"Watch out for the flame ball, luv," Albert shouted above the din.

Hannibal reached down into a crevice and felt around for something. "Got it!" he said.

'Bang!'

A bolt of lightning thrown from Escobar's nearby ball of flame struck his back. Hannibal winced with pain, but held fast.

"Ooh, that's gonna smart," said Albert.

The little monkey tugged at his prize. Leaning back for greater leverage, he strained with all his might, until suddenly he fell backwards onto his bottom holding aloft the Lance of Longinus.

"What on Earth? Said Albert."

Attached to the end of the spear was another blue ball of flame.

He stood up and stabbed the earth with the shaft end, planting it like a blue flaming Lollypop!

"Well done, Hannibal," said Mr White.

At that moment Vincent, Steve, Bandi, Garston and Maurice, still riding Sinatra, pulled up.

"What's going on?" asked Vincent, hot, wet and breathless, "And what's all that stuff on the ground and that stick?"

"You'll find out soon enough." Mr White replied.

"He's killed them all, Vincent, I saw him," Faith shouted from the balcony. "He's gone mad, look."

Vincent turned to Mr White who returned him an exasperated look.

"What can I say to that, other than, I haven't exactly killed anyone, have I? They are there in those balls of flame aren't they? She's prone to being a little dramatic I reckon!" he said.

Hannibal shifted over to Spike and carefully picked him up in his arms.

"Whiro," he whispered quietly, "it's time for you to wake from your slumber!" He gingerly walked back to the centre of the square and raised Spike high above his head. The ground beneath his feet began to warp and form a wide, deep fiery crevasse. He looked to the heavens and then at Spike.

"Hades," he called, "it's time for your prince to rise!" and then he cried, "Oolaballuh!" and with a shrieking scream, leapt bravely into the splitting earth, disappearing from sight. The two balls of flame that remained hovered luminescent side by side. The broomstick shaft belonging to the lance had long gone, burnt to flighty embers that were now dancing in the blustering winds.

"Where's Hannibal gone, what's he up to?" asked Garston.

Mr White returned him a shrug.

The rain suddenly ceased and the fierce winds abated. The ground appeared to reset itself as if nothing at all had happened and a deathly silence fell all around.

"Everyone," said Mr White whispering, "I suggest it's time for us to back away a little. Have you ever heard the expression, the calm before the storm?"

"Yes," replied Vincent.

"Well, that is the calm!"

The ground in front them creaked and split once more, but then, strangely, started to behave as if it were liquid, spinning and churning until it reached such a speed that it became a whirling vortex. Everyone just stared in wonder, as, from its heart, another ball of flame rose slowly into the air. It was substantially brighter and larger than the others and burned with twice the ferocity.

"Whiro! It's worked. It's all worked. Vincent, this is fantastic. You're about to witness something really quite extraordinary." said Mr White.

"You mean all of this isn't?" Vincent replied dryly.

"You are about to see the birth of three Gods," said Mr White.

"Been there done that," said Garston.

"Zo who have we got then, and where is Zeth?" asked Maurice.

All of a sudden, without warning, Escobar's blue flaming sphere ruptured into the moonlight. The crowd looking on, all momentarily forced to avert their gaze, were eventually able to readjust their eyes to the night and take a sneaky peek. However, to their astonishment an incredible, intimidating sight now faced them. Escobar had transformed! He stood gleaming, some 6 foot tall, pale green, crested and magnificent before them, with both human and bird characteristics His eyes were like radiant rubies enclosed in a ring of green emeralds and his beak had become a deadly, formidable weapon. His claws were something akin to feet and he had two powerful arms with long fingered hands and razor-sharp black nails. He strode forward, opening and fluttering an impressive set of wings formed of glorious shades of gold and brown that adorned a sign of Ankh at the centre of each feathered curtain.

"Karura," said Mr White, falling to his knees, head bowed, "I am your servant."

Karura looked down, and raised his crest before speaking in a soothing tone.

"Rise," he said.

Mr White got to his feet sheepishly.

"Have no fear, you have returned me to this world with actions of an honest heart."

Mr White nodded thankfully in silence, whilst everyone else just stood completely stunned. Karura turned to the group, beat his wings and rose into the air. Soaring high into the night, he let out a shrill call as his moon-cast shadow swept and climbed with the intermittent thermals. On his return back down to earth he amazingly, in a pulse of piercing light, changed to the form of Escobar.

"Showoff!" said Albert, a little envious.

Escobar glided in and landed on Mr White's shoulder, still displaying the sign of Ankh on his plumage!

"I am still Escobar, baroni's, your friend, but I am also Karura, the bird of life, mortal enemy of the dragon, Lord of Asia and Pangea. Within me lies the spirit of all birds, for each of them was born from me."

Tearfully, but full of joy, Albert flew up to Escobar and wrapped his wings around him with a big hug.

"Dad!" he said, overwhelmed.

Everyone had a brief chuckle

"Very funny, now get off me before you end up in a pie!" said Escobar.

Albert haughtily did as he was told and hopped back down to the ground, before another unexpected blinding flash forced everyone to cower.

"Whoa! Who we got now?" Steve asked excitedly, as if it were Christmas morning.

"This is just too weird," responded Garston, "and where are Hannibal and Seth?"

"Open your eyes," replied Mr White. "Seth is already with us."

The blue ball of flame that Hannibal had previously turned into a lollipop had vanished and all that remained beneath its once hypnotic glow was the smouldering head of the Lance of Longinus resting upon the gravel.

"Where? I can't see him," said Vincent.

"Oh, I am here Vincent, but not as you know me. Not as any of you know me."

"Is that Seth, but with a sore throat?" asked Steve.

Everyone turned to look behind, as that's where the gruff voice seemed to have come from. A gust of wind passed them by, but again, nothing was there.

"I am Tecciztecatl and I am Seth."

"Everyone bow please," said Mr White, "Tecci is extremely shy. There has never been, or probably ever will be again, such a beast to compare with what you are about to see."

"He speaks the truth, although, I am not bashful. I hide myself so as not to frighten you. Please remember I am your friend. Do not be afraid of me."

"Oh come on Seth, it can't be all that bad, you're just a rabbit for heavens sake."

"No Vincent, I am more then just a rabbit!"

And with that sentence another gust blew, and the strangest creature that once used to be just a fluffy bunny appeared in front them!

"Oh bonio, what is it? Seth, you're massive and your teeth are... and you have..."

Before Steve could finish, Mr White began to walk towards the newcomer, eulogising effusively!

"...The silky satin white wings of a butterfly, furnished with the sign of Ankh in shades of ghostly grey. Magnificent, muscular forearms whose gnarled, hardened, sharpened claws give you the ability to dig through even the toughest of granites. Great extended ears that allow you to hear the songs of the sirens from wherever you may be, and, of course, the marvels that are an armoured external spine and ribcage, which are formed to be as strong as the pillars of Hercules. They round off at your powerful rear haunches giving you the appearance, when seated, of a winged, long eared, giant snail like creature. You are a wonder, a moon god, Aztec in origin with the ability to fly at the speed of light. You are Lord of South America and Pangea. Tecciztecatl may I call you Tecci?"

"I prefer Lord Tecci."

"Sorry, Lord Tecci," replied Mr White. "Welcome!"

"Thank you Mr White," said the elephant sized beast, "I am sorry I lied to you all about my Peuja scan. I admit I didn't actually have one, I was too fearful regarding the consequences." He paused. "I was afraid, please accept my apologies."

Tecci shamefully bowed his head and in a flash of light returned to his Seth rabbit form, however, the sign of Ankh still remained, branded on his bushy tail.

"Seth, it's only natural to be afraid of the unknown. It's animal nature."

"Well said Vincent, very well said, very wise. Now, I don't quite know what to expect with this final character, but I can't wait to find out. I mean Tecci was relatively easy to find because of Seth's royal ancestry, once I had worked out the Aztec thing, I'll expand on that later, but this guy!" Mr White said excitedly. "Ooh, look, something's happening."

The ground beneath the last remaining ball of flame began to return to its normal state, and as it finally became nothing more than a plain gravel driveway, the sphere above it exploded into a million flecks of light, sending everyone diving for cover. A cold chill filled the air. The group rose to receive their remaining guest, but found they were standing in front of and eerie, mysterious mist. Steve, who was the first to his paws, brushed himself down and looked up. Immediately, he sensed danger and let out a bark as the hairs on the back of his neck stood up on end. A growling screech bellowed from the centre of the mist, everyone took a pace back.

Faith, looked down through the fog from her vantage point on the balcony. A massive fearsome shadow slinked within.

"Run," she screamed, "run!"

Like a rampaging prehistoric force of nature, Spike fearlessly burst into the open. The crowd all around momentarily froze, except Steve that is, who broke wind and rolled onto his back in submission.

"Run," called Mr White panicking, already some distance away!

Most of the group decided to take his advice and follow suit, all except, Seth, Escobar and of course Bandi, who until this point had remained silent and thoughtful throughout.

Spike was obviously no longer a normal iguana. He was the size of a whale, ornamented with Maori swirling tribal markings from head to tail. Where he stood, drooling and salivating, growling and shaking his head in anger at the world, a frost bleached the landscape. Cloudy, icy breath seeped from his mouth, whilst his puce tongue flicked back and forth tasting the air. With a barnacled and scarred hide as tough as steel and the colour of the night sky, and the sign of Ankh blazed down his muzzle between his large black eyes, he let out an immense roar.

"Whiro, now stop that! You're frightening everyone," said Bandi, firmly.

With a voice deep enough to carve the atmosphere, Whiro spoke.

"Hey, guys, stop running, I'm only messing with ya'll!" he said chuckling.

With a flash of light, everyone turned to see their old friend Spike still branded with the sign of Ankh between his eyes, standing on the drive.

"Oh, Spike, you nearly gave me a heart attack darling!"

"Me too, Albert," said Maurice, laughing with relief.

"It's ok guys, I'm still Spike although I also happen to be, you know, Whiro, the Maori Lord of the dead, Lord of Australasia and, of course, Pangea, blah blah, blah!

"Well, on behalf of everyone," said Mr White, jogging back from some distance away, "I welcome you too. Shall we get going then?" he said rubbing his hands together. "Avalon anyone?"

"How are we getting there?" said a familiar voice walking out of the front door of the Manor.

"Hannibal, how did you get in there?" asked a delighted Steve bounding over the drive up to his old mate.

"Chief, of course. Sorry Mr White, there's a couple of floor tiles up in the downstairs toilet and you might want to have a look at the drains!"

"That's fine, Hannibal, and well done," said Mr White as Hannibal took a bow.

"Bedivere, Jonas, bolt the roof rack onto the Mitsubishi Warrior would you? Karura will need something to hold on to as we are carried to Shepton Mallet."

"Already done sir," Bedivere replied.

"Oh, sorry everyone, this is Bedivere and that's Jonas. You've met them before haven't you Vincent?"

"Yes they threw me into a car once!" Vincent replied a little embarrassed.

Bedivere chuckled.

"Where are we going now?" asked Faith, walking out onto the drive in a strop. "Can't we just get there and get this, whatever it is, over with?"

"Yes Faith, that's the idea. We're off to Shepton Mallet, a 3000-year-old market town in Somerset that is steeped in history; it's not far from Glastonbury and the Tor. It has a secluded showground; by showground I mean a place where people show prize pigs and that sort of thing, anyway, it is not being used at present, so we can land there unnoticed and drive the rest of the way. It's about a 20 minute journey."

"Sorry sir, but what's a Mitsubishi Warrior? It's not some kind of ancient Japanese Sumo Wrestler, is it?"

"It's a truck Steve," said Vincent, "a lovely 4x4, a nice bit of kit; it's like a subdued, road-legal Monster Truck. But I don't think a roof rack will hold the weight."

"It's already been modified young sir," said Bedivere. "No need to worry, it's bolted to the chassis. Back in a bit."

Bedivere trundled off.

"Albert will guide you Escobar. Now, by my calculations, to carry all of us and the truck, I think a 12 foot Karura should be adequate," said Mr White. He turned to Jonas. "Jonas would you grab the thimbles, dish and velvet wrap and bring the head of the Lance please."

"Grab what?" asked Vincent, being ignored.

Jonas nodded and ran into the house.

"Zo can Karura be any size he wantz to be?" asked Maurice.

"Only to about 16 feet, I would say, but legend says 40, that's just a load of nonsense though, Chinese Whispers. Apparently he can breathe fire and block out the sun, too!" Mr White laughed at the ridiculousness of his statement.

"Hey, I am here you know. I would like to be included in the conversation if it's about me, ok, and yes, about 16 feet, and I don't like you using the word, nonsense, when chitter chattering about me!" said Escobar, frowning and a little disgruntled.

At that point Bedivere came wheel-spinning around the corner in a big black four by four with tinted windows, a double cab and covered flatbed.

"Right everyone, ready then, let's all pile in. I estimate the flight to be an hour or so," said Mr White.

He climbed into the front passenger seat leaving Vincent and Faith to jump into the back of the cab. The rest of the group made themselves comfortable on the carpet of the covered cabs flatbed. They all said their goodbyes to Chief and the rabbits, who had gathered in numbers, and sat back. Jonas was the last to jump in after locking up the Manor house, setting the alarms and miming Chief instructions. He climbed into the back with a tatty leather satchel and sat cross-legged. A shadow of a giant crested bird of prey soon cast its blanket over the moonlit drive and before the passengers could say, "what's the movie on this flight," the truck rose into the air. Hannibal looked nervously out of the back. His breath steamed up the rear windscreen. He could see Sinatra with Chief and his team getting smaller in the distance as they pushed his precious Monkey Bike back to the cottage.

"Wow, this is trippy. How you doing Steve?" Hannibal asked.

Steve looked up and then promptly enquired if there were any of those sick bags about!

THE TRUTH HURTS

In the early hours of the morning, the Tittytufts returned to their hotel suite at Claridges, after a strange couple of hours shopping for a limo!

"What is this splendid wooden box that you carry and why all of the costume regalia."

"This, sirs, is a coffin, one that has been handcrafted for a child and our clothes are undertaker uniforms. Do you like the traditional top hats?"

"Mrs Tittytuft, is tomorrow to be a fancy dress day and the day you swim the Thames without any arms and legs or, the day we finally become the greatest creatures *on the planet? What on this rock are you up to, you pathetic woman?"*

Jill slid behind her husband who further explained.

"Apologies sirs, I think my wife means, these are our disguises! We also have a very comfortable car, a hearse, waiting for us in the hotel car park. It's fitted out with all kinds of luxuries and is very powerful, too. It's the perfect vehicle for not getting stopped in! It is a driving shadow and it was the only thing we could find."

Yin and Yang turned to look at each other.

"FREAK!"

John spoke nervously, faster and faster until he found himself babbling.

"This coffin is for Freak to travel in. We've also drilled some air holes in it, added a pillow and there's even a rat thrown in for the journey. She'll be very comfortable and won't get bored. We've even bought a floral tribute that spells out the word, 'love' for displaying in the rear. It will tug at the heartstrings of humans, whatever nationality they are. All the guns and stuff will be kept beneath the flowers, hidden away. We've tried everything." John fell to his knees begging. "Please, don't rip my wife's arms off!"

"Oh get up moron, stop whinging. Very nice Mr Tittytuft and where do we sit in all of this?"

John chose his words carefully.

"Well, if you would forgive me for saying so, you do both look very much like automotive air fresheners."

"*What exactly are you alluding to?*"

Jill answered for her husband.

"The ones that sit up on the dashboard. You know, the ones people keep up front that smell nice, made by a company called turtle wax! You can see everything from there."

Freak started to giggle, but a glaring stare from Yin and Yang soon stopped that.

"*Well, if we have to be turtle shaped air fresheners for one day* in order to rule the *world for eternity then so it must be. At least I and I are not in a coffin!*"

Jill's mobile phone buzzed, she reached into her pocket and pulled it out.

"Sirs, your friends are no longer in Cheshire. They are somewhere near Stonehenge according to the locator programme."

"*How far is that from where we are now, Mr Tittytuft?*"

"Two and a half or so hours, sirs, give or take ten minutes," John answered.

"Then let's be off and don't knock the coffin gents, when that rat is dead this is going to be a fortress of solitude. So wake me when we get there. Would you mind popping it open for me? Shall we go, this is exciting?" said Freak.

Jill and John opened the coffin for Freak and then closed the lid sharply and sat on it as soon as she was inside. There was some scratching and bumping and then a noise like the last slurp of a milkshake through a straw and then, quiet!

"*Tittytufts*, check us out of this establishment that I's may pursue this pursuit*! I and* I will notify *our Russian friends regarding our pick up. Grab the technical* accoutrements we require, hand them to *the bell boy, put us in your jacket pockets and let us abscond this grandiose hostel of grandeur and* execute some old friends, Hahaaha!"

***

After flying a fair distance through the night with 'Air Karura' to Shepton Mallet, bypassing the pretty little town and landing in a quiet B road behind the showground, Escobar transformed to his Kite self and popped into the front of the Warrior and sat on Mr White's lap for the drive to Glastonbury Tor. There was little chatter during the remainder of the journey, just Steve asking, "Are we there yet?" a good number of times!

"This will do Bedivere, just park up over there behind those trees and leave the keys underneath the rear wheel arch would you?" said Mr White.

Bedivere did as he was ordered and parked up. Jonas jumped out and opened the tailgate. Everyone hopped out and took a look around.

"Look how the moonlight and creeping mist strike the ruins of St Michael's Tower at the top of the Tor. It's beautiful and so romantic isn't it, Vincent?" said Faith.

Indeed, the view of the gothic, architectural marvel, standing where the first Christian church of St Mary's had once stood, was incredible. To his surprise, Faith linked arms with Vincent and snuggled up. Bedivere gave him a smirk.

"The size of the Tor is actually really quite deceptive. We are still some distance away," said Mr White as he turned to the group. "We still have to walk over the fens and across the meadow to get there. Now please, I don't want to see any Gods until we are inside, is everybody clear? Even though many of you were once worshipped as ethereal beings from the minds of men, no one on the planet has ever seen an actual walking, talking deity, got it?"

Everyone nodded.

"How did we die?" asked Seth.

"Sorry?" replied Mr White, a little taken aback by the question.

"As Gods, how did we die? Are Gods not immortal?"

"Yes, yes they are Seth, but you are mortal in your animal form."

Everyone looked a little puzzled.

"OK then, if this has to happen here, then here it shall." Mr White tried to explain. "You were once all worshipped by early man, but when the sins of man became prevalent in society you were all soon forgotten and man began to worship Gods in his own image! However, once the belief in you died, the beings that you were, were lost to time. It was only those with a hankering for theological curiosity that spread the stories of your existence and blatantly, these have been watered down from generation to generation. You see, the spirit of the Gods, you are, has been hidden within your individual species, for thousands of years, passing through evolution like an ant marching tirelessly through flowing fields of grass."

"So the Gods were in us all the time, but just needed waking up!" said Spike.

"Correct Spike," Mr White replied.

"Does that mean I will be a special God, too?"

"I'm afraid not, Steve," replied Mr White kneeling and giving the little dog a stroke. "Each of you were selected, bred and genealogically pasted together, to give the greater likelihood of your return."

"So the rest of us, are quite normal."

"Normal Steve, normal! You are all far from normal, look at you."

Steve lowered his head.

"Don't be despondent about it all, little buddy, you all have a little of someone else within you!"

"Really, so who do I have in me?" asked Steve with his head up and ears pricked!

Mr White smiled broadly.

"Steve, you have within you the bloodline of a great dog, and you, Albert, a great pigeon and you Maurice, a great toad."

"What about me?"

"Garston, you're different. You, now don't be disillusioned, are a gerbil plain and not so simple!"

"Yes and...?" said Garston.

Mr White shrugged and smiled.

"Err, with a bionic tail!" he replied.

"Ruddy typical!" Garston replied disgruntled.

"So who's the great dog then, hey, hey?" asked the excited Steve.

"I'll tell you all once we get there, now we must get moving. We haven't got that much time until daybreak."

The group accepted Mr White's logic and trundled over the fen and through the meadow until they reached the foot of the Tor.

"Right, wait here," said Mr White turning to everyone. The group looked at him quizzically, but let him get on. He walked off towards a small rock poking out of the grass and knelt down by its side, he stroked it gently. The name Arturo magically glowed vibrantly within its mineral encrusted form.

"See you in a while old friend," he said quietly. He then turned to the patiently watching and waiting group. "Come on everyone, quickly, we have to get to the tower," he called.

The steep incline of the Tor stood ominously before them, but everyone strode up the slope purposefully without taking a break. As they neared the top and the ancient stone tower, a chill filled the air.

"Now, don't be alarmed, just follow me," said Mr White walking towards the tower's weather worn arched entrance.

"Stop right there," said Hannibal jumping in front of him and halting him in his tracks. "I'm not following you anymore!" he said, "not until you tell me who I am!"

"Yes, me too," said Steve standing firm, joining his buddy.

"And me," said Albert landing by their side.

"Yez me too," said Maurice hopping forward.

"Yes, and I want to know how Hannibal always knows what to do?" asked Steve.

Mr White looked down at them and then puffed out his cheeks in frustration towards the skies.

"OK, ok!" he answered.

The four friends stood in a line in front of the man in white. He addressed Albert first.

"Albert, you have within you the bloodline of the 'dove of peace, the Minoan dove!' It has appeared throughout history and mythology, time and time again. A messenger, a herald of hope, the wise, selfless bird that fooled the great Clashing Rocks and aided Jason and his Argonauts in their quest, and let's not forget that clever episode with Noah and the olive branch. The fact that you appear and guide saints, humans and Gods when hope and strength are needed is a testament to you and your species."

"Oh, love, I think I may cry, I've always felt special, different," Albert said sniffing. "But, I'm a pigeon, not a dove," he quickly realised.

"Oh um, yes, well, all of the above was actually carried out by a pigeon! Yes, hard to believe isn't it, but it's all been embellished over the years by romanticising writers who believe doves are more aesthetically pleasing to the eye, than pigeons!"

"How dare they!" said a horrified Albert.

Mr White hurriedly continued!

"Maurice," said Mr White quickly changing tact.

"Yez!"

"Within you is the DNA of Chan Chu, the money toad! In Chinese mythology you bring prosperity and wealth to those you reside with. You are usually depicted as having only three legs and your ugliness and secreting poisons are said to drive away evil. You are the perfect house mate for Vincent and the others in this fortune grabbing world."

"Did he juzt call me ugly? I am ze love toad!" said Maurice.

"Yes, you are baby and don't you ever believe otherwise," said Albert.

"Me now, me, me, me!"

Steve was jumping up and down and dribbling saliva.

"Hannibal," said Mr White turning to the little monkey.

"Fiddlesticks, I thought it was my turn," said Steve.

"Would you mind?" Mr White asked.

"Would I mind what? Hannibal replied.

"Haven't you worked it all out yet?"

"Obviously not!" Hannibal again replied. "Would you mind filling in the blanks?" he asked.

"Hannibal," he said looking into the little monkey's eyes, "within you lies something very special. You are, of course, a Lord of Pangea."

A gasp ran through the group.

"I am," he replied flabbergasted.

"And, Lord of the subcontinent of India," said Mr White.

"Wow, that's cool, that explains why I love Mangos and a good curry, so much!" replied Hannibal.

"You are studious, knowledgeable, a leader of men, brave beyond your stature and a scourge to all that is evil. You, my little furry friend, are the Hindu God, Hanuman, who was once the architect that led the building of a great bridge between the southern tip of India and Sri Lanka, and I bow before you."

Mr White closed his eyes, brought his palms together and bowed his head.

"Unfortunately, when I say 'are' I mean almost! If I had got it right then you would be like the rest of your godly friends, but I got it wrong."

"Got what wrong?" asked Hannibal a little confused.

"Your Reckoning. You were my first effort in returning the Lords of Pangea to Gaia and I made a mistake. You see you were not dead enough of this world when I attempted your transformation and, as I was nowhere near fathoming the circumstances in which it should occur, I ended the experiment, hoping to save you and the knowledge you would possibly possess. But a terrible price was paid. I did try to help though. I gave you Sinatra to hone your combatant instincts and a television to trigger your subconscious mind. They are the reasons you were confined to level five. Please, forgive me. I am so sorry."

"Do I change, or anything?" asked Hannibal.

"Well yes, it is said Lord Hanuman could transform his size and shape and, to a fashion, you can kind of do that when Lecter is released," replied Mr White.

"So who is Lecter?" Hannibal asked.

"Lecter is Hanuman and you, thrown together in a jumbled concoction of genetic mayhem. He is also the instinctual soul of you both."

Hannibal took a moment to digest Mr White's words.

"Apology accepted, you were only doing what you thought was best for everyone and everything," he said.

"Thank you, Hannibal, now can we get on with this? I mean we could natter, but shall we just get on?"

Faith and Vincent remained silent, just a little in awe of the entire situation.

"What about me?" Steve asked whining.

Mr White smiled.

"Come here, Cabal!" he said.

Steve ran straight up to the man in white and sat by his side and turned to face his friends, not having the foggiest idea why he had done so.

"You are my dog," said Mr White.

"Who is Cabal?" Albert quietly asked Bandi.

Mr White bent down and tickled Steve under his chin. Bandi spoke;

"The Internet tells me that Cabal is the great hound of Arthur Pendragon, a strong and fiercely loyal dog that is able to find his master wherever in this world he may be!"

Mr White stood up straight and spoke to the group.

"Yep that's right, good. Now we all know who we are, let's get moving on shall we?" he said impatiently. "The door won't stay open for ever." And with that, Mr White turned and walked through the imposing stone arched entrance to the tower and disappeared in a pulse of electrical brilliance.

"Well come on you lot, through with you all," Bedivere ushered.

Steve barked and bounded right through undeterred.

Faith and Vincent were standing arms still linked, gob-smacked.

"He's King Arthur. King of Camelot!" said Vincent dryly and quietly without any change in his expression.

"He certainly is, young sir; now get through this blooming entrance before I throw you all through by your various bits and bobs!" said Bedivere, losing his patience.

Faith was the first to follow orders.

"I'm King Arthur's PA," she said, smiling mischievously and turning to Vincent. "Not bad for a first gig I suppose, but who do I work for from here, hey?" she giggled.

One by one the group tentatively followed Mr White into the unknown, and one by one they vanished!

***

Jill nervously handed the tall leather clad, shaven headed, flat nosed man a plain brown envelope. He snorted, sneered and then looked down at the package. He tore it open sniffed it, peaked inside and gave Jill a look that made her feel like a lamb at a convention of wolves.

"Everything fine?" she asked nervously.

The man said nothing; he just gave her a grin that scarily exposed some fantastic gold-capped dentistry and slowly lit a cigarette. From the darkness of the service station car park, two other men walked over to the back of the hearse and handed John a bundle of guns and ammunition covered in grey flannel blankets. John thanked them with a nod and loaded everything into the back covering it with flowers. The two men said nothing, just turned and walked back to the darkness where they came from. The golden-toothed boss gave

Jill another smile and followed. Minutes later the hearse was humming down the motorway. Jill checked a palm top!

"Sirs, something has happened to the locator programme. It can't seem to find anyone. It's as if they have all just gone, disappeared!" said Jill, not really wanting to impart the information or face the wrath of her masters.

"Gone, disappeared! Now listen Mrs Despicable Demented... no, no, she's telling the truth, just don't get angry just handle this in a constructive manner. Where were they last dear Mrs Tittytuft?"

The Terrorpins were smiling sweetly at the subservient.

"Err, Glastonbury Tor, sirs," she replied.

"Then head for that location you dim-witted pea brain!"

"We'll be there in an hour Mr Yin," John said proudly.

"It's Mr Yang you numbskull. Dear, dear, at this rate I and I will soon have to use previously utilised insults!"

***

Mr White and the group were standing huddled together in the centre of a sizeable cavern that had eight tunnel entrances leading away from it. Natural light had somehow made its way into the huge space allowing glittering minerals and crystals to sparkle in the rock walls like pieces of mosaic mirror on a cracked uneven façade.

"Wow, err, what just happened?" asked Vincent.

"Nothing much," replied Mr White, "we have all just travelled through..."

"Ooh, ooh, let me guess. An interstellar viral cortex that enables carbon based conveyance! I love Star Trek," said Bandi delightedly excited.

"I was going to say, 'The Soil of Change.'"

"Cool name, which way now then?" Garston asked bounding towards one of the tunnel entrances.

"Stop right there, Garston!" said a very forthright Bedivere. "Those dirt tunnels will kill you. They are all filled with killer booby traps. Just one man has ever made it through them, and he is my little shaven headed mate here."

Jonas took a bow before being startled into a nervous grin.

"Name?" said an unfamiliar bellowing Irish accented voice that quickly made everyone jump to attention.

"Arthur Pendragon," replied Mr White.

"Oh what, Arturo not good enough for you now then is it? And I suppose that 'Bev the deer' and that 'Jo the nurse,' are with you?" the voice replied.

"Yes they are, and I know you can see us, so can we just get this over with," replied Mr White.

"Oh come on, Arturo, don't spoil me fun, I hardly get to tease anyone anymore, well, not for a few hundred years anyway."

"I know but we really haven't got that much time, so please, if you wouldn't mind appearing somewhere, please?

Now, don't be alarmed everyone, he really is just a big softy." said Mr White.

In front of the confused group, particles of dirt crept and shuffled along the ground and began to create two small mounds. Grain by grain the mounds grew, shifted and joined until they formed the huge rotund figure of, a bare-chested, dirt covered colossus, that stood a commanding 10 feet tall. The giant shook his head and a fine layer of dirt fell to the floor to magically reveal a being of flesh and blood. With curly ginger hair and bright green eyes, he looked absolutely terrifying. A pair of red braces hugged his substantial ale fashioned belly, which, of course, was not for decorative styling, but to hold up a huge green and yellow tartan kilt dressed with a brown leather sporran. He stood proud in the largest pair of leather sandals you ever saw holding an old gnarled driftwood club in his right hand. A tattooed sign of Ankh looped decoratively, around his belly button. He leant forward, grimaced and coughed and then roared at the group, spitting out dust and bad breath.

"I'm sorry," said Steve trembling. "Has anyone got a scoop?"

"And what on earth are you doing bringing a rat down here? I thought the plague would have turned you right off teaming up with vermin for all eternity," said the giant.

"Oi, man boobs, just because I'm a rodent it doesn't make me a rat. I'm a gerbil and one that can handle himself big boy, so if you fancy a rumble, let's dance ginger!" Garston replied.

The giant burst into laughter.

"You must be Garston, I've heard much about you."

"Well, forgive my ignorance, Mr Ginger, but who the fuzzy

sideburns are you?"

Seth stepped forward, "You're Finn McCool aren't you, the Irish Giant?" he said smiling broadly.

"That's right Seth, or should I call you Lord Tecci."

"Seth will do Finn, Seth will do."

The giant bent down and shook the rabbit by the paw.

"The roar was just to clear my throat, all the dust and stuff you know."

Seth nodded.

"Welcome all of you, especially you young Faith, we are truly blessed!" Said Finn, glancing a wink and a bow that made her feel decidedly unnerved.

"Look, this is just all a little too much, invisible elevators that travel through rock, animal gods, giants made of dirt." Vincent was finding it all hard to come to terms with.

"You're standing next to a talking rabbit, son," said Finn.

Seth smiled a cheesy grin.

"Yes, I know. I've heard that before!" Vincent replied, rolling his eyes.

"Well maybe you ought to open your mind up to new things sonny! Let's get going then shall we? You're all about to get a big surprise," gestured Finn.

"Well, it can't be much bigger than you, can it darling?"

"Oh yes it can, Albert, oh yes it can!" said Finn.

"He knows my name, he knows my name!" Albert chattered completely flustered.

"OK, we all need to hold hands, paws or claws and stand in a circle," said Mr White, "Jonas would you like to lead us all please." Everybody did as they were told and stood in the centre of the cavernous space linking hands. Jonas broke the chain and walked into the circle's centre; he bowed his head for a brief moment and then looked up and began an elaborate mime, gesticulating and moving around with great dexterity.

"What's he doing?" Vincent asked Faith quietly.

"He's praying, in sign language," she replied.

"Really, what's he saying, can you understand him?"

"Yes I can, I was taught this language when I was a little girl by the nuns that cared for me, they thought I might use it one day to help those less fortunate then myself."

"So, what's he saying?" asked Vincent.

"He's reminding Zeus to look after the souls of his brothers that gave their lives for the safety of the Cup, and to bless us all in our quest, I think!"

Jonas ended his prayer and rejoined the circle.

"Knock, knock!" called Finn.

"Who's there?" said a voice from the air.

"Finn!"

"Finn who?"

"Finnk you better let me in before I grind some bones to make my bread!"

Vincent turned to Faith disbelievingly. "You're kidding me right," he whispered.

In the centre of the man and animal made circle, the floor groaned and then, with puffs of hissing dirt and dust, fell away in massive blocks to create a huge downward spiral stairway.

"That's clever," said Steve, "So what are all the tunnels for?"

"Protection," replied Mr White, "You could walk them forever and never find 'The Pool.'"

The group walked down the brightly lit winding stairway until, after negotiating over 200 steps, they emerged through a natural stone arch onto a large clam shaped crystal shelf some 40 metres wide. Steve and Hannibal were bringing up the rear.

"I hope there's another way out cos climbing them stairs ain't gonna be funny!"

Hannibal nodded in agreement but then, found himself alone standing in a darkened, funky smelling, space.

"What's that awful smell?" he said.

"Oi!" yelled an angry Irish voice, "That's an Irish giants natural odour after a barrel of Pumpkin soup! And I wouldn't look up if I were you!"

Hannibal, realising where he was, darted out from beneath Finn's kilt.

"Sorry," he said cowering.

Finn growled a smile at him.

"You alright, mate?" Steve asked.

"Yes, but I feel the need to wash my hands, I feel dirty," Hannibal replied.

The rest of the gang were staring in wonder at what glistened before them.

The shelf clung to the edge of a huge subterranean void that boldly displayed walls made of millions of iridescent coloured dogtooth crystals. Some distance below, via a cut away staircase, a maze of jagged, razor sharp, crystal cluster formations, varying in size from sea urchin to garden shed formed the ground floor! Crystal splinters fashioned bridges and multiple levels beneath the 150 feet high ceiling that displayed its impressive wares like a peacock spreading its tail-feathers. The complete space gave the overall impression of an enormous bejewelled inside out Fabergé egg.

"Wow, it looks like Superman's house with disco lights in here," said Bandi.

"It's a giant Geode," Faith said reflectively.

"I didn't know you knew about geology," said Spike.

"What's a Geode?" Steve asked.

"Geode's are crystal formations mostly formed by gas bubbles in volcanic lava, but this one is truly massive, probably the largest on the planet!" Faith replied.

"Maybe or maybe not!" said Finn, shrugging a reply. "Now, don't get too near the edge, one slip and you're shish kebab. For your own safety, don't stray from the path!"

"Where's the path? I don't see one," asked Steve.

"You will," Finn replied.

Vincent turned to Faith.

"That's bad, whenever anyone anywhere says, 'don't stray from the path,' something bad always happens." Vincent voiced nervously.

"You're talking nonsense," said Faith.

Vincent backed up his statement.

"Every werewolf film I've ever seen has got that line in it somewhere."

"Oh, don't be so silly, there are no such things as werewolves," Faith replied.

"Yeah, there are no talking rabbits either!" said Vincent.

Faith glanced at Seth.

"OK, I see what you mean." Faith replied. "Everyone, stick to the

80

path, wherever it is!" she said uneasily.

Some distance away on a raised crystal plateau, a raven fluffed its feathers and cawed. It was perched on a marvellously equipped workstation, which had computers, monitors, and projectors set on crystal blocks in a horseshoe formation and, at its centre, sipping a Margarita from a cocktail glass and sat on a big, black, puffy comfy leather office chair, was a little old wizened man!

"Who's that? Steve asked.

To the astonishment of the group the chair rose silently into the abyss, hovered for a while and then glided over the precarious drop and landed safely on the shelf beside them.

"Merlin," said Mr White smiling cheerfully and wrapping his arms around the little man.

"Arthur, dear Arthur, you look so well."

Merlin was neatly groomed, grey haired and for some reason very hairy legged. He was dressed in a pair of three quarter length black linen shorts, a white linen shirt and a pair of brown crocs!

"But that's the police inspector that came to see Vincent at the house," said Garston.

"Inspector is that you?" asked Vincent.

Mr White turned back to the old man and threw him a knowing look.

"Have you been up to your old tricks again, Merlin?" he asked.

"Just keeping an eye on my investment my friend," the old man replied smiling.

Bandi wasn't reacting like the others. She was frozen to the spot, captivated and the fur down her spine was standing on end.

"Bandi, is there something wrong?" asked Garston.

"Ask Hannibal," she replied, softly.

Garston turned to Hannibal, but he, Seth, Escobar, and Spike were all standing in a line mumbling to one another, seemingly engrossed in something else.

"Well, come and say hello then everyone, this is Merlin my dear old friend."

Merlin turned.

"I take it from the look on their faces, you have succeeded," he said.

"What do you mean?" Arthur replied.

"You have done well, Arthur," said the little old man.

"Err, Mr White, or is it alright to call you Arthur?" Seth asked politely.

"Please, all of you, call me Arthur; Mr White is no longer necessary!"

"OK then, Arthur, how can I put this, this man that you know as Merlin, err, isn't!" said Seth.

"What are you talking about, Seth; I've known this man nearly all of my life."

"Prometheus, I think you might need to do some explaining!" said Bandi.

There was a silent pause as Arthur turned to the old man.

"Prometheus?" he said perplexed.

The old man grinned.

"Time to explain then! I am all of what you think I am. I am Merlin and also, Joseph of Arimathea and any number of men that have appeared through human history at times when the human race has needed them most. Moses, Mozart, Michelangelo, Galileo, Lincoln, Martin Luther King, the police inspector and even a little man pulling Vincent from a canal. I have embodied all of these great men and many more. I have been martyred a dozen or so times and lived here for a human eternity. I even embodied the monk Rasputin for a time and tried to save the Tsar of Russia and his family. People tried to kill me countless times, but I wasn't having it. In the end I just couldn't be bothered and so, poor dears, I let them deal with their own fate!"

"What, how Merlin, what's...?"

"Calm yourself Arthur; you really didn't think I was an old medieval wizard did you?"

Arthur's expression fell to one of great disappointment and embarrassment.

"You mean it's all been a lie, our time at Camelot, you saving me, all of it. You've' deceived me for this long. Finn, did you know about this?"

Finn bowed his head with shame.

"Arthur, you have deceived as much as anyone. Don't worry, Camelot was real and I saved you to save mankind. So what if I'm thousands of years old and a Titan!"

"So what?" Arthur replied exasperated.

For the first time since encountering Mr White, the group saw his self-confidence drain of heart,

"I imagine to the Lords I look… actually err…Hannibal, how do I look? Go on describe what you see to Arthur and the others please, it might help. You have 'The Sight', what do you see? Now be gentle with me, I don't want to burst into tears or anything."

Hannibal looked around at everyone a little surprised at being asked the question.

"Tell him Hannibal," said Maurice ushering him on. "Tell me I want to know."

Hannibal took a deep breath and gave a nod.

"Well, I can see you as the little gent in shorts as can we all, but, I also see you like a misty vision, shadowing your own self! You're about twice as tall as Finn," the lords hummed and nodded in agreement supportively, "hunched and terribly bony. You're wearing a dirty cloth of some kind around your, err, privates, and you have a tail, a bit like Spike's trailing behind you. Your face is warn and gaunt, kind of human but not, and you have a prominent nose which could also be described as a small muzzle type thing, maybe!"

"Yes, I agree," said Escobar, "that's good, Hannibal, carry on."

"Your head's an odd shape, it's elongated like someone's grabbed the back of it and pulled it a little. You have no hair anywhere, as far as I can see, and you have two large, slanted, black reptilian type eyes. You're painfully emaciated with saggy pallid, almost translucent skin which in places is covered in sores, scabs, blisters and warts!"

"We'll get you some Wartner, darling, it will be alright," said Albert.

Hannibal dithered.

"Your ribs are prominent and your side is scarred and deformed as if it was once ripped and torn away. You stand on two very thin legs and have fleshy, saggy, arms, with long bony webbed fingers and toes and, well, to put it mildly, you smell bloody awful! You look as if you're starving, sir."

There was another brief pause.

"Well, thanks, Hannibal I knew I could rely on you to pull no punches and, you're right, I am starving, I am! My God self hasn't eaten anything for thousands of your years and as I haven't, my own body is eating itself and has been ever since the day that I was banished by Zeus. Now, you call me immortal, but I am not, nothing is, it is just a case of perception. I live a long time in comparison to all of you and almost nothing on this planet can harm me. A year in your lives is just a second in mine and that is the difference in our lifeline time frames. My kind can only die by the hand of our own, and as my body is eating itself, well, that counts too. The only thing I can eat that provides my God self with sustenance is Ambrosia, the fare you call the food of the Gods, but there is none on planet Earth. You see, Ambrosia grows out there in a galaxy far, far away, in the ether of space and the drive through is closed!" Prometheus chuckled at his own joke.

"Hello sir, I'm Faith."

"Yes, I know who you are," Prometheus replied curtly.

"Oh, ok, well err, are we all going to die then, on the 21st of December 2025? Are the Titans going to return? Why are we all here and what about the Mayan calendar and the Crystal skulls?"

The old grey haired man gave Faith a broad smile.

"The Crystal skulls are fossils that once belonged to the Titans who died in the wars. They have been discovered and dug up by man over the centuries. They are nothing special."

"Excuse me sir, that's nothing special to you maybe, but you have just told us they once belonged to a few dead Titans. I reckon that makes them pretty special." Faith replied demonstratively.

"Perhaps they are, but what I mean is that they are insignificant regarding the reason you are here." He paused. "Are you all going to die on that date? Well yes, unless we can stop proceedings, yes, you are. But not in a frozen wasteland at first, oh no, you will die with the cataclysmic movement of the continents. We are talking volcanoes, creeping glaciers, earthquakes, tidal waves, floods, famine, hurricanes, typhoons, the full 'Four horsemen of the Apocalypse' stuff, fire and brimstone, you know! And, if you survive all of that, then you will die by the hands of the returning Titans in a frozen wilderness. That's if the planet is still here and not blown apart by some nuclear missile wielding, crazy person!"

"Why," asked Arthur, "why is all this going to happen?"

"Because that is the day the game ends, it's Zeus's wedding anniversary!"

The group turned to each other, not understanding quite what Prometheus was going on about.

"Zeus loves his games and so he put myself and another Titan up against one another to see which one of us would come out on top. It was all Hera's idea, Zeus's wife!"

"What!" replied Faith dumbstruck? "Do you mean to tell us that Zeus is going to wipe out the human race because of a game he's having with his wife? And we are here because you brought everyone back to play in that game," she said angrily.

"To a fashion, yes! Because of my supposed tinkering with humans, you know, the fire thing. So, The Lords of Pangea are here because they are the only beings that can stop all of this nonsense! Let me explain."

But before he could begin, Maurice fired a question.

"Who on Earth iz your opponent?"

"Sorry?" Prometheus replied.

"I said, who on Earth iz your opponent?"

"It's Hecate isn't' it? It has to be, she's the only other Titan on the planet right!" Arthur said, striding up and down, "I can't believe you deceived me like this all these years. I can't believe I kil..."

He was abruptly interrupted.

"Arthur, whatever you did, you have done to save the planet as you know it, be this all because of a game or not."

Arthur felt his heart cry with guilt.

"I'll get back to the explanation in hand, shall I?" said Prometheus.

"Yes, you do that," said Faith crossly.

"Faith, we need to keep a level head, something tells me that this is all leading somewhere."

"Oh, don't be so naive, Vincent, of course it bloody is!" she replied snapping back.

The old man a little surprised at Faith's tetchiness continued.

"Hera, was always so supportive of my work, she loved the way my creations decorated Gaia. However, she did not take as kindly to Zeus's roving eye, and Hecate was so beautiful back in the day. Hera wanted and demanded Hecate punished for her flirtatious antics and Zeus wanted me, err, dead! And so they came to an agreement, well actually it was more of a wager. If I could direct humans safely through evolution, caring for the planet to the expressed date, then victory would be mine and the human race would survive. But if Hecate could manipulate man to the point where they are, once and for all, going to destroy themselves, then the results don't really bear thinking about!"

"So, what do you get for all of this?" asked Seth.

"The prize is a return to the heavens."

"This is all so you can get back to heaven then?" asked Steve.

"Yes and no, as I said, this is to save mankind and if you think about it, the planet too. After all, man-made nuclear power could shatter her into a billion pieces," Prometheus replied.

"What happens to you if you lose the game?"

"Well, I hate to think, but I imagine it will involve me and a torturous, horrible, forever lasting drawn out death of some sort, Seth. Anyway, we digress. I gave the end date handed to us by Zeus to the Mayans and they built a calendar and the mythology surrounding it and the skulls just snowballed from there. You see, I left them a crystal skull as a present; similarly to the way you would take a bottle of wine to a party. I had no idea the skulls or the calendar would become so popular over the centuries."

Bandi gave an understanding nod as Prometheus became more involved in his tale.

"So, through the ages I began to implement my strategy. You see Hecate and I have been playing this game for thousands of years, for every move she makes, I countermove and vice versa. However, Zeus and Hera do throw the odd spanner in the works every now and then. It's as if they play their joker card and we have to, begrudgingly, live with it. I suppose it makes their game a little more exciting."

"More exciting! This is not right, I don't like it, old man, I don't like it at all," said Faith furiously.

"I don't make the rules Faith, I just have to follow them, or maybe bend them, best I can! The rules of the game are simple, we can't directly execute one another and that goes for the humans we embody too."

Prometheus began to walk up and down like a schoolteacher in front of a blackboard.

"Let's say I chose to embody someone like the Prime Minister and Hecate embodied the, err, the Queen of, err, Bibbidi Bobbidi

Boo, well, I couldn't go out and smite her myself and even if anyone else did, her spirit would just find another living human being or creature and move on, as I did when Rasputin was killed. We can both embody whom we like, when we like, you see. Our spirit selves can just come and go as we please!"

"Bibbidi Bobbidi Boo? Where's that? Sounds Scandinavian! I'll have to check it out!" said Albert turning to Steve. Prometheus continued undeterred.

"However, our pawns on the other hand, are sanctioned to do what they need to succeed. And I, through a little piece of good fortune have been delivered four wonderful pawns; a giant, a king, a knight and a monk, that's a bit of a thief!"

Jonas blushed self-consciously and then smiled awkwardly at the group.

"Don't worry Jonas; I know you took the grail because you had to, and to tell you the truth, I'm happy you did?"

Jonas smiled at the little old man, flashing a grin that could light up a wake.

"Jonas escaped the grasp of Finn long ago, but not before taking a sip from the pool. Little did he know that that drink would cast him impotent and add centuries to his lifetime."

Jonas covered his face with his hands; utterly embarrassed at everyone learning he was impotent!

"It's fine, mate, I know how you feel," said Steve comfortingly.

"We're not all impotent are we?" asked a worried Vincent.

Faith raised him an eyebrow!

"No Vincent, impotence is selective and rare," replied Prometheus. "I imagine that the rest of you are fine."

"I imagine," Garston repeated worriedly.

There was an audible sigh of relief from the rest of the group.

"I think!" Prometheus chuckled. "Anyway, some thousand years earlier than the Jonas episode, Bedivere, severely wounded, brought his dying King and friend to Avalon and me, and I used the power of the Pool to heal them both. They slept for over 300 years but woke appearing not a single day older. I went on to tutor them for a while regarding their missing years and then, eventually, enlightened them to the world's predicament."

"What happened next Arthur?" Hannibal asked.

Arthur looked at the little monkey and filled in the blanks.

"Well, for the remaining 700 years or so Hannibal, Bedivere and I travelled the world, amassing wealth and knowledge, until we were asked by Merlin, sorry Prometheus, to search for Jonas and the Cup. We eventually found him in North America, with a noose around his neck hanging from a Joshua tree in the desert! We thought he was dead, but he was just hanging there sleeping, slowly baking in the sun. After cutting him down and giving him some water, he told us his story without speaking, as he couldn't, imparting it with mime, theatre and a finger in the sand. He was convinced that the Cup was the reason for his ageless existence and God had punished him for stealing it. Well, he was half-right, wasn't he?"

Jonas smiled again.

"He explained that he deliberately chose the Joshua tree because each tree resembles the hand of God leading the way. He hoped that his tree would send his soul to heaven, but it sent him to sleep. He travelled back with us to Avalon and along the way we, in time, gained his trust. We taught him, after several unsuccessful attempts, that suicide was not the way forward and he became the third amigo."

Bandi giggled a private giggle.

Prometheus continued.

"It all really started to take off when the first young Russell was given milk to drink from the Cup. Generations of very clever Russell's then followed. These brilliant, bright men began to wow the scholastic establishment and that's when the weird and wonderful Mr White came about."

Arthur gave a grumpy diminutive bow.

"Just like Edmond Dantes from Alexandre Dumas' wonderful story, The Count of Monte Christo, Arthur reinvented himself as Mr White and positioned himself amongst society and began, not to seek revenge like Dantes but, to implement a plan of befriending and manipulating the Russell men. The Russell men were a key, you see. Dazzling minds put to work on a series of conundrums which, when all solved, would lead us to resurrecting the Lords of Pangea. Who better to solve all of the problems of a time lost, than further evolved human minds, hey? I was left to carry on my creative work here at Avalon, whilst we all tried to save Mother Earth. With my knowledge, Arthur's charm, Bedivere's strength, Jonas' cunning, the intelligence of the Russell men and Mr White's mystery, the A team were born and I do love it when a plan comes together!"

Bandi stifled a giggle once more.

"Identities were either created or stolen from the dead every 30 years or so, and staged tragic accidents would permit Mr White's trust funds and inheritances to perpetuate on paper through the generations to a new, but the same, Mr White!"

"So how did the idea of resurrecting the Lords come about?"

"Well, Seth,'" Prometheus answered, "I'm glad you ask. It was Finn that planted the seed regarding the Lords. We were sitting around a crystal, he was having a drop of grog, I wasn't, when he asked me about the old Gorgon days and that's when the conversation came up about, 'Animal Gods.' I told him about the Lords and shazzam, that was that!"

Maurice turned to Hannibal.

"Did he juzt zay Zhazzam?"

"Yes he did," Hannibal replied dryly.

"I thought the Lords could be this group of world serving heroes. Leading and protecting mankind against Hecate's efforts and followers," said Prometheus.

"You said followers!"

"Yes, I did Bandi. Hecate has embodied humans and creatures throughout history too, and those humans, all women, have at times had their own followers. And occasionally, those followers have turned into armies and evil has tried to engulf the world."

"And I take it from your explanation that she can only embody females and you only males."

"Well deduced, Bandi. Now, as you already probably know, resurrecting the Lords of Pangea was always going to be trial and error, as only Zeus knew their identity. Species after species were tested and then there was an accident, which had an amazing result!"

"Accident! I'll show you an accident old man," said Faith.

"Is she always this demonstrative?" asked Prometheus turning to the group.

No one dared say a word. Steve just looked up what demonstrative meant!

"Anyway, the accident involved the one beast who had served

Gaia more than any other. This incredible creature, once upon a time, selflessly sacrificed itself and, as a reward for its service, its entire kind were given life on every continent and shelter in every ocean."

"Who's he talking about Albert? Steve asked turning and whispering to his friend.

"I don't know, but I'm sure we'll find out later," Albert replied.

Seth pondered the old man's statement, it didn't sit well with him, but he thought he'd pry further a little later. He didn't want to disturb Prometheus in full flow! However someone else also, wasn't happy!

"Follow me," said Prometheus, as he began to walk down the crystal carved stairway towards the lethally spiked lower level.

"Hold on!" said Faith curtly. Prometheus pretended not to have heard her.

"A quick tour anybody? Hungry, little snack anyone? I'm sure you want to see the Pool, the Lab, the Allotment and the rest?" Prometheus pried.

"Down there, with all the spiky bits, are you sure Promo?"

"Just stick to the path Garston," Finn said with a teasing glint in his eye.

"I wish I could see a path," Garston replied nervously.

"Stop! Before I go any further, I would like an explanation regarding the remaining Lords of Pangea." Faith had her arms folded like a petulant child wanting a sweetie, but being refused her favourite jelly baby! "I mean it, I want to know. It's not difficult to work out that we have five of the eight Lords of Pangea here and that must mean that there are another three yet to be resurrected."

The group kept quiet, they all just turned to Prometheus, waiting for an answer.

"I'm not just a pretty face you know!" Faith was looking a little smug. "Well, come on Prometheus, do we have to get back to the Manor and put shampoo into the eyes of another fluffy rodent, or should we be aiming to stab another helpless reptile with an ancient ethereal stick?"

Prometheus rubbed his hands through his hair and looked to the floor as if he was searching for an answer. He seemed forlorn, a little lost, but Faith wasn't going to let him off the hook.

"We are missing the Lord of Europe, the Lord of North America and the Lord of Antarctica. Who are they? Do you know? Has Zeus let it slip? Do they exist? Are you gonna say something before I lose my rag?"

Prometheus stayed silent.

"Are those little mental amphibians Lords, and why, and what are they about? Mr White says they're not, but are they, old man? I'm talking to you, how dare you ignore me." Faith started to bristle with anger.

Prometheus, perturbed, seemed to drop his eye level respectfully and answered as if he were a servant responding to a master.

"Faith, there are animals and beasts that, have and do, provide the Earth with such an essential service that without them she would be a very different place. As I am sure you know, the simple common Bee for instance, if wiped out due to climate change, would not be able to pollinate the flora and fauna that the rest of the world depends upon. But have you ever asked yourself about plankton? If there were a change in the temperature of the world's oceans, what would happen to sea life and the planet's oxygen supply? Yes, too awful to consider isn't it. The common cow on the other hand, is killing the ozone layer with methane gas because humans are over breeding them for greed, sheep too! This sacred isle used to be the home of, Bears, big Cats, Wolves and Jackals. They all used to walk this land freely and keep the food chain in check, but now, humans, with their gluttony, have exterminated those animals and because of this, the land suffers as it is overgrazed and over farmed. This has happened in nearly every country around the world. The food chain is a formula, a cycle that needs to be carefully balanced and that is why every living thing on this planet has a purpose."

"You slipped up with the, Wasp though, didn't you?" said a curt and smarmy Faith. "Didn't do much good there did you?"

"You think? Did you know that hundreds of humans die every year because of a little sting? Even humans need to be kept in check. In fact humans need to be kept in check most of all, and it's Mother Nature that does it, mostly," Prometheus replied.

"Mother Nature! What are you on about, you're just waffling." replied Faith.

"I am, what did you call it, waffling am I? Well then, the great earthquake that is to strike and demolish the beautiful city of Istanbul is just a scientist's whim and will of course, never occur and the aftershocks won't affect any of the enigmatic islands of Greece. The cluster of volcanoes that are rumbling beneath the skin of Italy's toe will not, of course, explode into life and destroy many of the coastal cities of the Mediterranean with colossal waves from Monaco to Beirut. Similarly, the faulted Canary Island of La Palma will not drop half a mountain into the Atlantic Ocean and cause the eastern cities of the Americas, including New York, Boston, Rio and Buenos Aires to be submerged by another huge wave. The slipping of the San Andreas Fault is all going to be harmless, too. California and the Western states will all be fine, so don't you worry yourself! Of course, Asia is also going to be okay and the trench and fault line off the west coast of Canada is not going to cause an oceanic plunge in the Pacific and hit the Orient with the largest tsunami's the world has ever seen. I'm not even going to mention the super volcano that is Yellowstone Park, USA; I mean why should I? It's not going to throw a splendiferous amount of dust into the atmosphere and cause a dramatic drop in world temperature, or indeed devastate the US and life on the planet. No, no, don't worry yourself. It's all going to be fine, let me allay any fears; humans don't have to be concerned because none of the aforementioned is ever going to occur!" He paused during his sarcastic angry rant. "Mother Nature, who by the way is Mother Earth or Gaia depending on whatever you want to call her at the time, is evolving like everything else!" Prometheus gave Faith a frightful stare as he filled with frustration. "And don't you ever follow the world's social and economic news? Oil is becoming exorbitant in price and vanishing, populations are rebelling against their governments because they can't afford to feed themselves or simply survive without dragging themselves into debt. People all over the world are suffering with famine, drought and pestilence, and the more they try to help themselves, the more they dig the planet an ecological hole. It's a domino effect; someone's life moves forward, another person's life takes a step backwards and, as a consequence Mother Earth takes the weight." Prometheus turned and wagged a finger at Faith. "So, you listen to me, you precocious, ignorant little girl, it is Mother Earth and Zeus we answer to, no-one else and don't you ever forget it."

Faiths temper flared!

"Don't you get all sarcastic and high-brow with me. God or Titan or whatever you are, I'll put you in your place. Do you understand me? Well, do you?"

Faith was standing her ground, shouting at Prometheus.

"Faith calm down babe, calm down," said Bandi trying to placate her as best she could. "Come, walk with me." She said trying to lead Faith away.

Faith's voice rose in pitch with anger. "He still hasn't answered the question concerning the remaining Lords and Yin and Yang. He's like this stuffy, evasive politician, schooled with this special useless vocabulary."

"The other Lords will show themselves when they feel they must, Faith. There are beasts that cannot be resurrected because maybe, they already are," said Prometheus somewhat knowingly.

"See, he's so infuriating. What does that mean? I could scream." Faith screamed!

"Look, darling, at least we know that the Gods don't live on a mythical mountain at the top of the Empire State building. Actually we don't know that do we! Remind me to ask him about that later. Sorry, I can't wait. Prometheus can I ask you a question?"

"Yes, Bastet please do."

"Please call me Bandi, Bastet is only here when I need her."

"Sorry, your highness, certainly," he replied.

Bandi sighed! "Are the sons and daughters of the Gods, you know their children's children, walking around the world?"

Prometheus didn't answer; instead, he just considered the question very thoughtfully.

"Let me rephrase that." she said. "Are there any human descendants of the Gods walking the planet, you know, like that Percy Jackson fellow from the books?"

Prometheus pursed his lips and tried not to look at anyone, He mustered a twisted smile.

"Oh heavens, there are!" said Bandi.

"Well," he said, "I would have to say yes. Many of the Gods partnered humans under various guises so there have to be descendants somewhere, but they just appear human I would assume."

"You mean they don't have massive translucent shadows following them about for all of us Lords of Pangea to see?"

"Well Bastet, sorry Bandi, from the evidence presented to me, I don't think so."

"So the Percy Jacksons of this world can exist?"

"Yes they can, didn't Arthur tell you the tale of Europa?" Prometheus replied.

Steve nodded.

"Yes he did."

"And what about ze Harry Potterz?" asked Maurice.

"Yes, they can too," Prometheus, replied.

"But he'z just a young wizard, from ze mind of an author," said Maurice.

"Yes but, I was once considered a magnificent wizard remember, and I had books written about me and I'm a Titan? The wizards and magicians and geniuses of this world could all actually be godly descendants and are all, maybe, blissfully unaware that they are! It's possible isn't it?" said Prometheus.

"It's possible I suppose, but let's face the facts shall we. Merlin actually existed and Harry Potter is a figment of someone's imagination," said Bandi. "There is no evidence of godly intervention, just a great deal of nurtured thought and imagination, unless, the author has some kind of inside knowledge?"

"Inside knowledge, that's brilliant Bandi!" said Prometheus. "OK everyone listen up. Hecate has disguised herself as JK Rowling and tomorrow you will find her and..."

"...And what?" said Garston interrupting. "Smite her! We can't hurt her, you said it's only your own kind that can do that. I couldn't hurt her, I couldn't hurt anyone, not unless I had to."

"JK Rowling is Hecate!" said Bandi. "Why didn't I think of that? She's rich and powerful. Hold on, every time I've seen her on TV, I haven't seen her being followed around by a translucent shadow. But come to think of it, I haven't watched much television since, 'The Reckoning.'"

"But I have, and I can tell you this, she's just a normal lady and you are all going mad!" Hannibal interjected.

"Damn, we were so close," said Prometheus delivering his line like an old ham actor.

INCY WINCY AND THE EMERALD KING

Whilst John drove the hearse steadily through Somerset's hedge lined lanes, with classical music playing wistfully from the stereo, his darling wife at his side and Yin and Yang perched up on the dashboard, Glastonbury Tor rose impressively out of the British countryside. The entire scene could have been interpreted as one that was 'serenely idyllic,' but for one thing, an ominous, disconcerting chorus of knocking, scratching and grinding coming from the coffin in the rear! It was starting to make everyone a little nervous.

"P*ull over this must be it. We* have to let Lady Muck out of the box before she does *it on her* own!"

The coffin was jumping around violently in the back, banging against the side windows and the rear door, mulching the flowers and smashing against the blanket wrapped arsenal.

Bang!

The sound of a sudden gunshot filled the hearse. John stamped down hard on the brakes. As the car skidded and swerved, narrowly avoiding a hedgehog and a roadside ditch, the back door flew open and the coffin clattered out onto the tarmac in a pile of guns and roses. Jill looked down at her left arm.

"I've been shot, darling," she said calmly.

"*You will be perfectly fine; it's* just a flesh wound. *Actually it isn't, the offending bullet has travelled straight through see; it's up here* in the dashboard. *Too close for comfort I'd say and I, it could have killed I or I!*"

"It's ok, darling, just tie something around it tightly, it will help."

"I don't feel any pain though, dear."

"*Of course you don't woman, it's mind over it doesn't matter! Now get us out of here. Tourniquet, tourniquet!*"

As John and Jill did as they were told and climbed out of the car placing Yin and Yang into a respective jacket pocket, the coffin lid unexpectedly burst into the air like a popping champagne cork, causing everyone to leap out of their skins. A second later Freak landed on the hearse roof with a bang. It buckled and bowed beneath her weight. Worryingly, she had grown!

The Tittytufts stood stiff like statues whilst Yin and Yang had a peek from their undertaker coat pockets to see what the heck was going on. Freak was staring at Jill and John salivating and bouncing like an angry rabid hyena.

"*My*, h*aven't you grown! Now, I know that* look. No, *don't you dare, I and I need* them. Go and run around for 5 *minutes, use the facilities* and come back, there is a ball of shuffling spiky rodent *around here* somewhere."

Freak responded with a deep throaty grunt and leapt into some nearby foliage. A squeal was followed by the sound of rustling undergrowth, and then a tree lost a branch, snap, creak, some snorting and chirping and then a blooded Freak returned.

"That wasn't enough," she said, in a voice that had become raspy and sinister.

"There will soon be more, so leave these two alone." Yin and Yang demanded.

John and Jill, rather relieved, collected the weapons and ammunition and loaded themselves up, donning shotguns and bullet belts crossed over their chests like Mexican bandits. Jill grabbed her little black handbag that contained their passports and any legal documentation they may, at some point in the future require, and then joined her husband. They stood ready for orders.

"Why look at you two. This is what would have happened *if Quentin Tarrantino had directed Oliver the Musical.* Hahaha. *Well, I thought* it was funny, I did too. Now enough frivolity, I *and I think I's should start at* the top by that tower up there, do I's *have a*ny thoughts on the subject?"

"Woof, woof, bark!"

"What was that?" Freak asked, senses alerted. "I thought I'd butchered everything."

"Yes, I have thoughts on the subject," said a little old lady wrapped in more wool than one could imagine walking out of the trees with a petite scruffy mutt.

"It's our getaway driver from the lane by the old cottage near the manor. She had the little red car and that's her little ratty dog. Where did they *come from*?"

Freak lifted her fangs and leapt at the little defenceless old lady. 'Thud,' a hit, but not the target she expected. Her eight legs were wrapped around a tree and her fangs were rooted deep in its trunk. Slightly bemused, she plucked them from their hold, jumped to the ground and turned to face the walking ball of wool. The tree's bark splintered and cracked and its leaves browned and fell to the ground like drops of rain, as a creeping poisonous death set in.

"Hello again spider, my, haven't you grown. Where are your friends the bird and the lizard?"

"They are no longer my friends, but they are here somewhere," Freak replied with a menacing tone. "How did you do that, avoid me like that?"

"Yes, how did you move that speedily, *I mean you're as old as Santa's beard?"* the duo asked.

"Oh, I didn't move, the tree did, I'll put it back later, and if your former comrades are no longer with you, then I know where they are."

"Hahahaha, isn't she funny. Why isn't she picking *her nose, lifting her skirt and singing, 'I'm just a girl that can't say no?'* Err, sorry I and I didn't catch your name Mrs?"

"Yin and Yang, hello again," said the little old lady smiling.

"No she can't be?" They gasped, *"You are another pretender, like that Mr White aren't you? Well,* prepare to meet thy *doom human."*

John and Jill, expressionless, raised their guns and pointed them at the old lady.

"Did I say I was human?" the old lady replied.

The Tittytufts turned to each other and then lowered their weapons slowly.

"This is preposterous, it's worse than I and I thought. *She really thinks she's a sheep."*

"Now, look at you all. I'm so proud," said the old lady.

The old lady was getting a bit mushy.

*"What are you ba*bbling *on about Missy?"*

"Oh boys, if it wasn't for me you two wouldn't be here today, and Freak, my dearest Freak, I am so looking forward to bonding with you."

"I don't think this ball of fluff is very well, gents," said Freak.

"Darling Freak, don't be so eager to dismiss me, I am very well," said the little old lady.

"She has definitely escaped from a local institution, but how can she hear us all?" the Terrorpins asked.

"I have always been able to talk to the animals, isn't that right Roxy?" her little dog barked with a smile. "It was I that embodied a young biologist and developed the double yoked terrapin egg that you two were hatched from and it was also I, masquerading as a cleaner, that took a young tarantula to the Russell boy. For many years you have been my children in the care of another. It was heartbreaking leaving you all, but I am so proud of you, you have become all a mother could wish for. Come and give me a big hug. Oh, come on lovelies, come to mummy!"

The Tittytufts didn't know what to do, which meant Yin and Yang didn't know what to do!

"Look, you are an old lady, they are amphibians and I am a spider!"

"Close dear, but wrong. They are amphibians yes, advanced, evolved and fantastic, but I, I am a Titan and you, and you, are not just any spider you are the spider!"

Yin and Yang fell about!

"Hahahahaha! Freak, kill her now, she thinks she's a Titan. Put the old dear out of her misery, would you please?"

"So, you all know what a Titan is?" asked the little old lady.

"Just kill her now; she thinks I and I are imbeciles."

Freak didn't need asking twice, even though she had been asked twice! She crouched and then, lifting her fangs again to strike, sprang at the old lady, however, once more she found herself gliding past her target, but this time rolling to a stop in the middle of the road. She turned and readied herself to pounce again.

"All right enough of this, we have a lot of work to do if we are going to eradicate mankind," the old lady exclaimed.

"Wait, Freak stop!"

John and Jill jumped in-between the old lady and Freak, both scared out of their wits but unable to run.

Yin and Yang turned in their pockets.

"Excuse I and I, dear mad aged ewe, but did you say eradicate mankind?"

"Of course I did, that's why we are all here isn't it?" she replied. *"I think I's may like her!"*

***

As Prometheus stepped off the crystal stairway, all of the shards within a ten feet radius of him retracted like the tentacles of an interrupted sea anemone to form a glistening smooth flat path to walk on.

"Follow me then," he said, "but stay close, remember we don't want any shish kebab!"

Prometheus turned to Finn who was still standing on the Crystal shelf.

"Finn, why don't you and the boys meet us in the kitchen, and, what about a snack Jonas?"

Jonas grinned delightedly.

"But Jonas before you go, the valuables please."

Jonas hurriedly ran to the bottom of the stairway and reached about himself. He searched his satchel and hideaway pockets and carefully pulled out the four thimbles, the dish, the black velvet bundle, the metallic bottle and a bubble wrapped old wooden bowl. The little old man took a plastic carrier bag from his pocket and held it open for Jonas to place all of the magical artefacts into.

"The Holy Grail in a plastic shopping bag, who would ever have thought it?" said Vincent.

"Come on Arthur, let's go and have a drink, they'll be fine, it might cheer you up a bit."

"You're right Bedivere, it won't hurt, what could possibly happen?"

Jonas joined Finn, Arthur and Bedivere and they all walked back through the arched entrance. Faith turned to Vincent.

"Something strange is going on," she whispered in Vincent's ear.

"We can all hear you if you whisper, Faith," said Albert, "and what on earth could be strange about any of this?" he said sarcastically fluffing up his feathers and adjusting his cravat.

"Now, the crystal shards conceal a number of entrances to smaller crystal bubbles in the rock, caverns that connect to the main space, and the only way to get to them is to be a descendant of Kronos. As you can see, wherever I walk the geode clears the shards and provides a path for me."

"Oh right, that's all very interesting Prometheus, but can't you tell us more about this so called accident that you mentioned earlier and the beast that was given shelter on every continent and in every Ocean. I'm more than a little concerned because, well, after searching through the Internet I can only conclude that you mean Arachnids!"

"Yes, of course, sorry Seth. Know thy enemy! Good strategy. Inkomen, remember that name, Seth, Inkomen was a monstrous giant spider that lived deep within the bowels of the earth millions of years ago. It was she that held the eight land masses together beneath the Earths crust with her eight powerful legs and it was she who sacrificed herself so that Pangea could become the continents, as we know them today. This enabled evolution to continue at the differing rates it required on each landmass, giving birth to all of my alchemised creations. Now, Inkomen's exoskeleton meant that she could withstand the heat of Gaia's core from where she hung upside down beneath the earth's mantle. However, when she was asked by Zeus to sacrifice herself, she willingly let go and fell into the burning furnace below to her death.

"Then, who the blighty is Inkomen?" asked Steve.

Everyone stopped and looked at him disbelievingly.

"What, what did I say?"

"Think about it Steve, how many deadly SPAFF spiders do you know?" Hannibal whispered in his ear.

"Oh right, got it!"

"But Arthur could have killed her a long time ago by splitting her into a thousand pieces," said Spike.

"But he didn't, did he, and the question you have to ask yourself is, could he?" Prometheus replied.

"Freak is unlike all of you. You can all choose when to release the Gods within you, but she cannot. She is Inkomen, reborn when electrocuted during your escape from the Grid. The other little accident of shutting her leg in a cupboard door and Vincent replacing it with one made of metal was ultimately responsible for her amazing resurrection! That is when I knew it had all started."

"And is there anything else we should know?" Maurice asked.

"Well, she will decimate life on the planet when she drags and pulls the continents back together to reform Pangea. Nothing will be able to stop her, except that is, of course, all of you. You must stand in her way and keep her from reaching the sacred entrance to the catacombs that lie hidden beneath the Earth."

"Where is that?" asked Vincent.

"That's a question for the Emerald King."

"And who on earth is the Emerald King?" asked Seth a little perturbed by Prometheus's nonchalance.

"He's the giant chopping veg in the kitchen, and before you ask, he has no idea where it is. I've asked him a thousand times myself!"

"Does Freak know about any of this?" asked Garston.

"Who knows?" the old man replied.

"How large are we talking Prometheus? How large will Freak grow?"

"The more she feeds, the larger she will grow, I would estimate somewhere around the size of Switzerland, Seth!"

"Wow! So what now?" asked Steve.

"Now you get the tour!" Prometheus replied. "Up there, where I was sitting earlier, is of course the nerve centre of the operation where I can talk to Peuja and vice versa."

"Peuja!" said a surprised Seth.

Why, of course.

Did you think I was going to let you have all the fun?

"Peuja, it's good to hear your voice, how are you, is everything alright back at Camelot?"

Well Seth, Chief and his team are repairing everything that needs repairing, but in general we are all ok, but somehow my files were hacked and...

"...Don't worry about all of that now;" said Prometheus, "it's time for you all to see this great wonder."

Prometheus led the group to the face of the far wall and then magically seemed to disappear straight through it.

"In here," he said.

The group turned to each other mystified. Prometheus's head popped out making everyone jump. The rest of his body was missing with just his head being visible! He laughed and stepped out from behind a wall.

"It's just an optical illusion, I've been waiting to do that for over a thousand of your years. You should have seen the look on your faces, come through," he said having a chortle.

"This bubble in the rock is about the size of a tennis court and the pool is in the middle."

Garston jumped up onto Vincent's shoulder and whispered in his ear.

"Vin, he's not right this bloke, he's a nut nut! I'm a little worried."

Vincent had already secretly thought the same. There was a light-hearted madness to the old man he just couldn't work out.

One by one the group stepped through the concealed entrance, but once again they found their route blocked; this time by a simple brick wall. The wall had no air gaps from edge to edge, and stood just inside the concealed entrance. A sliding viewing trap was built into it at human eye level and a steel flap 10 inches or so wide, like the small coal-oven door on a steam train, was built in at floor level.

Prometheus faced the group.

"The wall is here for everyone's protection. The Pool shines so brightly that it could damage your eyes if you looked directly into it. You can only view it through this sliding flap that is backed with thick, black glass. Now, from here, the Pool illuminates the entire facility. Light escapes through the crystals at the sides of this wall and then dissipates from crystal to crystal and abracadabra, we can see the light."

"Did he just zay abracadabra, Zeth?"

"Yes, Maurice, he did!"

"This geezer thinks he'z the Great Zuprendo!"

Vincent lifted each member of the group one by one to have a look through the viewing glass.

"It's like looking at a black and white film negative," said Seth. "The Pool looks magical, like a glorious puddle of mirrored glass, and I can see the two trickling streams leading to and from it, they just disappear at the walls."

"Well described Seth. But look at the collectables set around the Pool and on the walls, what do you think of those?"

"Are they what I think they are?"

"Yes, they are. Priceless mythological artefacts, which I suppose are actually historical artefacts. And this steel hatch down here at your feet is the only way in and out, it's the door to the vault!"

"There isn't a handle," said Garston.

"Not on this side," Prometheus replied.

"What was that?" asked Escobar, turning his gaze from the viewing trap and looking rather startled. "I think I've just seen a ghost."

His curiosity got the better of him and he took another glance.

"It's a lady but, I can see right through her, she looks like the shadow that follows you Prometheus, but without the human body alongside her, and she's gliding not walking, oh and she's, oh err, naked!"

"She's there, where let me see. She must have sensed a delivery. I haven't seen her for years. OK, everyone turn around and stand back."

Prometheus put on a pair of protective, tinted swimming goggles that were hanging on the wall beside him on an old rusty nail, and knelt down and knocked on the steel hatch. He placed the carrier bag down handed to him by Jonas, which was full of the precious relics, and stood back.

"Turn away everyone," he said.

Seconds later the hatch door opened, curiously morphing in size and shape to the exact dimensions needed for the bag to slide through. A ghostly, long, fingered hand slowly reached out. Prometheus gently gave it a stroke. It stopped moving immediately when touched, but then, it abruptly snatched away the bag and the door slammed shut. Prometheus stood up and removed his protective goggles. He peered again through the viewing trap.

"Now wait a minute," he said, "this is the bit I like. It's like getting a Christmas present, you never know what you're going to get. Here she comes, close your eyes." Prometheus slid the goggles back on.

The trap door opened once more and a small twig was thrown out.

"One package in, one package out, that's the rule," he said.

The group opened their eyes.

"But it's just a twig."

"Well, it might appear to be so to you, Vincent, but obviously it's not! Triope decides if the object is worthy or not. We will look it up later if we can. She has very kindly written me an, 'Anthology of

Artefacts;' unfortunately she keeps it in there! She is so beautiful though, isn't she?" he said.

Vincent stepped forward, "Can I see?"

"No you can't," said Faith pulling him back by his shirt. "She is naked!"

Faith took a step forward and took a look herself.

"She is beautiful, you're right."

The ghostly figure looked straight back at her, tilting her head as if inquisitiveness and reflection had both struck her at once. Suddenly, she let out a scream, dropped the shopping bag to the floor and began to fly wildly around her crystal walled vault, vexed with anger.

"What's happening?" Faith asked.

Triope maddened, ripping and tearing at her own ghostly body she horrifically transformed in appearance into the most terrifying fanged and clawed hag and then flung herself at the viewing wall. Prometheus quickly grabbed Faith by the scruff of the neck and threw her to the floor. "Close your eyes," he shouted.

The steel door banged open, and a sinewy pair of blistered hands reached out and grabbed at Faith. Faith felt her ankle taken. She screamed and scrambled backwards kicking out. The hatch slammed shut. Faith had lost a shoe!

"What did I do? Why didn't she like me? Who is she anyway?" Faith was shaking.

"What the hell was that, what just happened, are you alright?" asked Vincent. Faith threw her arms around him.

"Well, Vincent," Prometheus answered, "Arthurian legend knows her as the Lady of the Lake but I and the ancient Greeks know her as Triope. She is incredible don't you think? An ethereal water-based elemental undine, a nymph and a changeling. Enchanting isn't she? But beware; she'll kill you with a kiss if you fall under her spell. She prefers a singular, uninterrupted existence and obviously doesn't get many visitors. Some are born to a life alone, and some are dead to it, too."

"Yes, err, well, she sounds lovely, whatever that all means!" he replied a little bemused.

Triope held the shoe close to her chest like a coveted trophy. Subdued by her prize, she returned to the beautiful ghostly creature, she was before.

"You weren't kidding when you said the 'Pools' were well protected were you?"

"No Vincent, I wasn't kidding and it is she that protects them all."

"How on earth did Jonas get to drink from the Pool, without getting his head ripped off?" asked Faith.

"He was offered one, a drink! And to this day I have no idea why," Prometheus replied.

'Clonk!' The steel hatch sounded to open once more.

"Avert your eyes again everyone," called Prometheus, "remember one for one, that's the rule, so a gift for the shoe!"

"Whose rule?"

"Her rule, Vincent."

The hatch opened and a tatty old Greek sandal was thrown out. Faith peered through the viewing trap and Triope grinned straight back at her.

"A tatty old Greek sandal! That was an expensive training shoe," said Faith.

"I imagine that's not just any old sandal," Prometheus replied.

"Yes, yes I know," she replied slipping it on.

"It's huge," said Faith.

In a cloud of mist, the sandal magically transformed to match her other shoe and fit exactly to size!

"Oh wow," she said. She peered through the black glass, smiled and said, "thank you."

Triope returned a bow, graciously.

***

"And that's who you are darling, Inkomen or if you like Armageddon, the end of the world as we know it," said the little old lady. She was sat up on the bonnet of the hearse holding court with her little dog Roxy.

"Well?" she said expectantly, waiting for someone to say something.

"*So we are pawns in a game* and not the '*Chosen,*' and she, our dearest eight *legged assassin, is* the most important thingy on this god, sorry, Zeus forsaken *rock?*"

"Yes."

"And that cat is an ancient Egyptian God and as far as we know there may be more animal gods running around trying to save mankind, and they just may be our past Grid-mates! And the idiot that is the Russell boy is a further evolved human being and Mr White is actually Arthur Pendragon? Oh, I and I forgot and you *are a* Titan?" They paused. "Hahahaha! *Well it's a fantastic story, one* that would need the imagination of someone drinking a brew of surgical spirit and a dash of lunacy to compose and therefore *I and I still don't believe* you!"

"But you saw the cat?" said the old lady.

"Filming trickery," replied the terrapin duo indignantly.

"It was live!" the old lady insisted.

"A delayed feed," was the riposte.

The old lady, exasperated, turned to her little dog.

"Roxy, darling, you wouldn't mind giving us your party trick would you sweetie? These two seem to be as stubborn as a constipated walrus!"

"And Twice as watertight, madam!"

Roxy jumped down from the hearse and, like a superstitious weightlifter following a choreographed ritual before a lift, had a yawn, stretched and gave her head a quick flip-flap. A brief stillness waltzed through time and then her eyes strangely misted over and frothy spittle balls formed at the corners of her mouth. She winced, yelped and cried and began to sway hypnotically under the shadow of the moon. The swaying gathered momentum until, sickeningly, her tiny fragile torso viciously snapped and crunched, shuddered and broke. Maggots seeped a weaving dance from her cute, pointy ears, and weeping pussy boils formed on her skin through the hairy, fluffy curls of her coat, as if she was made of dead flesh.

"Ooh, that's disgusting!"

Roxy convulsed and vomited a mass of slimy black worms, which swarmed around her and engulfed her miniature frame.

"No, no, forgive I and I, that's disgusting! The maggots seem to have just been the appetiser!"

Jill and John took a step back.

Roxy's bones visibly cracked, formed and reformed before her audience as she roared and grew into a terrifying monster.

"Finally, a beast worth slaying," said Freak.

"What the big furry is that?"

"This is my Roxy at her best. She is a Warg, the result of a wolf that has mated with a werewolf during its time of transformation."

"Err.... sorry?"

The old lady sighed.

"Imagine a man, becoming a werewolf during the full moon, getting a little tipsy on the blood of an alcoholised human, walking in the woods, coming across a she-wolf that looks a bit saucy, doing the deed and…"

"Sorry, doing the deed?" the terrapins were confused.

"Making the beast with two backs!" the old lady answered with Shakespearean terminology.

"Whatever does she mean?"

Yin and Yang were ignored and the old lady continued.

"Then, the werewolf changes to its human form after a few hours sleep, but is then unfortunately killed and eaten by the she-wolf, which then goes on to give birth, several months later, to a beautiful Warg."

"So she is human, werewolf and a wolf?" Yin and Yang enquired.

The old lady smiled and nodded.

Roxy was now as tall as a pony. Her lithe muscular frame was cloaked by a tight, steely grey matted coat and her upper and lower canines were like those of a Sabre Tooth Tiger, deadly and in clear view. Her giant tufted paws were armed with long fearsome ripping retractable claws and her eyes were a piercing bright yellow, but she did have a cute unusual fur pattern that resembled some kind of cross between her eyes! Drooling, salivating and grumbling a low guttural growl, she stepped forward and sniffed the Tittytufts.

"Hello Roxy, good doggy! I liked her as she was before," Jill said whispering nervously. "You know, just before we became dinner!"

"Oh, shut up Gelfling! No-one's going to eat you. She's not is she? *Anyway the Interweb says that if you don't die and are just mauled by a Warg you would walk the* earth as one of the undead, *so things* wouldn't be that bad or different *see! In fact, almost as they are now!* Hahahaha!

Dear old lady, question! How does the little dog stay as a little dog, *why does she not remain a Warg always? Good question, like it, well it is mine!"*

"Witchcraft obviously!"

"Yes, of course, and you know this because you are a blah blah blah, Titan!"

The old lady hopped off the car bonnet with an angry look in her eyes and turned her back. She, shook, crouched and doubled over but then, in complete silence, unravelled herself to a height of some 14 or so feet, turning to reveal herself as a beautiful beast of great wellbeing, a creature like no other, a huge three-headed, two-legged Titan. The head on her left was that of a black, coarsely fur covered, wolverine, foul breathed and bad tempered, the second, to her right, a black, smooth haired, proud and noble, panting horse, but, the third, the central head, was truly terrifying, a huge, powerful, hooded serpent! She had hands with fingers that were thin and bony, housing deadly claws and the parts of her torso, that could be seen, had a skin of mixed origin that appeared to change in form under the moonlight, as if it were made from a combination of the three beasts. Her arms were toned and yet feminine and she was doglegged, but without a tail. All of her faces had bright fiery eyes and her woollen clothing had become a cloak that had a fleece of gold sewn to its centre!

The serpent head motioned forward.

Yin, Yang, John, Jill and Freak all stared at her, petrified like marble statues.

"I am Hecate," she hissed and seethed in a terrorizing voice. "I am a Titan and the Goddess of Witchcraft, thanks to my dear Lord Zeus, and you will do as I tell you or you will die together with this pitiful planet. She may support your puny existence and be the mother of us all, but that holds no favour with me. I belong in the heavens and if I have to destroy her as well as mankind to get there, I will. This cursed needy rock has, in some way or another, been the catalyst of all heavenly conflicts since the dawn of time, and you know what, I've had enough! If this life-caressing orb was never here, there wouldn't be any quarrels and home would be at everlasting peace. A home for my darling Zeus and I to rule together in eternal bliss."

"Isn't Hera the wife of Zeus?" The terrapins enquired confidently!

Hecate snapped back.

"That conniving tramp will get what she deserves when I get up there you'll see."

Seeming to calm herself she took a deep satisfying breath, swayed and, almost regally, returned back to her little old lady disguise. Roxy, however, remained in her monstrous canine form.

"Freak my dearest, I do hope you are hungry," she said.

"Famished, ravenous," was the reply.

"Now, let's get to the crest of that hill. Tittytufts, bring that bottle of water with you from the car, it's under the passenger seat."

Jill ran to the car and picked up the bottle of water.

"How did you know that was there?" Jill asked.

"I put it there, now let's be on our way," said Hecate.

"Yes, whatever you say oh great, err..."

"Queen of Darkness or Hecate." The little old lady said turning away.

"Yes, err, oh Queen of Darkness, of course! Now Tittytufts, follow that Titan!"

The weird and wonderful group set off up the grassy knoll towards the tower. Whilst they marched, the little old lady waved a hand and the hearse they left behind burst into flames. She conjured herself up a shepherds crook from a blade of grass and strode on with the big, bad wolf prowling at her side. The Tittytufts, with Yin and Yang in their pockets, brought up the rear with Freak.

"Freak, darling, not you. You need to skirt around down there and find a rock, not just any rock, but a lock, it will be the one that looks as if it has been there for thousands of years. Just give it a gentle stroke and then back to us as fast as you can. I imagine you'll find it poking out of some tuft of grass or something."

Freak did what she was told somewhat begrudgingly, but then again anything she did for someone else, she did somewhat begrudgingly! Her heightened arachnid senses didn't take long to find Arturo's rock. She looked at it wondering what on earth made it so special and then reached out and tapped it with a claw. Its crystalline structure magically glittered and the name Inkomen appeared spellbindingly across its face. She paused in thought, still feeling a little uncertain regarding the unreal realism that she was now facing. A squelching, rustling, sound teased the air. She spun around and vigilantly scoured her surroundings. No one, just her and a little unfortunate, tasty, earthworm spaghetti snack. She returned her gaze at the rock. She was finding it difficult to comprehend that she was the most important creature on the planet and that in her fangs stood the fate of the world. She drifted into a daydream, a montage of memories. She remembered a time when life was simple, when all she had to do was worry about what time of day she was to be fed fat beetles by a robot arm sliding out of a tile on the Grid. She wondered how Vincent was doing and what he was doing, and reminisced about the entertaining times she used to have teasing her friends at the Manor House. And then her thoughts turned to her beautiful palms. She recalled a time when she was sat on top of them watching the spectacular sunsets glide over the endless Pacific Ocean. She felt a longing, an empty feeling in her abdomen and realised that her heart was yearning for the fun she used to have back in Arcadia's garden with the vibrant and intoxicating exotic plants and all of those lovely living juicy treats. She missed them. She missed them all.

A voice in the distance snapped her back from her land of contemplation.

"Come on love, we haven't got all night."

Hecate disappeared through the stone arch in a burst of light.

Freak suddenly remembered the reason she was standing in the middle of the countryside. She had a murderous rampage to get on with. And so, pulling herself together, she bounded up the hill, through the sticky dewy grass, veering her course only once to skewer a bold sparrow, until she came to a stop beneath the tower's moonlit shadow. Something felt strange. Her eyes welled up with tears. She knew that something was coming, something eternal! She turned to look at the world as if it was the final time she would ever see it as it was, and then, she turned back and scuttled through the arch. 'Flash!' She was gone!

AN AGE OF PRUDENCE LONG FORGOTTEN!

"Now before we go in the kitchen hollow, I want you all to close your eyes. I've been doing the place up a bit."

"Oh, come on Finn we're not children."

Finn gave Arthur a sharp glance.

"Alright, alright, we'll close our eyes."

"Now hold hands, you take mine Jonas."

"Hold hands? Alright we'll hold hands!" said Arthur.

Finn led the boys into the crystal hollow.

"Right, you can open them now," he said.

Gone were the rustic oak benches, crystal shelves, inglenook fireplace and worn cushions and in their place was a magnificently equipped, state of the art, Italian designer kitchen with a natural gas range oven, granite worktops and more utensils than an Iron Chef's trinket box. Jonas welled up with happiness and gave his big Irish friend a loving hug. Bedivere and Arthur just stood flabbergasted, staring at a huge robust, circular oak-ring table that was in turn surrounded by a set of 25, splendidly carved, oak dining chairs, in the middle of the crystal walled room.

"I can't believe what I'm seeing. It's been a while since we've seen that hasn't it, Arthur?"

"Yes Bedivere, but it still looks as impressive as the day we first sat around it."

"It's not the original boys," said Finn, butting in. "Merlin, sorry Prometheus, told me what it used to look like and I thought it would be a nice surprise for you all when we all met up again. I've been giving it a regular oiling to give it that aged look; you know, to keep it from drying and splitting. What do you think?"

Arthur dreamily ambled over to the table. His eyes told a nostalgic tale of a time loved and long past. He ran his fingers over its chunky reddened grain and breathed in its earthly aroma. But then, out of the corner of his eye, he caught sight of his chair, his perch of leadership. He walked to it and gently sat himself down on its velvet red cushioned seat, savouring every moment.

"I sit here," he said reflectively.

"Yes you do, my Lord," answered Bedivere.

"Finn it's majestic, thank you."

"It's my pleasure, King Arthur." Finn replied bowing graciously, "I really don't condone lying and so I wanted to make up for all the fibbing I have had to do over the centuries. I was never comfortable with it at all. He should have just told you, it's inexplicable really. So, here it is Arthur, your great, 'Round Table.'"

Arthur raised his head and smiled.

"Apology accepted old friend, really, thank you," Arthur was truly touched and full of sentiment.

"Now let's all cook some grub, hey? There's some lovely seasonal fruit, veg and herbs in that cupboard in the corner Jonas, and some mutton, fresh from the moors last night, in the fridge. Prometheus will bring 'em all up for some food after he's shown 'em all the allotments, bunk rooms and stuff."

"Right you are Finn," said Bedivere, "However, let's leave the preparation to Jonas shall we? I'll only burn it, and Arthur would only poison us all and the truth is I'd like to see my old chambers, wrestle with a few memories and have a ten minute snooze me thinks, 'cos I'm knackered!"

"Yes!" Arthur said quickly agreeing with his old friend and jumping to his feet. "We'll be back in half an hour or so, so you two catch up and Finn, I think mutton may be a little heavy on the stomach for breakfast."

Bedivere and Arthur shuffled out of the kitchen making their excuses, leaving Jonas and Finn with the job of breakfast preparation.

"Just like old times hey buddy, just me and you cooking up a storm? They're still sloping off with something better to do when there's work to be done, hey?"

Jonas gave Finn a grin and walked over to a cupboard where he grabbed a vine of tomatoes and carried them to the sink for a quick wash before slicing and dicing them on a worktop. He was in his element!

***

Prometheus had finished presenting the group the sleeping quarters and the allotment and was now crossing a crystal shard bridge to his horseshoe shaped technological hub.

"This bridge wasn't here earlier, you used the chair."

"Oh yes, Seth, thanks for reminding me."

The chair rose from its position on the other side of the Geode and floated towards the technical plateau where it landed effortlessly.

"The bridges appear wherever I need them to, but I don't like to use them too often just in case I leave them out. It confuses Finn all the time!"

Steve changed the subject.

"How did you do it Promeotheseus? How did you create everything?"

"Good question Steve and it's Prometheus," said Albert.

"Cheers Albert!"

"Well Steve, I just did the science bit, I'm not the designer. All of the creatures on Earth are all based on the Gods or Titans in some way or another and then it's down to Zeus, evolution and blind luck, how everything turns out. I took all of our genes, mixed them with the essence of the elements from all over the universe and dropped in miniscule amounts of the differing concoctions, with the use of my trusty pipette into one of the, 'Pools of Life,' under the instruction of Zeus. As the Pools are all connected within Gaia's frame, life spreads via the pure blood of Mother Earth. I just stood back and watched evolution happen and I still do, new species are born everyday!"

"You mean you didn't use this Pool of life?" asked Garston.

"No, this Pool is where I chose to place myself and store the world's sacred objects. The hospitable climate above on the surface makes life here a little more pleasant than if I had placed myself with another Pool."

Vincent stifled a laugh; he couldn't believe that someone could think the United Kingdoms climate was ideal!

"And that's why I used the Pool at a place you know as, Shangri-La."

"Shangri-La exists?"

"Yes, very much so Albert."

"Where is it exactly?"

"Exactly? Well, I don't exactly know, I'm afraid. Shangri-La is indeed somewhere in the mountain range of the Himalayas, but the crystal encased utopia moves around within the mountain chain of its own accord and thus, remains safely hidden away. Think of it akin to Mother Earth having a moving heart."

"Why would Mother Earth move around something so well protected from all living things by her own forces of nature?" asked Vincent.

"Zeus wanted its whereabouts to remain hidden. Shangri-La's Pool of light is also a gateway, a very special gateway, to the heavens! We don't want any unwanted intruders, do we?"

"Of course, it all makes perfect sense. Now I understand why Shangri-La's Pool of Light is actually better known within the realms of human mythology as the, 'Fountain of Youth,'" said Seth.

"Because when you get to Heaven you live forever?" said Steve.

"No Steve, because drinking from the Pool sustains longevity. In fact drinking from any of the Pools does this, but no-one knew about the existence of the others, now you can understand where all the myths come from regarding its power," Prometheus replied.

"But what connects it to the heavens?" asked Bandi, "There isn't an invisible elevator or something is there?"

"No Bandi, it's the elements! Anyone or anything can walk out of the Pool and remain a living, breathing, lifeform. But, when you take a leap of faith from its… anyway, an elemental reaction is started that transports you to the gates of Paradise, unless, of course, you are a creature that has stumbled upon the whereabouts of Shangri-la completely by accident within the hidden peaks of the mountain range and then just taken a drink! After that you're just cursed with longevity." He paused. "Of course, if you're a water based Elemental, then you react according to your make up, which I imagine will usually involve some form of transference."

The group looked at him blankly.

"An Elemental? You've used that word before?"

"A being made from one of the four elements, Steve, like Triope."

Steve changed the subject again.

"Oh right, so what is SPAFF then? In, let's say, 10 year old human speak?"

"Oh, I like that question a lot, Steve, love it darling, you're on form."

"Cheers again Albert."

Prometheus smiled wryly.

"It's liquid from the Pool, which is without question, a thousands of times purer than water... blended with a drop of Titan DNA, mine and Hecate's and mixed in a test tube."

"And that's it?" Garston asked, not too convinced. "Just the three ingredients?"

"Well," he said evasively, "maybe a little of the Nanteus Cup too, which, of course, has Zeus's DNA within it, Christ's DNA and a bit of plant matter."

"So not just three ingredients then?" Garston replied.

"Err, no! So what do you think?" Prometheus asked.

Everyone else walked around the scientist's playground.

"Amazing, this is all just mind-blowing buddy, sorry, may I call you buddy?" asked Vincent.

"Not really, Prometheus is better," the hairy-legged little man replied.

Vincent, embarrassed, tried a little chitchat.

"That looks like a liquid crystal monitor," he said.

Prometheus walked over to a keyboard and pressed a few keys.

The wall appeared to flicker and then moving pictures appeared. Footage of Vincent's unbelievable escape from his Canal Street apartment ran on the massive crystal-wall screen.

"I want this TV," Bandi said excitedly.

"Ooh, watch this, it's Vincent's leap into the canal dears," Albert said excitedly.

Faith, still grumpy, was still pondering Prometheus's creation explanation.

"How did you get Hecate's DNA?" she asked inquisitively.

"Yes, how on earth did you get hold of that?" Seth repeated.

"Yes, how on earth did you get hold of that?" repeated Escobar.

"I just asked that. Wait a minute, so water from the Pools that curses people with longevity is an ingredient in SPAFF, as is your DNA and you're as old s time! So I can conclude..." said Seth.

"...You are all going to live a very long time! And as for Hecate's DNA, well, I had it in store Seth," Prometheus replied.

"Great I'm going to be the world oldest cam eyed, super tailed, Scouse gerbil!" said Garston drolly.

"In store! Where, top shelf of the larder?" Faith asked sarcastically. "You were chained to the face of a mountain for thousands of years, not many supermarkets about, I imagine!"

"Oh, we've met on occasion since my release; all it takes is a strand of hair you know," Prometheus replied.

***

"What just happened, that felt very odd; did I and I just *do that science fiction B Movie* thing of fizzing to *nothing and then appearing somewhere very obscure?"*

"No darlings, you just walked through a front door, that's all, a door that you can't see," Hecate replied.

"And what's happened to the fearsome drooling canine?"

Roxy had returned to her little cute doggy appearance.

"Isn't that obvious?" Hecate replied once more, a little tired of all the questions.

"Yes err, so what you a*re saying is that we are* now standing *in the entrance hall of something!"*

"That is an excellent way to put it, and these eight tunnels lead down to the main space within the property. It is extensively developed with many bedrooms of individual styling, the latest technological gadgetry and, of course, no audacious crib would be complete without a luxury Pool!"

"Sounds fantastic, so what's the plan? Jump in, stand behind the *Spider, watch her kill everyone and* then rule the world?"

"Something like that, just follow my lead and all will be well." Hecate replied.

"So which way now, what tunnel do we take?" asked a salivating Freak.

The group watched as Hecate closed her eyes and muttered an incantation. She tapped her shepherds crook on the dusty ground and magically it transformed to a flaming torch. The Tittytufts, feeling movement beneath their feet, leapt sharply to safety as the floor beneath them dropped in blocks to reveal the massive downward spiral stone stairway.

"I'll go first, then you Roxy, Tittytufts and Freak you bring up the rear, sweeties, and I'll take that bottle of water please," said Hecate.

I believe I is right to think I and I are not quite as in command as one thinks I's are!

***

"Take a seat everyone, but not those two, they belong to Arthur and Bedivere," announced Finn.

The table was laid out for a breakfast banquet with fruit, nuts, breads, vegetables, salmon, cheeses, juices, cereals and flowers for decoration, unless you fancied a nibble of one that is. Everybody had a quick shuffle about and sat down at the table in little clusters with Faith and Vincent taking a seat either side of Prometheus. All the shuffling soon turned to silence as Arthur and Bedivere arrived and stood at the kitchen's crystal framed entrance. They were dressed in traditional court clothes from their medieval past and Arthur was wearing a simple golden crown.

Finn cleared his throat.

"Ladies and gentlemen, Titan, Gods and creatures, will you please all rise for your King, Arthur Pendragon."

Everyone slowly stood where they were, and bowed their heads, as Arthur made his way to his chair at the head of the round table.

"Please, my friends, all of you sit. It is strange and yet comforting that our first meal together should be around this great table."

"It's not the original!"

"Even though, as Finn insists on reminding me, it is not the original."

Arthur cleared his throat.

"Long ago," he said, "from far and wide, a group of men joined me in saving civility and making history. These men became my brothers and their families, my family. We fought great battles together against foes from the south, north, the east and sometimes even the west. Isn't that right, Finn? Anyway I digress. What I am trying to say is that these men, my dear friends, became heroes, and now their names reside in this country's folklore, sorry, this world's mythology. From the gatherings we held around this table, sorry Finn, a table very much like this one, the first true English council was born, a council of upstanding men that spoke for everyone and vanquished evil doing. The Knights of Camelot became legends and now, it gives me great pleasure in once again filling the void left behind by their passing, by welcoming you, the new Knights. You are all this planet's future. Even though some of you are more immortal than others, around this table we are all the same. You are the Knights of Camelot and I toast you all with this, um, fine glass of apple juice. To the Knights of Camelot, to you." Arthur raised his glass and the group toasted one another.

"We are Ze Knights of Camelot! I knew we were," said Maurice.

"Yes, Maurice, together you are. Now let's eat." Arthur replied.

"Shouldn't we thank Zeus first, for what we are about to receive?" asked Hannibal.

"We don't have to thank him all of the time. Zeus knows that we are each thankful because he knows each of us like we know ourselves. So eat, my friend, eat."

"Can I do it, anyway?"

Arthur smiled at the little Monkey.

"Yes, Hannibal go ahead." he replied, "Every living creature has the right to worship who or what they want, whenever they want."

"Cool, ok then."

Hannibal jumped up onto the table and raised his fists in the air and, like a power rock icon with a throat full of growl, sang. "For what we are about to receive, 1,2,3. May the Lord make us truly thankful? Oooh!"

A raucous round of laughter and applause followed a second of stunned silence. Hannibal took a bow, but then stopped moving, freezing suddenly to the spot.

"Did you feel that?" He asked nervously.

"Yes, I did," Vincent replied, "What was that Prometheus, sir?"

The shuddering happened one more. The table began to shake, a rumbling filled the Geode, an apple rolled across the table, a glass fell over and Finn jumped out of his seat.

"Keep it together everyone. It's time. The shield is rising, that's all," said Prometheus.

"The shield is rising! It's time? Oh for havens sake, what does that all mean?" said Faith, completely fed up of Prometheus's cryptic riddles. "You're speaking in tongues again old man!"

The whole room shook once more, with a deep grumble. Pots and pans began to teeter and fall from the shelves and everybody grabbed at what they could for stability.

"Under the table everyone, take cover!" Arthur called.

"Now, don't overreact, it will all be over in a minute Arthur, there is no need to get your tunic in a twist," said Prometheus.

At that point a large crystal shard fell from above and smashed onto the table, scattering crockery everywhere.

"Twist, twist! Under the table everyone," Prometheus called, sliding under the table for cover as smartly as he could.

"Good strong table Finn," Bedivere shouted cowering beneath the hefty oak top as the noise roared.

Finn was on all fours with his shoulders and massive head under the table but his bottom sticking out.

"Yeah, not bad, Bed!" he said smiling.

"I can't change!" Escobar yelled.

"You can't what?" Seth replied.

"I cannot become Karura."

"Me neither, you're stuck with me as Spike."

"None of you can change," said Finn above the din, "didn't Prometheus let you know, you have to be granted metamorphoses by a Titan for your powers to work in here."

"What in the kitchen?" Steve asked.

"No, Steve, in here, in the Geode."

The rumbling tremor soon fell away allowing everyone to breathe a welcome sigh of relief. Prometheus gathered himself and ran to the entrance.

"They're here," he said delightedly looking out. "Come on!"

He waited patiently on the crystal shelf for lengths of crystal to slide out of the sidewalls of the Geode to form a glorious Cinderella stairway that swept down to what was once the sunken, deadly spiked floor beneath.

"Just follow me."

Where the treacherous floor once threatened, a gleaming smooth gently concaved surface had risen to the same height as the entrance shelf, and now greeted them in the form and shape of a giant octagonal shield. A different hieroglyphic symbol was scribed into the face of each cornered edge and a large sign of Ankh adorned its centre. The entire space now looked like a beautiful shimmering ice rink. The group pulled themselves out from under the table and followed Prometheus down the stairway.

"Wow, where did all the skewering crystal clusters go to, darlings?"

"Well, I have no idea Albert," Spike replied, "Has anybody else?"

"Something is really out of sorts here, my tail is buzzing like a bee in a Poppy field!" said Garston.

"Just play along for now everyone, follow Prometheus's lead, alright!" said Seth.

Hecate and her group walked into the centre of the shield. She waved delightedly.

"Hello Promey!"

"Hecate, my darling, what an unexpected pleasure," Prometheus replied with a twinkle in his eye!

He ran down the sweeping stairway and across the shield to meet her with a lifting, squeezing cuddle. She wrapped her arms around him and kissed him as they spun like reacquainted young lovers! After staring into each other's eyes for a moment, he put the old lady down and nervously turned to Arthur and the group.

"Well, where are your manners? Come and say hello then," he said beckoning.

Everyone looked on a little stunned.

"But Freak is there," said Steve nervously.

"She won't harm you, loves, I promise," replied the little old lady. Come on!"

"Yes, come on, come and see your old friend the Spider!" said a taunting Freak, crouched, drooling and swaying menacingly.

Hannibal took the first steps and led the way, followed by everyone else other than Escobar who leapt off the stairway and glided down.

"It's Mr and Mrs Jenkins dressed like undertakers, Vincent," said Faith becoming aware of the Tittytufts.

"Is it really?" he said, " Hi, I'm Vincent Russell, I'm a friend of Faith's, and it's really nice to meet you."

Vincent offered a hand to shake, but was answered by Jill lifting a shotgun to his face.

"Shut your trap boy, we know who you are," said John,

"Yes, we do, but stop calling her Faith? She is the subhuman we know as Clipboard Girl?" Jill stated.

At that point Yin and Yang popped their heads out of their pocketed mobile homes.

*The Jenkins' no longer exist. J*ust the Tittytuft assassins here, mongrels!

There was a brief hiatus.

"Are we all present?" Hecate asked breaking the silence.

Escobar landed on the surface of the shield and was soon to be followed by a raven that perched on Prometheus' shoulder. "Yes we all are!" Prometheus replied.

The raven hopped to the floor.

In an instant, magic began to turn the known world of science upside down. The shield seemed to almost come alive as members of both parties found their feet, paws or claws being encased by millions of tiny crystals. It was as if they were being fitted for a pair of crystal clogs!

"What's happening to me?" Seth shouted.

The little clogs were becoming boots!

"Tail, remove Seth's, err, crystal booties." Garston whizzed over to Seth. His tail poked and chipped away the crystals now firmly covering Seth's shins, however, as quickly as the tail toiled, the crystals restored themselves.

"Just accept it, it's all ok," said Hannibal perfectly relaxed, also standing with his feet covered in crystals, "it's only happening to the Lords. Look around you, it's Mother Earth saying hello that's all."

Seth, Bandi, Escobar, Spike, and Hannibal were all stuck fast to the spot in crystal boots, however, so were Freak, Roxy and the raven.

"Who's the pretty little bitch then?" asked Steve, "and why does Freak also have her legs covered like that?"

"Yes, Steve, I'd like to know that, too, and who's the raven? It's been watching us since the day the Grid died, so what's going on?" Garston asked.

"It will all make sense in a few minutes everyone, don't concern yourselves too much. Now Finn come and meet Hecate," said Prometheus.

Finn strolled over to Hecate and knelt at her feet. She was

standing in the centre of the loop of the sign of Ankh.

"Dear Hecate, welcome to my home," said Finn.

"Thank you, sire, you are most gracious. Please do not kneel. It is I that should kneel before you."

Finn raised his head and looked at the old lady a little embarrassed.

"Don't be silly madam," he said, "I am but your humble servant, nothing special, just a larger than life Irishman."

"Oh, Your Highness, you do jest." Hecate retorted. "You are Finn McCool, King of the Giants from the land known as the Emerald Isle are you not?"

"I am my lady," Finn answered.

"Then I apologise," said Hecate.

"Apologise, for what?" Finn again replied.

At that point the old woman pulled the bottle of spring water from her pocket, opened it and liberally poured it all over Finn's head.

Finn instantaneously began to dissolve like a sand castle in the rain.

"Oh dear, I see," he said, as he became a mound of mushy dirt on the glistening surface.

"What on earth is going on here, Prometheus?" Arthur asked angrily.

"Take it easy Arthur, just relax would you. Finn is fulfilling his destiny."

All of the creatures held to the shield by crystals were now entranced by a captivating spell.

One by one they began to glide around the shield without bending their knees as if they were each travelling on their own crystal rail track.

"I have a bad feeling about all of this, as have I. Let I's abscond to the entrance, which I's assume is the exit. What a great idea, well, it is my own."

The Tittytufts, guns aloft, walked backwards slowly to the edge of the elevated shield and stepped onto the crystal shelf from whence they came.

"Right let's sort this out," said Arthur as he Bedivere and Jonas walked towards Prometheus.

"This is trippy, Arthur, it's like the 60's and hanging out with that

Jim Morrison again!"

"No, Bed, this is like home, with Merlin conjuring tricks all around us again!"

Prometheus raised a hand and as he did so, Bedivere, Jonas, Arthur and Vincent all rose into the air and were removed to the crystal entrance shelf and placed some 10 feet above ground level against the wall close to where the Tittytufts were stood. Not knowing which way to point their guns the Tittytufts turned them on each other.

"Not I or I, them you, peabrains!"

"Prometheus put us down now before I lose my temper," said Bedivere.

Prometheus closed his fist and Arthur and his fellow men fell, mute.

"Sorry, everyone, there's just too much to be getting on with," he said.

"Now Garston, Albert, Maurice, Steve; time for you to leave the floor and go and watch the big screen, Peuja is going to explain everything in a minute."

Steve turned and trotted off towards the horseshoe tech hub.

"Well, come on then you lot," he said.

He then sat down excitedly wagging his tail like a good little doggy.

"What about me, what do I do?" Faith asked mystified by what was going on around her.

"You just stay here dear," said the old lady, "and here, take this would you."

Hecate took off her woolly coat and placed it around Faith's shoulders. At once Faith's eyes misted over and the woollen coat transformed to a Fleece of gold. The shield lowered some 30 feet to reform the crater as if the Fleece of gold's return had been the trigger. Bellowing and creaking like a creeping glacier it marooned both the tech hub and entrance shelf. The giant crystal screen flickered.

"Something's happening to the shield and look a film's starting," Steve said excitedly.

Albert, Maurice and Garston, peered up at the giant monitor. Garston's senses began twitching madly, he knew something was afoot or apaw or even aclaw! A bursting crescendo of Mozart's Requiem filled the void and as the lights dimmed, Peuja's unmistakeable tones began to waffle!

LIFE IS WHAT YOU MAKE IT!

Ladies, gentlemen and critters, I welcome you to the premiere and also, final showing of the glorious epic;

'LIFE IS WHAT YOU MAKE IT!'

The title appeared on the huge screen, with sweeping thunderclouds providing the backdrop in moody shades of blue and grey. As the title faded, the clouds turned to CGI and the movie morphed to animation. Screening like an old fashioned fairytale, Peuja's forthright tone changed to provide a wondrous soothing, hypnotic commentary that filled the Geode. Like Cinderella, our leading character appeared, tired and over worked, but, instead of holding a mop, he, brandished a test tube!

A long, long time ago, somewhere in the corner of the expansive universe, a poor, handsome, young Titan named Promey, was working in the Foundry of Life that belonged to an oppressive Overlord.

A strings laden underscore emerged to provide emotive accompaniment to the lyrical narration.

Day after day he laboured, grateful for his position but, for little reward, other than board and lodging. To others this may have seemed a tragic step beyond terrible, but to the young Titan it was recompense for a glorious existence, for he knew that at the end of each day, when his work was done, he would journey out into a world that was nothing short of 'Paradise.' In the dreamy depths of his pensive mind, the clever Titan yearned for nothing more than an accepting smile from his master, but all he ever received was enduring criticism.

One day, whilst toiling hard in the forge, he was ordered to create a special beast, a beast that would give his master years of endless amusement and aid his benevolent mother, Mother

Earth, in her ageing fortitude.

"This is good, how long is it on for?" asked Steve.
"Just keep watching, not too long," Prometheus replied.

The young Titan, set to task and laboured for what would amount to thousands of years. This may seem a long time to you or I, but to the youthful Promey, the years seemed to fly by. Why? Well, because he wasn't alone. He enjoyed the company of an assistant, his twin brother, Epimetheus or Eppi to his friends. Eppi was very different to Promey, he was impetuous, lacked wisdom and indeed, was in and out of trouble all the time. He was often thought of as a fool and was always being punished for bending his master's rules, indeed, working with his brother in the forge was supposed to be a punishment for a previous indiscretion! The two young Titans however, made the best of their circumstance and their brotherly bond grew as they lived, laughed and worked together. Eventually, after a couple of close, hairy calls, the brothers produced their greatest ever creation and released it in a magical Pool of Light upon Mother Earth, a sacred place where all offerings were released so they may spread throughout the lands. Their master was so delighted with the result of their efforts that he held a great festival to mark the beasts unveiling and there, he named it, Man.

"Ooh, a bit like the unveiling of that King Kong fellow and we all know what happened *there, not a single memorable tune in sight, detestable behaviour! Shut it and let's get nearer those stairs, I fear skulduggery is afoot or a* flipper, I'm with *you!"* said Yin and Yang.

The brothers were introduced to many distinguished guests including, of course, the Overlord's wife. However, there was one particular guest that took Promey's interest, a beautiful, young, flirtatious Titan called Hecate. The attraction was instant; it was as if Promey and Hecate had both been struck by Cupid's arrow and they just chin-wagged the night through!

"Chin-wagged!" repeated Albert. "For heavens sake a more

romantic vernacular please, who's the writer?"

From that day forward their love grew and flourished like a bud being fed the purest of waters and, as a result, their relationship went on to become the talk of the town. The two young Titans became instant celebrities, the 'it' couple of Paradise. But, with the growth of the couple's popularity, came envy! Eppi found himself surrounded by others, due to his success, but alone within his heart. With a confused, tainted, mind he began to covet his brother's beautiful love and jealousy swept through him. The young couple's newly found stardom also displeased their Master, for he too also craved the touch of Hecate's beguiling beauty!

"Ooh, luv's, a romantic twist!" said Albert.

Upon the surface of the shield, the pile of earth that was once Finn sank through the crystal floor, like lava through ice, and created a hole the entire size of the marked loop of Ankh. Hecate and Prometheus stood watching for a moment before turning to each other and taking one another by the hand. Quietly and ignoring everything happening around them, they walked across the shield towards the hollow that housed the Pool of Light.

One day, whilst Eppi was relaxing and watching Man struggling to survive in his environment, from his vantage point in Paradise, he realised that many of the beasts that had been previously created, and even Mother Nature herself, were indeed a threat to Man's very existence and so, mistakenly, impulsively, and without permission, he handed Man his Overlord's secret of fire! Upon discovering this wrongdoing, the Overlord became vexed, but then, thought things through and despicably and cunningly came up with a plan that saddled Promey entirely with the deed! Eppi, full of shame, and unable to stand by and see his brother blamed for a crime he didn't commit, pleaded to his master not to punish Promey. However, his words fell on deaf ears. The Overlord, you see, saw the entire episode as a gift of good fortune! He decreed that Promey be banished to Mother Earth and shackled to the side of a mountain in lightning forged

chains, where he would send his own pet eagle to feast upon the young Titan's liver, every night, as part of the sentencing! The Overlord believed, you see, that time would clear him a path to Hecate's affections!

"I know this bit, it's horrible," said Steve.
"Hush, we all know it darling, just keep watching," Albert replied curtly.

However, not wishing to appear completely heartless before the rest of his throng, the master shrewdly rewarded Eppi for, and I quote, 'falsely trying to admit to a crime he did not commit in order to save his brother,' and promoted him to Governor of the Forge at a banquet for the Gods in his honour!
Distraught, embarrassed and riddled with guilt, Eppi returned to the solitude of his work.
Time passed and passed some more and the Overlord put his plan into practice and tried to sooth Hecate's broken heart by bestowing gifts upon her. Hecate, of course, refused them all and remained inconsolable. One morning, tortured by the sounds of Promey's screams and still overcome with grief, she ran to Eppi and asked him to join her in pleading with their master to end Promey's harsh punishment, but Eppi knew that their words would do no good and explained what had really happened with their Overlord's secret of fire. Hecate was outraged and set about conceiving a plan of her own to free her love without, raising suspicion or having to face any repercussions.

"Ziz is getting good; it'z got zome myztery about it."
"Yes Maurice, and perhaps a little bit of familiarity too," replied a concerned Garston. He turned to look at his friends on the shield who were all in one way or another stuck fast where they stood.

Hecate told Eppi to convince the Overlord that he needed to protect the location of Shangri-La and to impart the idea of empowering a select few animal lords to do so! This, Eppi did, whilst adding that it would also give his master more time to perhaps develop the other planets, or play some more Golf! The real reason was, of course, so that Hecate and Eppi could help Promey when the Overlord wasn't watching!

"Golf! This is getting silly!" said Garston.

The Overlord looked on this idea favourably and so, took it as his own. He stated that the location of the magical Pool of Light that connected Paradise to Mother Earth, the Pool known as Shangri-la, should be kept a secret from Man. Therefore a safeguard for the protection of the location of Shangri-la and, thus, Paradise had to be put into place upon the Earth! But, to appear to be fair to Man, he left them a puzzle! He proclaimed that an animal Lord from each separate continent would act as part of a combination, a key, to unlocking the whereabouts of Shangri-la, and these animal Lords he named the Lords of Pangea. He decreed that the gateway to Shangri-La, and thus the doorway to Paradise, could be revealed on Earth when all of the Lords were brought together around one of the worlds, Pool's of Light! However, like any good engineer, the Overlord also created a protective failsafe should this gathering of critter deities actually occur! He stated that once the Lords of Pangea had met, they would never be able to meet again, as death would intervene! With a million and one combinations of creature gods possible, and only he knowing the true identity of each Pangea Lord, the Overlord remained extremely confident that no one would ever break the cipher, especially as he also previously decided that he would move Shangri-La around from time to time! And so, he announced that if anyone upon Earth did discover Shangri-La, they would deservedly be welcomed into Paradise.

Hence time became Hecate's enemy. She knew that all she had to do was create a chain of events that would bring Promey and the Lords of Pangea together around a Pool of Light in order to return him to the heavens, sorry, Paradise and, that she had to do this, of course, before Promey perished of starvation, as Titan sustenance did not exist upon the Earth. She set about conceptualising and then implementing a well thought out plan and, much to Zeus's, sorry, the Overlord's delight, she flirtatiously offered herself to him! However, she also deliberately prepared to have this meeting discovered by the Overlord's wife, Hera, sorry Mrs Overlord! Subsequently, on finding her husband in the hands of another, Mrs Overlord got a little angry and insisted upon Hecate's immediate exile to Earth. Hugely embarrassed, the Overlord begrudgingly obliged and dispatched Hecate to Earth on the stipulation that she would be given the title of, 'Goddess of the Crossroads and Sorcery.' He thought this would convince the other Gods of Paradise into thinking of her relocation as a vital placement. He also made her the earthly custodian of the Golden Fleece, a magical regenerative artefact that would sustain her life without the fare of Ambrosia, the food a Titan, slash God, needs to survive.

This though, was not enough for Mrs Overlord who, had conditions of her own. She felt that sending Hecate away was not enough retribution for her husband's indiscretion and so, she stated that Hecate, in her words, 'a victim of the Overlord's lust,' should be allowed a reprieve and handed a return to Paradise if she manipulated her husband's beloved Man into destroying itself by a named date! She knew that this proposal would devastate her husband, as his treasured Mother Earth would suffer as a consequence. She furthermore stipulated that Promey should be given the right to return to Paradise if he succeeded in preventing Hecate from completing her task. Another dagger in the Overlord's heart, she thought, as Promey's return would be terribly humiliating.

And so the rules of the game were set and, as you already know them, I'll move on.

"How does the film maker know what we know already?" asked Steve.

"I have an unnerving feeling about all of this," said Albert.

"Yes, I suspect this movie may have been made, 'in house,' and is an autobiographical non-fictional docu- type animated yarn," said Garston.

"Err yes! What?"

"Never mind Zteve," said Maurice.

And nothing happened for thousands of years until Fate had a say!

Hecate's servant a priestess, named Medea, used a little wooden cup and a rare flowering bud to grind and prepare a potion, and then, one of the Overlord's sons, named Heracles, set Promey free for telling him the way to a tree of Golden Apples!

"Well zats something new!" said Maurice.

Down on the shield, The Lords Of Pangea were now almost completely encased, from head to toe, or claw, in their own personal crystal wraps, just the last remnants of their faces remained. All except for one, one who just happened to have a claw of steel, one whose eighth appendage was not made of flesh, one whose crystal encasement bore cracks and fissures, one who was deadly and in her current state already a living God!

"Look, Freak's not being covered like the others. I can speak," said Vincent, surprising himself.

"Well, if you can then so can I," Arthur replied. "Bed, you with us?"

"I'm here Arthur! Jonas? Oh sorry, forgot!"

Jonas nodded assuredly.

Arthur took the bull by the horns.

"Well, it is time for us to do what we do best boys and that's get down from here and fight some evil. It seems we've all been taken on a ride for some centuries, or so, and now it's time to get off the merry-go-round!"

"Great Arthur, now how do we get down from this wall?" asked Bedivere.

"Don't worry about that, just be ready to move as soon as you're released, it seems that every action has a reaction around here and I'm pretty sure that Prometheus has something in mind for us all!"

Now, Promey and Hecate would often secretly convene under Mother Nature's natural shrouds, as birds in a migrating flock, or as butterflies within the heart of a swarm, or even as fish within a giant shoal, wherever Mother Nature gave them sanctuary, that was where the two lovers would meet, prepare their strategy and remain safely hidden, from the prying eyes of

the Overlord. They thought this recourse best as an early discovery had delivered them a dangerous revelation! And so, Promey laid the foundations to finding the Lords of Pangea by chasing the bloodlines of man through time and by utilising his own knowledge of science and the elements, whereas Hecate did so, but by means of conjuring and sleight of hand within the realms of magic. All of the time, however, as both created mythical legends, they of course, pretended to be at war with one another! Regretfully, however, whilst enacting out their plan, they had to sacrifice many friends and enemies along the way, as they embodied various humans and beasts alike.

"What was the revelation then? I can't bear it. This is so exciting. I just may poop myself right here!" said Steve.

Well Steve, the answer is on the face of the giant crystal shield just to your left!

"How come the film's answering me?"
"That's a great question, which can only have one answer Steve. Someone wants to keep us occupied whilst they prepare for an imminent event. It's time to stop watching this drivel and save our friends. If I remember rightly, this up itself, hoity-toity, softly voiced narrator said that death would intervene and I don't want anyone to die, come on!" Garston said, running to the edge of the tech hub.

It has nothing to do with Roxanna the Warg, last of her kind and descendant of the Capitoline she-wolf that the founders of Rome, Romulus and Remus suckled from. She is Lord of Europe and Pangea.

"Wait, we've got to listen to this, darlings, it's important," said Albert.
Maurice, and Steve were already sniffing out a way down to the shield.

And it also has little to do with the Overlord's declaration that Inkomen should become the Lord of Antarctica and Pangea.

"So that leaves the Raven."

Yes, Albert, the Raven revelation! Hopi, Red Indian God, Lord of North America and Pangea, was a spy!

"Hopi?" Albert repeated, squinty eyed!

Yes, you see after the great biblical flood, Noah prayed to the Lord of all, Zeus the Overlord, for help in finding land, and in answer to his prayers he handed Hopi the gift of his own sight. In fact he gave every raven this gift, but only one raven could be the 'Eyes of Zeus,' at any one time.

"Oh, really?" said Albert disbelievingly.

In Norse mythology, the raven was known to be the eyes of Odin, the 'bringer of life,' and we know that Odin is the name for the Norse Lord of the Gods. And thus, whenever you see a raven anywhere, it could be Zeus watching you!

"Is this much longer? Any chance of a brew, I really fancy a cup of tea!"

Sorry Albert, there isn't time! Anyway, moving forward!

The Narrator was getting stroppy!

When Noah released Hopi, he flew until he found a land of grain and pasture. When he returned with an ear of corn, he discovered he was too late. Noah's great Ark had already run aground in the mountains of, Asia Minor, Ararat, Turkey. You see, Hopi had been away for so long that Noah had lost heart and made the decision to pray to the Gods for help, once again. However, this time it was Athena, daughter of Zeus, that answered his prayers and it was she who guided a different bird to a land of heat and dust, Ararat, and this bird returned with an Olive branch!

"The dove of peace, or the pigeon!" Albert retorted sarcastically.

Yes, Albert the dove, which was actually a pigeon!

"So, Noah released the pigeon and followed it to Ararat?"

Yes Albert, of course he blooming did! Now, this episode in history led to the survival of all the creatures of the Earth, including Man, except for Unicorns, who were too vain to believe that Zeus would ever destroy them!

"He Killed the Unicorns? Blaggard! How terrible?" Albert shrieked.

Now, after this sequence of events Man often, mistakenly, chastised the raven for what they saw as his, 'failure to deliver,' and so, in many cultures, the raven became a dark, much maligned and mysterious character. In return, the raven itself decided that man deserved little respect, as he found him to be a beast lacking in understanding and patience, and thus, he now treats Man with contempt.

"And so he should!"

Yes Albert! Moving on:
Now finding Hopi was easy, as Zeus had sent a raven to keep an eye on Promey! However I bet Zeus didn't expect Hopi to become such a great friend to Promey!

"Good on him!" said Albert.

The rest is pretty straightforward really. A few mishaps, a bit of luck and the fact that the entire world's creature reserve developed from the genes of just two subjects of each species due to the great flood. Well, that helped a bit. There was also Arthur and his men, the building of wealth, the Cup, creating, prolonging and obviously embellishing myths, Roxy's discovery

in the Troodos Mountain range, the military being oh, so gullible, the discovery of Finn, our Lord's placement of Triope and the wonderful acting and deception skills of Prometheus and Hecate themselves. Let's face it, a little while ago everyone here thought the pair either wanted to save the world or destroy it, and that they were great enemies, and life, as we know it, was going to end on December 21st, 2025, which, by the way, it still might! Well, now that you're here, you probably want to know the truth, and the truth is? Well, the truth is?

'Life is what you make it!'

Fluffy storm clouds returned to the screen in a crescendo of classical music and the titles ran!

"Not a bleeding tap number in the entire movie, nor a soppy irritatingly catchy, "I will blow up the world," disneyesque love duet! Shocking, absolute *rubbish! I's need to* watch Godzilla to cheer I's up!" Yin and Yang were very disappointed!

The End.

"What, that's it, no more? Oi, Peuja, what you playing at love?" asked Albert angrily.

Peuja tried to whisper, although obviously everyone heard her.

That's it Albert, act three of the film finishes here tonight and the whole project now becomes live theatre! We may talk about this later!

"Why may?" asked Albert whispering in return.

There was a pause.

And now I pass you over to the writer and director of this film, Mr Prometheus himself.

Albert clapped gushingly, alone!

"Why may?" he repeated.

You may be dead!

Albert stopped clapping!

Hecate turned to Prometheus and looked longingly if not tearfully into his eyes.

"It's time to go home," she said softly.

"Yes, yes it is. Are you ready to face them all again?" he asked.

Hecate smiled and squeezed her loves hand. Prometheus took a deep breath and looked around the Geode one last time, and then his voice filled the void.

"We have to leave now Arthur, all of you. You have all been wonderful companions and we thank you all for your service." He sighed heavily holding back the emotion filling him with sadness. "This is a wonderful Planet. Gaia is magical. I do wish you all the very best of luck." His lips pursed. "Man is a funny thing," he said smiling. "I am very proud of what you have achieved as a race, but your destiny is now out of my hands and those of my true love. We have brought you all to this point and now your fate lies with you. Gaia will live on, unless she is broken apart by Mans nuclear dreams. She may become an icy, cold rock or a dusty, arid wilderness for eons to come but let's keep the faith, hey. Hmm faith," he reflected. "That's a funny thing, too. It's something out there that is often unattainable, a far reaching abyss of thought and dream!"

Anyone not covered in crystals listened intently.

"You're a charlatan old man, a liar," yelled Arthur.

"I am a Titan," replied Prometheus, proudly bursting into his withered form.

Hecate turned to him and followed suit.

"I did what I did to survive and, of course, for love. You remember what love is, don't you Arthur?"

Arthur said nothing, Prometheus continued.

"I could have ruled this rock with an iron fist, but I chose not to. And what about you Arthur, are you not a liar, too? It was you and your servants that did all of my bidding. It was you who carried out the murders of the Russell men, whenever we needed to push a generation, it is because of your deception we stand here today proudly beside Vincent, the future of mankind."

Arthur bowed his head with shame.

"We did what we had to Arthur, for the greater good, remember? Don't listen to him, Vincent, he's messing with your mind." Bedivere shouted.

Arthur looked up at Vincent, his expression filled with deep sorrow.

Vincent stared at him, silent and empty of life.

"Your Father was," Arthur paused, "an amazing man and friend, as was his father and his father before that, and so forth. They were all wonderfully loyal friends, gentlemen with gentle hearts. What I did to each of them broke my soul. I know that no amount of apologising will bring them back and I recognize that depriving you of parental guidance and love is a guilt that I must bear alone. I ask you never to forgive me Vincent, just understand me. Sometimes in life we all have to suffer burdens that are irreplaceable by moments of understanding. Believe me when I say, I will never feel whole again. I have done what I can to watch over you not because of shame or guilt, but because I knew that nurturing you would do more for an ageing world than I could ever accomplish. Your ancestors achievements live on in you and their ghosts, well, they torment me. I'm sorry, so, so sorry my boy."

A stunned silence ran through the Geode for a brief moment.

"That's beautiful Arthur," said Prometheus, "I couldn't have said any of that better myself. Yes, Vincent, to get to you we encountered many obstacles, but none as forceful or as emphatic as time. But don't despair young man, Arthur is now the wisest of his kind and we leave you in his guiding hands."

The old man turned to walk away, but then stopped as if remembering a forgotten piece to a puzzle.

"Forgiveness is something that Zeus's son taught us all, and he passed for Man's sins. Demigods walk the earth Vincent, yes they do and no doubt you will one day face them or even befriend them, but as for now, you are Man, all of Man, the best of Man, remember that lad."

Prometheus stopped and smiled at Hecate.

"We have also left you something else," she said excitedly. "We just hope it all works!"

The two Titans smiled, but their happiness was soon subdued by the sound of a cracking crystal casement.

"Ooh, well time to leave!" Prometheus said hurriedly, "Goodbye everyone," he said waving and pulling Hecate towards the hollow that housed the Pool Of Light. The steel door transformed and became their exact body shape in preparation.

"Watch the screen all of you, it may be the only chance you get to see Shangri-La. I will let you see it through my eyes, and tell Finn that all the shards will forever move, so to watch his step!"

"Say goodbye to Roxy for me, kisses, mwah!" said Hecate as she walked hurriedly through the steel door alone!

'Creek, scrape, a burst of light and thump,' it shut behind her.

"Well that's going to make life interesting. You'll be receiving two gifts from Triope now instead of the one! Female Titans hey? Can't live with them; err well, because they usually kill you! See you all in Paradise!"

And so with an explosion of light and a clonk of steel, Prometheus, too, was gone. Arthur, Vincent, Bedivere and Jonas instantly fell to the floor from their wall hanging positions and the deafening sound of an unforgiving, deep thunderous roar soon followed. It was Freak, or rather, Inkomen raging at the world. She shook herself free of quartz, like a wet dog would the rain.

Arthur turned to Vincent.

"Vincent, read between the lines, don't dwell on the past, fight with us. We've all been duped, but we are all mankind and this Planet have got left!" he said.

Arthur grabbed Vincent by his arms, Vincent turned away.

"Vincent, look at me, look at me boy. If we don't stop that spider crawling into that hole, then we will all die and so will this world, as we know it. Do you understand? Do you understand me?" Vincent remained silent, his emotions scattered to the winds. Arthur changed his tack.

"Jonas get to Triope's and see what she throws out of the hatch. Bedivere get to our quarters grab swords and shields and whatever else you can. Vincent, stay out of the way!"

Bedivere nodded and disappeared through a nearby tunnel and Jonas set off for Triope's hollow. Like a Parkour champion flipping, tumbling and running over rooftops, he skipped around the edge of the Shield, tracked all the time by the eyes of Freak. Arthur turned to the Tittytufts.

"It's time for you to leave now," he said assuredly. "This is not a place for you. You must forget all of this and go back to your lives."

Arthur heard a sound like a cracking whip and turned sharply to find Jonas struggling, tangled in a web attached net against the sidewall.

"Great! She can do that, too!" he said.

Yin and Yang had been quietly observing the evening's entertainment from the relative safety of their respective pockets, but they were not going to let anyone spoil the party.

"Get lost White, these repulsive humans belong to I and I, they only depart when we say it's time to abscond, we are not leaving before the third Act of this tale concludes with our victory."

Arthur raised a hand and as he did so the terrapins left their pockets and became suspended in the air in front of him.

"Look boys," he said, "I do love you and so I won't kill you. Besides you are not the most powerful beings on the planet, The Lords of Pangea are and therefore I doubt very much you will be of any threat to the human race." He raised them up to his eye level. "It's time for you leave this party. Goodbye lads, it has been some fun. See you later!"

"Freak help I and I, give them all some ballast" they cried, powerless under the command of Arthur's telekinesis.

Freak turned to answer the call of her friends and then she remembered Clipboard Girl and the aroma of sweet revenge. With a calm assurance and without remorse she scuttled over to Faith and thrust her metal claw deep into Faith's shoulder, twisting it in order to induce the maximum amount of pain she could.

Faith's trance like state was broken. She screamed a shrieking scream and fell to her knees, Arthur turned swiftly.

"Don't you do it Freak, don't you dare. You'll regret it. I promise you that," he called.

Freak fervently struck again, as if she were taunting him, but this time thrust her claw deep into Faiths opposite shoulder, ripping at her flesh as she retracted. Faith wailed a sickening cry. Freak her venomous fangs exposed, hissed and salivated with the scent of her victim's impending death. Loosing consciousness, Faith slumped to the floor in a pool of her own blood. It glowed against the iridescence of the giant crystal shield.

"Come and get me, White, come and save your treasured little Clipboard Girl." Freak goaded.

"Stop her," cried Vincent, "She's killing her. Use your power."

Arthur closed his eyes and raised a hand. In his deepest thoughts he imagined Freak torn limb from limb and gave course to that action, but on opening his eyes he discovered that Freak still stood before him.

"She has grown too strong, but I swear this to you Vincent, Faith will never die on my watch."

He raised a finger and made a swirling gesture. In seconds the terrapins had glided to the exit, flown up the block spiral staircase to the 8-tunnelled cavern, travelled through the, 'Soil of Change,' exited the tower's grand arch and landed with a bump on the grassy knoll that was Glastonbury Tor.

"Oh bugger, better get on the radio mental! Calling all Tittytufts, calling all abhorrent Tittytufts, run up those ruddy stairs!"

Down below the Tittytufts dropped their guns and ran for the exit.

"Garston can you hear me?" Arthur shouted across the void.

In the blink of an eye Garston appeared on Arthur's shoulder.

"Thanks for the lift Albert, err, yes, I can hear you." said Garston.

"And zo can I," said Maurice instantly appearing on Arthur's other shoulder.

"Yep", said Steve appearing in Vincent's arms!

"What now?" asked Albert, standing on Vincent's head with a mean grimace!

Arthur looked at his platoon and summoned a rousing speech.

"Whenever I went into battle, I would turn to my men, look into their eyes and see their trust and belief in me. I see that very same look in all of you."

"Great, so what's the plan?" asked Vincent.

"Garston!" asked Arthur. "Tell us the plan?"

Garston took a stance, raised his tail and held it like a knight would his lance and said:

"Save the cheerleader, save the world!"

The group looked a little puzzled.

"Err, what did you say?" asked a confused Albert.

"Sorry, couldn't resist." Garston replied. "I mean, save Clipboard Girl, save the world!"

"Oh for heavens sake, and kill that psychotic spider too," Albert paused. "Wow, look at the screen."

"We've no time to watch the screen. If we dither Faith is dead, so listen up this is the plan," said Arthur. The group took a knee!

***

On the huge crystal screen, the emergence of Prometheus from the Shangri-la Pool of Light played out like a silent fantasy flick. Hecate was standing patiently waiting for him; she smiled and took him by the hand. They were alone in a brightly lit, tunnelled cavern, blocked by natural rock at one end but open to bright daylight at the other. The hollow sparkled gloriously with pearlescent minerals but was diminutive in size in comparison to the Geode that housed the Pool at Glastonbury. In fact the entire anomaly seemed as if it would be the perfect sleepy hideaway for a tired hibernating bear.

The Pool itself was also very different from the Avalon Pool. A two-foot high ornate marble wall displaying the sculpted tale of Zeus's ascendance to power ran around its edge. It rippled within, like a puddle of diamonds glistening on a bed of silver sand. Surrounded and covered by creeping burnt yellow leafed vines and sprawling pale-feathered ferns, it was without equal in its humbling yet dazzling setting. It truly was as a paddling pool made for the Gods! A break in its structure allowed for two thin meandering streams to trickle away from its grandeur towards the sun, like retreating serpents dancing around pebbles. Prometheus followed their flow to a ledge where the land fell away and the tiny streams came together and miraculously became a cascading waterfall!

Albert, the only one watching the footage, gasped, captivated and enthralled.

With his love beside him, Prometheus stood at the edge of the precipice, thousands of feet up the side of the snowless escarpment, and looked down upon the hidden land of Shangri-la. Its vast never-ending valley was comprised of lush, deep-misted forests overflowing with giant-leafed, broad trunked soaring trees. It was breathtaking. Above, lay the blanket of a Himalayan ice crystal cap. Rays of sunlight broke and split the air, and radiant coloured shafts of light illuminated Mother Earth's vestige of wonder. Prometheus looked down to the sandy floor at his feet and, with an outstretched bony finger, wrote something in the dirt.

$Nc + He + P + Fl = F$

"What the Hades does that mean?" Albert thought, unable to fully understand what he was watching.

    Prometheus stood up and turned to his love. Hecate returned him a kind smile and gave him a look that said she was ready for anything. He took her by the hand and took a few steps forward and then, that was the last of it, everything just turned to nothing!

IT WILL ALWAYS RAIN

"Alright, have we got the plan clear?"

Everyone nodded reassuringly at Arthur. He picked up the shotguns left by the Tittytufts, checked they were loaded and handed one of them to Vincent, "If they come back kill them." He paused, "remember it's for the greater good." Vincent looked at him terrified. Arthur tapped him on the shoulder reassuringly and then dashed down the crystal stairway unloading blast after blast at Freak. Closer and closer he strode towards her like a courageous soldier fronting his foe, but his efforts had little effect. The lead shots just bounced off Freak's tough exoskeleton with some, indeed, striking a lifeless Faith.

"Damn," he said to himself throwing his guns down.

"Albert, Garston," he called, "get Jonas down from there."

At that point Bedivere came running in, "Arthur," he yelled, as he tossed a short sword and a plain circular wooden shield towards his friend.

"Isn't it time for you to kill me yet, Freak?" Arthur called, rolling to a knee and grabbing the sword and shield in one fluid movement. Bedivere, also armed with a sword and shield, joined him at his side. He gave Arthur an excited glance.

"Just like the old days, hey?" he said. "Lets tie her up in knots. Two pronged attack, I'll circle round the back."

With no restrain, they then yelled and charged at Freak with Bedivere suddenly peeling right and circling behind her. Valiantly, they battled and fought but with little impact, however, their duelling did hand Albert and Garston the opportunity to snip Jonas free! Well, as fast as they possibly could, anyway. Freak's webbing had grown in toughness.

"Slice Tail, Slice!"

"I fancy a bit of Pizza after all of this, what do you say, Garst, luv?"

"Ooh, yes, Albert, with added walnuts," Garston replied.

Jonas looked at them both with a sense of panic.

"Yes, some Quattro Formaggio, yummy," said Albert.

"Yes great idea, four cheese! And what about some garlic bread, too?" Garston added.

"Ooh, garlic bread! Good call!" Albert replied.

Jonas couldn't believe what he was hearing. He gestured them to hurry up. The sight of a fraught toad riding on the back of a Jackahuahua bounding towards the eight-legged monster had made him a little anxious!

From his not so comfortable position, 'Sheriff Maurice le Toad,' flicked out his tongue and managed to wrap it around a pair of Freak's back legs.

"Great shot Maurice," Steve hailed, as he pulled as hard as he could and ran around a vertical shard near the edge of the void. Maurice returned a croak and took the brave step of leaping from Steve's back and sticking himself firmly to the wall with his sucker feet. Steve, seeing Maurice was ok, belted for cover as fast as he could whilst Freak began to totter and lose her balance! Bedivere, looking on, seized the moment, dropped his shield and ran at the eight-legged beast holding his sword in both hands raised above his head. With a warrior's yell he attempted to bury it deep into Freak's thorax. But she was too nimble. She flipped onto her back and fired off a strand of web. Bedivere was instantly disarmed. 'Spurt,' another strand struck him around his throat. He grabbed at it and fought to get away, but Freak pulled him in. She struck out. Bedivere peered down. Freaks poisonous fangs had pierced through his gloved right hand. A horror thrashed through him, but then, he remembered something, and a sense of relief washed over him. He grinned!

"Unlucky! You know, you really should have read up on your Arthurian history before battle. If you had of done, you would have known that this one," he said, as he pulled a stump away from Freak, leaving his gloved hand attached to her fangs, "was taken many hundreds of years ago and what you have in your mouth is some wonderful modern technology, rather similar to the tail that our little friend Garston possesses. However, this one," he said, raising his left arm aloft and clenching a fist, "is all mine!"

He smiled again, and with gritted teeth, threw an almighty overhead left cross into Freak's eight eyes. Freak winced, "How do you like tha..." suddenly, he fell silent and looked down to his stomach. One of Freak's legs had run him clean through. He looked at her, numb of feeling and then turned to Arthur.

"Sorry my friend," he said softly and falling to his knees, "it's time for me to finally visit Elysium."

He reached down for the hilt of his sword and with his last breath of life, grasped it to his chest. Freak gave a satisfied groan as he slid backwards from her hold, collapsing to the floor in a bloody heap. Arthur, looking on stunned, felt his heart shatter into a thousand pieces. After centuries of an exceptional, wonderful life, death had finally and mercilessly, claimed his friend. Around the Geode everyone stopped for a split in time. Still entwined in Freak's strands of webbing and with his eyes full of tears, Jonas bowed his head and muttered a silent prayer for his great, lost friend. Freak broke the silence with a hissing tirade.

"That's one of you down, White, and your Clipboard Girl will soon join him unless you can stop her bleeding to death," she taunted.

A screaming rage filled the great king. He tossed away his shield and with little regard for his own life ran at Freak, but once again she was too fast. Her front four legs danced dextrously like the blade of a Samurai master. Her deliberate defence and a slicing riposte followed Arthur's every frenzied attack. Cut, bloodied and struggling to fight a battle he obviously couldn't win, Arthur courageously fought to his last ounce of strength, until exhaustion finally took hold of him and eventually, the inevitable happened. Freak, too strong and too quick, tripped and pinned him down by his arms and legs. She snarled with satisfaction in anticipation of her kill. Drooling and salivating, she carefully engraved the letter 'I' into Arthur's forehead with a single venomous fang. Arthur's shrieks filled the Geode as the deadly, potent, venom burned through him. Freak stepped back.

"I am Inkomen, White, and you will die slowly and with as much pain as the universe can afford you," she said, sneering delightedly, "Remember, I told you I would kill you!"

But then unexpectedly, and with a show of belligerent arrogance, a young gerbil seized the moment and entered the fray, leaping onto the top of the great spider's head.

"Hey remember me? Well, if you don't I'll give you a few pointers. Tail, blind the spider," he ordered.

Garston's tail coiled and then poked and stabbed Freak's eye upon eye. She squealed, yelped and stumbled backwards, throwing Garston off before he could finish the job. Partially blinded, she bolted for the hole in the centre of the shield. Maurice however, stuck fast to the wall and still with his tongue wrapped around a pair of Freak's legs, stopped her in her tracks. She turned and tried to free herself by slicing through Maurice's tongue with her remaining claws. However, the slippery-tongued Frenchy was too quick for her! He would unwrap from one leg and then rebind around another faster then she could act. Again she stumbled, but this time it was over something on the on the ground. It was Faith. Freak made herself busy. Fixing a strand of webbing to Faith's arms, she dragged her lifeless body across the shield leaving a blazing trail of smeared blood in her wake. Engulfed by the pain of her pierced eyes, she took cover behind a crystal cluster at the far edge of the Geode. Still hampered by Maurice's tongue, she composed herself and then brimmed and roared with anger.

A familiar burst of light was followed by a clonk of steel.

Jonas reinvigorated by circumstance, wriggled free from his silk bonds and dashed for the vault. Lying on the floor, in front of the steel hatch, was Arthur's mighty sword, the sword that hundreds of years earlier he had taken from the heart of a stone, the sword that history knew by the name of, Excalibur. However, it was not alone. By its side, battered, but shining, was the helmet of a Roman legionnaire! Jonas peered through the viewing trap and was greeted by Triope. She smiled at him and ushered him to take both and go, which he did with reverence and thanks, before running over to his friend. Arthur was still lying on his back shivering uncontrollably where Freak had left him. Jonas knelt down and gently set the hilt of the sword in Arthur's palm. Arthur, quivering, turned to face his faithful servant. Jonas mustered a sympathetic smile and then took the battered brass feathered helmet, and placed it on the head of his king. A tapestry of over 700 years of memories suddenly shot through Arthur's mind, before clarity eventually came to visit.

"Help me stand," he mumbled, "Help me."

With Freak's inexorable poison coursing through his veins, Jonas helped Arthur to a bended knee.

"It may be time to die, my old friend," Arthur said softly, "and every warrior should die with his sword in his hand, thank you, now get Vincent for me."

Jonas looked up to the shelf where Vincent was standing, dazed with horror and beckoned him over. Vincent, stumbled, dropped his shotgun and ran across the shield as fast as he could. He knelt down beside Arthur, taking him by the hand.

"Save Faith, Vincent, she… is something special, …I don't know what, but Man needs her, Man needs, Faith." Arthur paused and spluttered, struggling to hold onto life. "Now get Bedivere and me to Paradise, my lad, whilst the doorway still remains open. We can at least cheat an eternity in Hades for our crimes, hey?" Arthur fell forward into Vincent's arms. "The family solicitors, you must visit them once more boy, do this for me. It's regarding your…"

Vincent nodded.

"I will," he replied. "Save your strength. And Sir, I know you've done what you had to, to save us, to save us all, I know!"

It was at that moment, with a dying king staring into his eyes, Vincent became a leader of men.

"Now, we've got to get that spider's attention and get Faith clear and straight to a hospital, Albert!" Vincent called.

"Err, I don't think we are going to need a doctor," Albert replied, landing at Vincent's feet. "Not unless they now conduct exorcisms!"

Vincent turned to his friend with a look that said; 'what the begeebies are you on about?' only to see Albert raise a wing and point. Faith, lifeless and surrounded by a golden glow, was floating to the centre of the shield several metres up in the air. Like a wonderful motionless, wireless, marionette she dragged Freak along behind her by the strand of web that tied them together.

Commence the Reckoning, sounded through the Geode, startling everyone.

"What's going on Peuja?" Vincent asked, but with know reply.

Freak cut herself loose and retreated cautiously. The light in the void pulsated and the Geodes crystals sparked and crackled as if they were alive with electricity. A singular shard slid down from the ceiling directly above Faith's halted, floating position, which was over the hole created by Finn's dissolving, above the sign of Ankh. Around the void sparks entwined and intensified and soon became zipping, flying bolts of threaded lightning. Dancing and prancing from crystal to crystal, they slithered along the walls to the protruding shard, which dazzled until it could store the massive charge no more and then, from its tip and with an almighty crack, as if thrown by the arm of Zeus himself, it blasted a blinding bolt directly at Faith! A bright blue electrical sphere instantly formed around Faith's suspended body and she began to writhe and shudder within its heart.

Vincent turned to Jonas,

"You know, about a year ago I would have thought this to be pretty strange, but now," he shrugged, "soy off a Peking duck's back!"

Jonas looked back at him obviously petrified.

"That look you're giving me doesn't fill me with optimism, Jonas!" said Vincent.

Albert, slapped by a moment of clarity, solved Prometheus's equation scribed in the dirt at Shangri-la.

"Nc + He + P + Fl = F. Oh my Lord. Nanteus Cup + Hecate + Prometheus + Fleece = FAITH! She's being reborn, I'm going to be an uncle," he said, tearing up and wiping an eye with his cravat.

"Albert if you know what's happening, please would you explain it to the rest of us?" Vincent asked impatiently.

"You didn't see it, you were all listening to Arthur's plan." Albert took a breath. "Prometheus wrote an equation in the dirt before he left, to err, wherever he went to, and I've just solved it, darlings!"

"Well?" Vincent pleaded.

Full of pride, Albert replied.

"We few, we privileged and humble brigade of misfits, are witnessing an event not seen for a million or so years," he paused. "Friends, I give you the birth of a Titan. Faith is a God, well, a Titan, which is a God, before they were called… Oh, you know what I mean!"

The Golden Fleece seemed to sweep and twist about Faith, until they both became almost indivisible from each other and then, magic! Curly ram-like horns began to appear from the side of Faith's skull as her facial features changed to somewhere beyond human. Her clothes withered and dissolved like grains of salt in water, leaving her naked to the world except, that is, for her gifted sandal, whose leather strapping climbed her calf like a vine winding around the trunk of its host, as it altered in size and shape to fit one of her now fur lined cloven feet. A pair of glorious white and golden-tinted feathered wings sprouted from the blades of her back and spread spectacularly, glittering at their tips like the burning embers of a spitting log fire. Where her skin was not covered by short, twisted, fleece like knotted body hair, it transformed and become dusky and burnished in appearance. She shimmered like satin and shone as brightly as the heart of Mother Nature herself.

"Oh heavens, isn't she beautiful?" Albert whispered a gasp.

Maurice, for some reason, possibly momentarily distracted, let his tongue grip slip and 'slap,' it quickly drew back into his mouth, setting Freak free.

Project Theacate complete!

"Theacate huh, predictable but surprising to the end. You've got to hand it to the pair of them, Prometheus and Hecate that is, they fooled everyone in their quest to get back to Paradise, even Hera and Zeus and now, they've left mankind with something to help him survive himself! They weren't so bad after all, just adoring lovers in an uncontrollable world of romantic notion!" Albert reflected.

The sizzling sphere surrounding Faith exploded into the ether and she dropped to the ground, landing crouched on all fours. Slowly she tottered up onto her two legs like a newly born fawn and revealed that she was now some ten feet tall! Her eyes flashed open and exposed their captivating deep blood-red hue. She stared at the world around her for a moment and then stretched out and flapped her wings and then, launched herself into the air like a brave fledgling taking its first flight. Everybody watched in wonder as she dove and spun around the vastness of the Geode with childlike, mischievous joy. After a little while she came to land beside Arthur, Vincent, Albert and Jonas, her wings beating to a halt and folding away behind her. She looked at them all with an expression that told them not to be afraid and then knelt down by Arthur's side. Reaching forward, she removed Arthur's helmet and took Excalibur from his grasp. She handed them to Vincent before placing her arms around her dear Mr White and standing, effortlessly, with him cradled in her arms. She turned to Vincent, who looked up at her, mesmerised.

"Take the sword, helmet and Bedivere to Triope, there is something I must do," she said in a wondrously, soothing controlled tone.

Vincent, speechless, nodded and then turned to Jonas who smiled back at him nervously. Arthur, hearing a familiar voice slowly opened his eyes.

"Faith is that you?" He muttered in his dazed state.

"It's Clipboard Girl to you, sir, and don't you forget it," she answered cheekily. "Now, come fly with me."

Faith stretched out her wings once more, gave them a beat and rose high into the void. She swooped around its walls briefly before heading out of the entrance, up the stone spiral stairway, through the 'Soil of Change' and out through the open top of the shell of St Michael's tower, high into the crisp night air. The chilled autumn winds watered Arthur's eyes as he looked down at the night-lights of Glastonbury town glimmering beneath him like jewels in the blanket of the English countryside. "I'm flying. I'm flying!" He whispered,

A joyful tear rolled down his cheek as the pain within him began to fade.

"Time to rest now," he muttered stroking Faith's arm. She remained silent, but returned him an understanding look. Gliding with the thermals, she turned towards the Tor.

Jonas, Vincent and Albert, laid Bedivere, Excalibur and the Roman helmet gently down in front of Triope's door. They rested Bedivere's sword in his arms across his chest and took a step back. They felt the air around them beat as Faith came to land by their side.

"I thought the power of the Fleece might save him, but it appears he is too weak and beyond saving. Inkomens venom is…" she paused, "it is time to finish this. Here, take him." She handed Arthur to Vincent and took flight.

Vincent laid Arthur down beside Bedivere.

"Thank you, boy," he said. "Paradise calls."

Albert jumped up and hovered at the viewing trap, Triope looked at him curiously.

"Triope," he said, "I know these two men are not antiquities of historical significance but they are human relics of a great time past. They are, if you like, walking artefacts of mankind and they deserve a place in the heavens for all they have done for Mother Earth and their own species. Please will you open the vault door and drag them through. I know you can, and will, because I know you are an extraordinary err, thingy! Please luv, take them to Paradise?"

Triope returned Albert an understanding smile and a few seconds later the trapdoor began to alter its shape.

"Wait!" Arthur said, grabbing Vincent's arm tightly.

"Hold on Triope, one second darling," Albert called raising a wing.

"Cabal," he said with a whisper.

From where he was hidden behind a crystal, Steve's little ears pricked up and without hesitation or fear, he ran across the shield to the group and sat down beside Arthur.

"Cabal, I have lied to you, and I must confess." Arthur said gasping for breath.

"You have a past that you know nothing of." Steve tilted his head to one side. "You too have lived almost as long as I. It was I that placed you on the Grid and not Prometheus. Your memory was removed so that you would not be confused in your task of protecting those around you, and you have done well, my boy. You have done very well. You have been my eminent, faithful friend for as long as I can remember. You are the bravest and most loyal of your kind. Promise me, you will trust Vincent and guard him at any price, promise me."

Steve barked as if to answer and then whined.

Arthur raised his hand and gently stroked the little dog.

"I love you, boy," he whispered, "Vincent is your master now, love him," and with those words Arthur drifted into an everlasting sleep.

The group fell silent as a tidal wave of loss engulfed them all. Steve whimpered and gently licked Arthur's face. It was only the sound of the steel latch turning to release Triope's side of the hatch that brought them back to the task in hand. They closed their eyes and listened out for the sound of the door closing. When they opened them again, Arthur and Bedivere were gone and in their place was the black velvet bundle that held the head of the Lance of Longinus.

Vincent peered through the viewing trap into the Hollow. No one was there.

"What's in the bundle?" he said turning and bending down to unwrap it.

Jonas quickly jumped in and pushed Vincent to the floor. He looked at him and motioned a deliberate no with an outstretched index finger.

"Is it dangerous?" Vincent asked

Jonas nodded.

"Can it kill Inkomen?"

Jonas shrugged a shrug that meant, I don't know, maybe!

"Well that's good enough for me," Vincent said getting to his feet and running out of the vault cavern to the shield.

'BOOM!'

A sound of rolling thunder filled the Geode. Billions of minuscule, powdered crystal particles had burst into the air like puffs of flour. A cry of 'Oolaballuh,' could just be heard above the din and an eerie ball of mist formed at one point on the shield. The Lords of Pangea were free and each was transforming! Faith landed in front of Freak and fluttered herself free of the crystal blizzard. Freak growled and stamped threateningly, but Faith just calmly returned a smile and, after a moment of thought, leapt once again into the air. Freak turned sharply as, strangely, she felt a gust of wind blow through her silvery sheen, she saw nothing, nothing was there, but then 'Smash,' she was sideswiped and sent tumbling and crashing against the outer wall as if struck by a rumbling rolling boulder. Stunned, she tried to stand but found one of her eight legs to be broken at a joint. Staggering, she looked around half-blind to see what had hit her, but again she found nothing. She turned to run to the hole near the centre of the shield, but found it to be heavily defended. Roxanna the Warg was standing in her way drooling and howling and ready for a fight, she beckoned the monstrous spider on. In a breeze blown flash, Tecciztecatl was at Roxanna's side hovering and darting hither and thither. They bowed to each other in a show of mutual respect and then turned once more to face their enemy.

'Look, they're guarding the entrance," said Albert.

A roar, grabbed Freak's attention, she turned. Bastet in her fiery lioness form was stealthily crouched on a small crystal ledge. Freak took a stance and unleashed a volley of webbing, but it merely disintegrated upon striking its flaming target. Bastet prowled forward purposefully, her appearance inducing Freak's nervous, scattered memories of the Earths burning core. A screech from aloft returned her to the present. She looked up, Karura was hovering high above her, menacingly sounding his intent. He expanded his chest with a deep intake of breath, opened his beak wide, extended his neck forward, and from the depths of his throat launched a spectacular jet of flame. Freak's silver hair instantly set ablaze, causing her to scamper and panic wildly. She dived to the ground and rolled around trying to put it out, but then, suddenly, she just stopped and rose to her feet. She had realised that the pain she associated with the burning was only in her mind and she allowed her once beautiful hair to sizzle away to nothing and expose her tough dark brown exoskeleton. Scorched and furious, she retaliated with a barrage of webbing, but it, too, missed its target as Karura just eased to one side and watched it fly by. Freak screamed with frustration.

Faith, sat perched on a ledge, watched inquisitively, giggling gleefully like an amused child enjoying every minute of a wonderful game. Hopi landed on her shoulder. He looked no different from his normal self, but for the fact that his eyes now appeared to be pearlescent. Faith stared at them, looking at her own reflection. She gave the glossy raven a respectful bow and then returned to viewing the gladiatorial spectacle that was unfolding before her.

"I think it's best we all stay out of the way for a little bit," said Vincent turning to Jonas and his friends.

Garston muttered something in scouse that no one could understand!

"Oh hello, Maurice, come for a front seat?" said Steve.

"Zis is all very exciting."

"Isn't it just Maurice," Albert replied, transfixed.

"Don't move a muscle any of you!" Garston suddenly shouted, "We're getting a visitor!"

Lecter was bowling up towards them.

Everybody, of course, knew that Lecter wasn't just Lecter but also Hanuman, the great battle scarred general and Lord of the sub-continent of India and Pangea, but that didn't stop them feeling very nervous! He ran up to Vincent and climbed up his trousers and top to Vincent's face. He twitched and snorted, ruffled Vincent's hair a bit, checking for knits, and then grabbed him by the ears and pulled him in until they were nose to nose. His eyes darted madly from side to side as he prodded and sniffed the human face.

"Vincent," he yelled delightedly, his jaw still wired shut, "Kisses!"

And with that the little monkey slobbered a great fat one all over Vincent's face!

"Shouldn't the timer be putting that helmet back to its original position by now?" said Vincent.

"Oh Vinnie, you iz zo behind ze times, in it! Hannibal iz self-governing now thanks to Zeth. Hiz voice recognition now workz both wayz."

"Thanks Maurice, that's great to know," he said sarcastically! "If not a little late!"

Lecter leapt away and with his bizarre gait, ran around from cluster to cluster frantically searching for something until finally, after much studying, he grasped the root of a thin 6-foot shard and shook it with all his might, as if it was a palm and he was shaking loose the world's last coconut. With a final grimace, it snapped away cleanly in his hands and instantaneously began to glow. He bounced towards Jonas, who was still holding the velvet black bundle, looked at him suspiciously and then pointed towards something high in the air behind him! Jonas turned to see exactly what had grabbed Lecter's attention and, as he did so, the mad monkey snatched the bundle from his grasp and turned his back to the group. A split of hair in time and some cracking noises later, Lecter revolved to reveal a wired crazy grin and a glowing futuristic spear, a Lance of Longinus, looking as if it had travelled from a galaxy far, far away! He gave Vincent a salute, which Vincent tentatively returned, and then Lecter headed towards Freak. He slalomed left and then right and then he'd crouch and then jump!

"Wat'z he doing?" asked Maurice.

"An assault course in his own mind by the looks of it." Garston replied.

Lecter did indeed look very peculiar. With the stealth of a cold war spy keeping out of sight, he ventured forward. Freak was too preoccupied to notice the little monkey; the strange mist slowly crawling towards her had alerted her senses. Taking cover just off the edge of the shield behind a wide crystal, Lecter planned his attack, visualising his actions in his own head, whilst waving a hand in the air! He took in a sharp breath and then took a quick peek. Freak was facing the opposite direction. He wiped the beads of sweat from his brow and then turned the tip of the lance downward. One last minute glance, a garbled chat to himself in a mysterious dialect, and then he ran towards his target, once again skipping right and left, side to side. However, to the astonishment of Vincent and the rest of the group he did not attack the eight legged beast, but chose to frantically prance around her with the tip of the lance scratching and gouging a thin trench into the face of the shield. His manic endeavours, of course, aroused Freak's curiosity. She watched him intently with interest, and a little confusion, as he toiled!

"What's he doing now, luvs?" asked Albert.

The shield seemed to bleed a translucent liquid from its wounds.

Lecter raised his head, smiled and waved endearingly at the spider and then scuttled off back to the relative safety of a crystal barricade at the shield's edge. His heart thumping like a drum in his chest, he looked up, and signalled, with a, 'thumbs up!'

Bastet immediately sprang from her ledge and landed not aside Freak, but within her. She strode through her as she would a wall, roasting the great spider's internal organs. Freak shrieked and tore about, bewildered and disorientated. Unable to defend the attack, she dashed for the hole in the shield where Roxanna and Tecci braced themselves for trouble. However, there was no need for any undue concern, for upon Lecter's command Karura released another jet of flame. The gauged trench oozing the translucent liquid instantly ignited. A wall of fire, some three metres high and burning a bright blue flame, stopped Freak in her tracks and obscured her view of the world around her. Karura let out another burst of flame, but this time directly at the spider; Freak's torso began to glow with the intensity of the heat. Lecter once more peeked out from behind a crystal and again raised his arm aloft. From the ghostly creeping mist, a vociferous roar sounded and filled the void and then Whiro's hulking great fearsome frame erupted into the field of battle. The branded, war scarred monstrous iguana, with his icy breath and powerful jaws, let out another guttural bellowing roar. This was the signal for Bastet to stride out of the circle of fire. She strode up to Whiro and bowed her head regally as she passed. He flicked out his tongue, shook his head and then charged at the wall of flame. As he entered the circle steam hissed from his torso. Vincent caught a glimpse of Freaks glowing exoskeleton.

"Did you see that?" he said as the curtain of fire closed behind

Whiro. "She looks like the inside of a furnace."

No one answered; they just looked on, silent. All of the Lords of Pangea, other than Hopi who was still sitting with Faith, slowly gathered around the flaming circle and one by one transformed back to their normal selves. Only Lecter stood as a God, well sort of! He turned and beckoned Vincent and the rest of the throng over to his side as the uncomfortable, disconcerting and heartbreaking sounds of an animal screeching and wailing in distress filled the air. As the cries died away, Whiro, head down, exited the circle of fire and walked over to Vincent, transforming back into Spike. Lecter turned to Bandi and motioned her to cut the wire holding his jaw together. She obliged by pinging out a claw and putting it to good use. Lecter grinned and yawned and then walked over to Spike and knelt down before him.

"Young Spike, nay Whiro," he said in a comforting tone. "You have done what you have had to for the good of all the living creatures of this planet, those who without, we are all nothing." Lecter paused. "Destroying something that breathes a life for the reason not of food, is a terrible thing, and to be one of our own too, well, my heart doth cry with the shame you must feel. However, you must remember this, when we were given this servitude we carry, we all knew that one day, this day might come upon us and, you have done well my, Lord."

Lecter turned towards the curtain of fire and watched the flames quell and die away. Freak, broken, mangled and frazzled lay on the shield twitching. Some of her legs were ripped from her torso and she was bleeding heavily from a vicious bite to the side of her thorax, but she was still alive.

"Why did you leave her like that? Why didn't you finish it?" Albert was overcome.

"Because we must all say goodbye." Lecter replied.

"But the pain…"

"…Is so much to bear, pigeon, that she is near numb, come," Lecter replied.

The group, led by the little mad monkey, congregated in front of Freak who raised her head slowly. Her eyes were now so damaged that she could hardly make out those who stood before her.

Lecter began; "Lord Inkomen, you have been a magnificent Lord of Pangea, an adversary who has performed her duties with dignity and efficiency. You were both dedicated and dependable and shall be missed by those who love you and those who worship your kind. You have done Lord Zeus's bidding and no doubt shall be rewarded in the afterlife."

He dropped to one knee still holding the Lance of Longinus and peered at the others, they followed suit.

"Is there anything you would like to say, Lord Inkomen?" Lecter asked softly.

Disorientated, with her face battered and broken and dripping with her own blood, Freak looked up at the group. Struggling to hold onto life she murmured with great sorrow, breathing a whisper.

"Sorry! It was just my nature!" She said.

Albert sniffed a whimper and wiped away his tears.

The group were all stood stunned in a respectful silence and filled with remorse.

Lecter got to his feet, muttered a prayer beneath his breath and raised his lance. With fleeting speed and accuracy he lunged at Freak like a matador administering a coup de gras.

"To Paradise," he said.

Freak squealed and quivered briefly and then, peace and darkness took her spirit. Lecter looked to the skies; "Lord Zeus, take Lord Inkomen your servant home. It is finished."

"No, no!" Albert cried, "covering his face with his wings."

Lecter turned to Vincent; "It is time for me to abscond now," he said. "This century is not a time for me and my work here is done. But do not be too concerned; our little friend can call upon me whenever my service is required." He turned to Jonas; "Monk, this Lance needs to be returned if you please."

Jonas nodded, took the Lance and covered the spearhead with the black velvet cloth and ran over to the Vault. He put on the safety goggles, tapped on the steel door and placed the bundle down. To his surprise, the door opened and then shut with lightning speed. A plain looking key, made of iron that was obviously many hundreds of years old, had replaced the bundle! He peered through the viewing glass, Triope returned him a smile and again, ushered him away. He took the key, placed it on his key chain and rejoined the watching group.

"Now before I retire, I do have a small request." Lecter grinned. "If you wouldn't mind, dear lady."

He walked up to Bandi and somewhat strangely, and more than a little awkwardly, lifted her up onto her hind legs and danced a waltz with her whilst humming a tune.

"I haven't danced with a lady in years," he said.

Lecter then stuck out his tongue, and blew a raspberry at the group.

"Remember," he said, "to live your life as if bathed in sunlight! Because, it will always rain!"

The group turned to one another with a look of uncertainty. Lecter placed Bandi down kissed her paw, turned to the group once more, gave them all a massive grin and yelled, "Hullabaloo!"

Unlike the terrifying shrill of transformation belonging to Hannibal, Lecter stood with his arms wide and roared with ecstatic verve as his joints and bones cracked and popped. Finally, his little bright red glossy helmet slipped over his face and, like Elvis, Lecter left the building!

Hannibal crouched, turned sheepishly. "Did I miss anything?" he said.

Albert burst into an explanation that to any normal critter would have seemed ridiculous.

"Oh Hannibal, it's been terrible, Mr White's dead, Bedivere's dead, Freak's lying in hundreds of pieces just behind you, dead, oh, and I forgot to mention that Faith is a flying coat from Harvey Nicks and apparently, it will always rain!" his sobbing rant was cut short.

"Welcome back buddy," said Steve, "I'll tell you all about it when we get home to watch some reruns of Dallas."

Hannibal smiled kindly at his old friend.

"So what happens now?" asked Garston.

No one answered; they were too preoccupied with the fact that Faith was swooping towards them. She landed a little distance in front of the group and then in a malaise of pulsating luminescence, changed back to her human form. The Golden Fleece glittered magically and transformed into a long plain beige woollen cardigan, gratefully hiding her blushes, and her footwear became just an ordinary tatty ancient Greek sandal! She stroked Vincent's face tenderly, staring into his eyes as if something deep inside of her had been woken for the very first time.

"We go home," he said softly returning her gaze, "all of us."

Faith put her arms around him, like a lost child found, and hugged him tightly.

A familiar voice called to them across the void.

"Well, I don't know about you guys but I'm still hungry, and that spread in the kitchen isn't gong to eat itself." It was Finn holding a heart of celery!

"How on Earth did...?"

"Exactly, Vincent my boy," he replied, "Earth! From that hole, to the entrance and anywhere else I want to be. When I'm not transformed by the magic of knowledge and circumstance that is! Eh, Roxy would you like some ham? Got some lovely honey roast in the fridge. Come on girl, hold on, where's Arthur?"

Albert suddenly appeared on the giants shoulder.

"Finn," he said sadly, "I'm really sorry, but Arthur and Bedivere, they didn't survive the fight."

Finn bowed his head and then lifted it and smiled at the little pigeon.

"Then this is indeed a great day," he said, "the day they've been dreaming of for centuries. The day that they see their loved ones again. One thing I learnt from Prometheus, actually he taught me many things, but importantly, he taught me that death is just another part of life, the final part of a trilogy. Our spirits, or for those of you with a religious nature, our souls, all meet again in the onward realm of Paradise. So Albert, don't be sad, Arthur will be with Guinevere somewhere, laughing about old times and talking about forgiveness and Bedivere, well, he will be playing with his sons at last. It's a day to rejoice and not grieve. Celebrate how people live and never how they die, that's the philosophy a great Titan once taught me."

Catching the group by surprise the shield once more behaved as if it were alive! A creaking grinding noise came from its centre as the hole in the Sign of Ankh began to close and the smooth surface started to grow clusters of razor sharp crystals.

"Quick to the stairs, up to the ledge," said Vincent in a panic.

"No need to rush," Faith said calmly. "Just walk close to me."

As the shards split the air around them the group huddled together and walked over to the edge of the shield and up the stairs to the entrance shelf where Finn was stood with a smile.

"Are you going to be alright Finn, with Prometheus gone?" asked a concerned Albert.

"Alright, alright? Course I am. First thing, I'm going home for a brief visit, see how that old Causeway looks now. I'll sit there at night with a barrel of stout and watch the sunset over the sea. Then I'm going to travel the globe and sample every country's version of porcine that I can find. Then I'll take in a few sights, the wonders of the world and the other 'Pools of Light' and stuff. I can't wait. It's going to be fantastic. Freedom to leave Avalon at last, no ties."

"That sounds fabulous," said Albert excitedly, "I don't suppose I could join you every now and then could I? I have a little bit of wanderlust in me myself. Just email me and let me know where you are, darling, and I'll be there in a instant."

"It would be my honour, Albert."

"Look!" said Maurice, "what iz Hopi doing?"

The group turned.

Across on the other side of the Geode, Hopi was perched on Freak's shattered carcass picking at her remains like a wild vulture feasting on carrion. Garston used his cam eye and zoomed in. He watched closely as Hopi pulled something from the back of Freak's skull and took flight, just before the shield's crystal clusters engulfed and swallowed up Freak's remnants leaving no evidence of her existence.

"He's got Freak's Microchip in his beak," he said.

"What? In the wrong hands that could be disastrous," Seth replied.

"He's flying right at us," said Hannibal.

"No he's not. He's flying for the exit that's what he's doing." Garston replied.

Hopi swooped past them but then changed direction and flew straight at the wall of the Geode and then miraculously straight through it.

"Hopi can become anything he comes into contact with, be it stone, crystal, water, anything at all and therefore he's already above us flying through the air to his destination," said Finn. "Prometheus tutored me in each of your ways you see, and as Hopi is the eyes of Zeus he got the greatest gift of all. He can go anywhere and be everywhere! This isn't over, it seems someone up there isn't happy!" Finn breathed a deep sigh and led the group up to the kitchen hollow where he and Jonas cleared and wiped down the round table.

"I think we should leave Arthur and Bedivere's chairs empty, retire them as a mark of respect," said Vincent.

"Agreed young man," said Finn, "that way they will always be remembered by their absence. You're going to make a fine leader my boy, Arthur would be proud. He and Bedivere would have wanted us to rejoice their lives by raising a glass of juice," he said, "and as I said, I'm absolutely starving!"

***

A pair of dishevelled undertakers sitting on the back of a trailer that was being drawn by a tractor down a country lane holding a pair of white terrapins in their hands, may be seen as a strange sight!

"Oh woe is I and I. Thrown out of the party for merely having the nerve to rise up and try to extinguish mankind. It has come to pass that I and I have been hoodwinked all along by a pair of Tights! The sad thing is that thine knows nothing of the significant events that have unfolded within the cavernous abyss. Henceforth I say it's time to go home and lick said wounds. Find myselves a good patch of seaweed to rest I's weary selves upon and take a miniscule moment to rethink and reformulate. For one day, I and I may venture to rise again! Hahahaha! Oh, I's cannot be bothered!"

"Where are we off to now, masters?" Jill asked sullen and exhausted.

Yin and Yang ignored the question.

"Is there any chance that we may see our children again? I miss them terribly," she said stifling a snivel.

John put his arm around his wife.

"I do too, Jill," he said comforting her. "Please don't cry."

"Oh heavens, the human race can be so repellent. Yes you can, but only in a few months time after you heal."

"Heal?" Jill enquired.

"Well, due to your continued service I and I have decided to

161

purchase thee both a gift, Plastic Surgery!"

"But I don't want Plastic Surgery!" Jill replied.

"You're both dead. Appearing from the grave to your children will make things very messy. Thus if you want to see them again, facial restructuring it is. There is also the little point of continuity!"

"Continuity?" John replied a little confused.

"Yes, you see when the film of I and I's lives, 'The rise of the great Terrorpins', finally reaches production, your roles can be played by a younger more virile pair of actors when I's get to the sequel! You know for the ratings and box office, someone like Bradley Gosling or Angelina Knightly! It's a win-win situation. The stars get to meet I and I, and you get to look ten years younger."

"But our kids won't recognise us," said Jill.

"Isn't there just always something to moan about? Humans are so repugnant and self absorbed, always thinking of themselves. Anyway that's enough, bored of that conversation now, so moving on or back, whichever you prefer! To answer your earlier question I's are going home. We have a plane waiting for us at a local airfield and from there we are being taken to a larger airport where once again Customs have been taken care of and our private chartered 707 awaits. You will use the facilities at the airport to clean up and, of course, you will have time for some retail therapy in order that you may re-clothe yourselves from the many outlets available at free of duty once you are through passport control."

"But, sirs..." said Jill

"Don't but sirs I and I woman! Have you forgotten who I's are? Would you like your husband to lose a toe? No! Good, then shut it!"

AMMOTHELLA SYMBIAS, BLANC, ASPRO, AND ABYADH!

"Vincent, would you like to lead the toast?" asked Seth.

The group were all sat around the round table in the Kitchen Hollow.

"I think that honour should be left to Faith," he replied noticing how sad she seemed.

Faith looked up at the group, as if prompted to return from a land of notion, and pulled herself together.

"To Arthur," she paused and raised a glass, "my Mr White, and to Bedivere my friend, our friends and friends of Mother Earth. May they live forever in our thoughts and watch over us from their place in Paradise always."

"Hear, hear," said Finn. The gang all raised a glass, cup or mug best they could.

"May I be so bold as to propose another toast?"

"That would be absolutely fine, Albert," said Seth.

Albert climbed up onto the table and took his cup of fruit juice in both wings.

"Comrades," he said proudly, "please raise your vessels or just face your bowls, for the greatest minds ever to grace this wondrous, majestic world. To Prometheus, who is responsible for everyone's gifts and set us on our way, and to Hecate, his love, who introduced us all to beautiful Roxy," Roxy let out a little bark that triggered a universal giggle. "And, of course, thank you to them both for delivering us Faith."

The troop jeered heartily.

"A wonderful toast of sentiment Albert," said Seth.

Albert fluffed his feathers and took a sip of juice before the group settled down and tucked into some grub. In Maurice's case, it really was some grub! One of the group however, had his mind elsewhere. Spike, immersed in pain and remorse, dragged his claws along the plate that lay in front of him.

"We forgot someone," he said with his voice filled with regret.

He raised his eye line and nudged a bowl before him.

"To Freak, my friend and companion who gave her life because she was created to know, no different. She was truly one of the greatest beasts to ever grace this world, and when we meet again, may she hold forgiveness in her heart."

Silence filled the room.

"Please eat," he said. "This is my guilt to bear. I just think she should be remembered as much as anyone."

Vincent turned to his friend.

"Spike," he said, "this place, everything around us, this world even and all the Pools of Light that illuminate its hidden secrets, are monuments to all of our lost friends. You are right to remember her and celebrate her life. She will never be forgotten, She was amazing."

Spike tried to give Vincent a smile.

"So what do we do now, I mean after going back to Little Budworth?" Escobar asked.

"Well, simple really, we become what Mr White, sorry Arthur, wanted us to be," replied Bandi.

"What'z zat zen?" asked Maurice.

"Saviours!" Seth replied.

"What?" asked Albert.

"I think what Bandi is saying, if I may be so bold, my lady, is, that we should use our incredible gifts to fight for the survival of Mother Nature and all around her." said Seth

"Exactly," Bandi added, "despots, evil oligarchs, dictators, drug barons, crime lords, terrorists and anyone else who does anything remotely stupid to the creatures of this world or Mother Earth's environment, or their fellow man for that matter, well, they're going to come face to face with something quite surprising."

"You mean uz."

"That's right Maurice, all of us," Bandi replied.

Steve, with a sudden thought blurted out a question.

"So what does all the stuff we got from Triope do then?" he asked.

"Yes, this sandal's very peculiar," said Faith, munching incessantly as if she hadn't eaten for a hundred years! "What?" She said spitting out a mouth full of cheese. "Anyone got a problem?"

"No, no, not at all," Vincent replied nervously on behalf of the group.

Jonas rattled his chain and brought out his ancient iron key!

"That's new, or rather, very old! Well, anyway, I have no idea and I'm not asking for the book from Triope, so you'll have some fun finding out won't you. And I'll get you a pair of Prometheus' slippers Faith, although you'll only need the one!" said Finn.

The group ate and chatted for a little while and then were given licence to have a further look around. They all got to see Arthur and Bedivere's quarters, where they had a little weep, and Seth got to go through some of Prometheus' notes. But, more importantly, they all got to have a sleep. Saving the world from impending doom had taken all night and now they had eaten their fill of food too, well, they just couldn't keep their many eyes open. Finn, Faith and Vincent, one by one, put all of the little ones to bed before Finn handed Faith a singular purple corduroy slipper, which was actually a little too big, but soon transformed to a perfect fit! Vincent and Faith thought a gentle stroll to walk off supper around the tunnels of Avalon, would be a good idea, and so, pottered off!

"Stick to the crystal tunnels, the dirt ones will kill you, full of booby traps remember?" said Finn.

He decided to take this peaceful time to sit down on the Internet for a while and have a look at where around the world he would like to visit. His massive frame looked very peculiar hunched over a little keyboard over at the Tech Hub, and his fat fingers struggled to find the keys on the keypad as he typed, but he looked at the enormous screen with satisfaction as his searches reeled out success!

"Mardi Gras, great they'll think I'm in a costume there. Borneo, see the Orangutans, should be plenty of foliage to cover me up there. The world heritage sight in Marrakesh! Hmm, now that one will be a little tougher!"

***

"So you're a Titan, huh?" said Vincent, with the hint of an upward inflection as he and Faith dawdled through the sparkling, crystal walled labyrinth.

"Yeah, I guess I am," she replied blushing. "I wonder if I've got one of those shadows following me around? I must ask Bandi."

There was an awkward pause.

"And you're the next step in human evolution, the future of mankind!" she said.

Vincent smiled shyly. There was another pause as Faith took him by the hand.

"I'm going to miss him terribly, you know?" she said sombrely. "Arthur really was a great man, a clever, loving, generous man. He was so committed to good causes; he gave money to everyone that asked for it, when it came to saving animals and the good of the planet. Many of the world's endangered species are actually being saved because of his charity. You know, everything he did was for the best."

Vincent remained sullen.

"It's just all a little tough for me to take in right now, with what happened to my parents and everything."

"I know Vincent," Faith replied, understandingly and affectionately.

There was another awkward pause.

"So will you come and live with us then," Vincent stuttered, "I mean we have a spare room at The Cottage?"

Faith smiled.

"I would love to, but we will have to see. There is Jonas to think of," she replied.

"I'm certain something's been arranged. When I get to see the family solicitors, I'll have to ask about the Manor and Alcatraz Island," said Vincent.

Faith stopped walking and reflected for a moment. She raised her hand to her face and strangely drifted into daydream. "I hope something sensible has been sorted!"

She felt herself come over a little tired; she gave a stretch and had a satisfying yawn.

"I'm a little pooped, I think I should get back for a lie down before we toddle off."

Vincent nodded in agreement and they both turned to stroll back, however, there were tunnel entrances and exits all around them.

"Which direction did we come from?" asked Faith, "We've been walking around for a while now, I don't suppose you kept track did you?"

Vincent's face said it all. They were lost in the maze of tunnels and didn't have a clue which way to turn.

"We could just yell out! Someone will hear us," he said.

"But they're all asleep. I would feel horrible waking any of them up. Everyone has gone through so much today." Faith had a glint in her eye. "We could just sit here and wait until someone wakes up and comes and finds us. It's a little cold though. We may have to snuggle up to keep ourselves warm," Faith teased with a giggle. "Don't worry, I wont bite you, not unless you want me too!" she said.

Vincent felt his face flush with embarrassment.

"We could just send them a message via JR. Or just tap our heels together and say, 'I wish I could find a way back to Finn?'" Vincent said smiling.

A sudden buzz sounded around them. It was coming from inside Vincent's pocket. He reached in and pulled out the twig that was put out by Triope from the vault. It was vibrating so much that he dropped it to the floor. He gave Faith a puzzled look.

"How did that get there?" Vincent said.

The twig then proceeded to flip and turn from one end to the other and oddly travel along the long narrow corridor.

"Well, that's something you don't see everyday," Faith said.

"A walking stick!" said Vincent.

"Well, let's follow it, we should, shouldn't we?" Faith replied.

In no time at all, the stick hopped and bounced through the catacombs, easily conquering every obstacle in its path. It finally stopped travelling and vibrating upon reaching Finn who was still sat at the computer keyboard on the Tech Hub.

"Oh, hello you two," he said. "Anything wrong?"

"No, not at all Finn," Vincent replied bending down to pick up the twig at the giant's feet. "I think I know what this does now, though," he said. "We were lost in the tunnels and I said, I wish I could find a way back to Finn and lo and behold this twig began to vibrate in my pocket. I took it out, dropped it, and then it flipped along on its own and found its way to you. Hard to believe, I know."

"Did it? No, it can't be! Well, it must be? No it can't possibly be, not a chance! Well it has to be?" said Finn assuredly! "I have heard Prometheus talk about this twig before. It's Theseus's stick!"

"What?" Faith asked looking for a slightly better explanation than the one offered.

"Theseus, as in Theseus and the Minotaur, you know the ancient Greek myth," he replied.

Vincent and Faith turned to one another and then gestured for Finn to continue.

"Theseus used a ball of twine to find his way out of the labyrinth after slaying the Minotaur below the Palace of Knossos where King Minos of Crete kept the terrible beast. Well, Prometheus used to tell me that it wasn't really the ball of twine that was special, but the stick it was wrapped around! I never used to take much notice; I mean he had a story for everything. Tell you the truth, he could be quite boring sometimes, full of this fact or that. The amount of general knowledge he possessed was ridiculous. Very well read he was. You know that thing must be from around 1430 BC!"

"Wow," said Vincent, "we better get a little box for it, then!"

Finn chuckled.

"Yes, now you better get some kip, both of you, before you totter off back to The Cottage tomorrow. You can use Arthur's quarters Faith and you Bedivere's, Vincent. They are both very comfy. They'll be none of that sharing a room business while I'm in charge, so behave yourselves and get to bed!"

Vincent, as red as beetroot, nodded his head, said goodnight to Faith and sheepishly skulked off. Faith giggled, wrapped her arms around Finn, gave him a big kiss on the cheek and skipped off to bed.

***

John and Jill Tittytuft had been kept in a mind controlling daze from the moment they got to the airport until reaching their destination. However upon arrival, Yin and Yang allowed the usual state of semi-control. The Tittytufts drifted out of their haze and opened their eyes in astonishment, metaphorically speaking that is. They found themselves standing before a huge glass window facing the ocean. There was no land, no garden to speak of, just water.

John turned to his wife who was standing beside him wearing a slickly styled yellow and brown pinstripe suit, green Wellington boots and a red and white bobble hat.

"Now that is an astonishing view," he said.

Jill turned to John and looked him up and down. "That's an interesting ensemble you have on there, dear," she said sarcastically.

John was sporting a blue frilly dress shirt, tan checked plus fours and a pair of black leather air-soled, high-calf, walking boots, with woolly beige socks rolled down over their top. He looked at himself and shrugged his shoulders and raised an eyebrow in suggestion that his wife should take a look at herself.

"Where are we, sirs?' Jill asked.

"Nonsuch!"

"Where?" John asked.

"Nonsuch, This is your new home, I and I's masterpiece. *You are still resident upon the Island of Alcatraz.* Sorry no, one must refrain. You are now resident within the Island of Alcatraz. It's perfect, no one, in their mind of rightness, would think I and *I would have the cohoness to return. Hahaha! Now, above I and I lies a scalded patch where the cindered remains of the dwelling once branded as Arcadia stood and below, well, not a lot. Alcatraz itself is now a protected* Nature Reserve so, 'let our cousins live!'"

"Nonsuch?" John repeated.

"Yes, you preposterous minion, the name of this cliff encased residence *is Nonsuch. For the reason that nonesuch property exists anywhere else. Hahha! King Henry VIII once had a palace* called Nonsuch, it was a paragon of luxury and taste. He eventually gave it to *a mistress who dismantled it and sold its parts to pay off her gambling debts. But this abode is never* going to be dismantled, unless Superman *himself appears and crushes this villainous Bondesque Island in its entirety."*

John turned and took a look around. "This is absolutely astounding. So this is carved into the cliff face?"

"It is moron! The matt non-reflective glass is also tinted with the same tones of colour that are seen from outside, which makes it virtually invisible from the ocean. *These veritable,* gargantuan windows slide horizontally into the surrounding rock to open when all is clear regarding radar readings. This room of course is the only room *with natural light. When you go through those* connecting doors *the facility becomes an extravagant subterranean abode with all the bells and whistles you pair may require."*

"How did you get all of this done and how did we get in here and what on earth gave you this idea?" Jill asked.

"Money you imbecile, lots of it. In fact humungous amounts distributed and toyed with, *with verve and reckless abandon and of course, watching the unrivalled Gregory Peck destroy the Guns of Navarone!* Oh, don't look at I and I so blankly. You know, the battlements that belonged to the *Germans during the second great human war! No? And how did we get up here? Well, that's via that elevator over there."* Yin And Yang gestured towards a couple of well-camouflaged doors nestled into the wall*; "It connects us with the smugglers sanctum below, where you moored the Dark Shadow. The jetty* and the stairs on the *cliff face have long gone, lemmings!"*

"The Dark Shadow, what's that?" asked John.

"Oh for Hades sake. It's the vessel once known, as the White Mistress now painted a shade of opulent iron!"

"But you set fire to the White Mistress!" said Jill.

"CGI idiot! Take and make thine own, just like the pirates of old. Hoist your own flag and terrorise the seas. PS, there are also some armament alterations on board! Hahhahhhe!" Yin and Yang paused having surprised themselves! *"There is a he at the end of I and I's ha! I's like it!"*

"So Arcadia's burning was also CGI was it? I mean it's really still above us right?" John asked.

The Terrorpins sighed a heavy sigh.

"No, no, no, I and I have already said, it is burnt to the *ground for sure and I and I kept the footage for prosperity and giggles upon said DVD. Why don't you load it, the said DVD machine is over there woman, let's have a snigger!"*

Jill did what she was told as a well-placed 50-inch screen came to life whilst sliding out of the wall! After a brief buzzing and snowy interlude, footage from Arcadia's security cameras ran scenes of the fire.

"See look, there's the pool house flaming up, I's do like a flambé, and there's Mister White's balcony ablaze, which means only one thing for his bedroom. Hahaha! There's the garden *there, where that reptilian traitor spent so much of his* time with that renegade bird sizzling *in the sun and there's a nice close up of Freak's palms. Ah, bless her and her murderous self. I and I wonder if her quest succeeded. Well, will know soon somehow I's do suppose. Look there she is there on her palms, look at that close-up. Stop! Stop, pause it! Ooh, look at her, she looks so cute, quite small in comparison to as I's left her. Will have to show her this for old times sake if she ever returns! Wait! Wait! Stop, rewind. Can I and I really be seeing what I and I think I's is watching?*

Jill frantically grabbed the remote control.

"Oh, by the rings of Saturn, look at what she is doing. She... is that a ball of...is that a...? Oh my and my!"

***

After a few hours sleep, a hearty breakfast of freshly baked bread, butter, preserves, fruit and Jambon, a morning in the subterranean allotments and an afternoon tea, the Avalon posse said their goodbyes to Finn and Triope and left the Geode sneakily through the tower's grand arch in the evening, so not to be seen by amazed human eyes. They took the leisurely stroll across the meadows back to Shepton Mallet and the Warrior, where Jonas drove to the train station so that Vincent could catch the express to London to meet the family solicitors that evening. Albert, however, decided to fly home just to let Chief know that everyone was en route, although he did stop off at the beach in Durban, South Africa for a little sun first! The journey back for the rest of the group was strangely subdued, there was little conversation, no fun and games. Everyone was just sat in their own little world drowning in a mixture of emotions. Even the pee breaks were quiet! It was clear that everybody's life had changed again, forever. Faith rubbed Jonas's shoulder reassuringly.

"Don't worry," she said, "it's all going to be alright. Like Finn said, let's remember how they lived, hey?" She paused, putting on a brave face. "I bet you have some crazy stories to tell. I mean, all the things you must have done and have seen together."

Jonas smiled a wry knowing smile and then lifted a finger to his lips, as if to say they were his secrets, he gave a sorry sad look.

"Oh, don't you worry about any of that, I can keep a secret."

Jonas grinned.

"As I can speak sign language, we can sit down together loads and you can tell me everything. I want to know the lot, from the discovery of the Americas to the Industrial revolution! You must be a walking encyclopaedia!"

His expression quickly changed to one of concern!

"We can also talk about carrying on Mr White's, sorry Arthurs legacy regarding helping the environment!" she said.

In the back, Seth was sitting quietly with his own thoughts; He contemplated the new dynamic of the group and made a mental note on his personal document file on his microchip.

Dear Diary,

Thus far, I think everyone has listened to me and everything is fine. I am their tried and tested leader after all! However, that was before they had tasted the power of their other selves. Was their experience in the Geode going to change anything? Who knows? There is also the reality that little Roxy is not just a cute furry pup. She is an extremely powerful Warg, able to transform whenever the fixation so takes her and she also just happened to be the long-time companion of someone who called herself, 'The Queen of Darkness!' No good can come from that, me thinks!

Having an adolescent Titan on our hands also concerns me. After all, she was born an adult and that means she has all the facilities of a grown up, but none of the wisdom that comes with age and experience. I also note that in her human form she can fly off the handle quite easily and she is, quintessentially, a temperamental little minx at the best of times. Then there are Spike and Escobar, friends that were able to deceive us all for so long. There are also the other more immediate questions to be answered like; where will everyone live or even sleep tonight for that matter? Jonas, a lovely man, but what is going to happen there? And, of course, there is Vincent, supposedly the future of mankind, but unable to choose socks that match in the mornings! There is also something else niggling at me, but I just can't put my paw on it.

Regards Seth.

He told himself, he worried too much, and then closed his eyes for a doze. As he began to drift into a world of warrens and Bunsen burners, he suddenly jumped up wide-eyed banging his head on the inside of the Warrior's roof. This in turn caused everyone else to leap out of their skins and for Jonas to swerve into another lane!

"Hopi," he blurted, "What about Hopi?"

***

Hopi had, peculiarly, flown across the great ocean and was happily tucking into the remains of dismembered crustaceans and picking at fish skeletons that were surrounded by empty seashells on a small, hidden, sandy beach, inside the smugglers grotto below Nonsuch. He seemed oblivious to the world around him as seawater swashed and bathed the secluded sands. In the rock behind him there were two matt black painted elevator doors and in front of him some fifty feet away, rocking gently, was the moored, Dark Shadow. He was totally at peace, until an unusual ripple in the water suddenly caught his attention. He twitched, stood aware and stopped eating straight away. Letting out a squawk, he picked up the Microchip that he had placed on the ground beside him a little earlier, and turned to face the water. He stretched out his wings, as if to make himself larger than he was, and then in the blink of an eye, a strand of spider silk shot out from beneath the water, fixed itself to his glossy plumage and pulled him under. The water settled quickly and returned to being tranquil, but then, with a burst of air bubbles, it began to churn violently as if something beneath it was thundering around at great speed. A few seconds later, Hopi rose from the water in a fountain of salty foaming droplets and flew out of the cavern into a sunbathed world. He swooped and turned and in due course came to land on the small table where John and Jill Tittytuft were sat having a long cool drink in front of their giant window which was wide open to the world.

Startled, they just stared at the raven and then at each other.

"Now, on any normal day that would seem a little strange, wouldn't you think darling?" said John.

Jill giggled and replied, "It's just a bird. Look it's hungry, it must have spotted the plate of olives and crackers."

Jill leaned forward and offered the raven a piece of broken cracker. He hopped up, crowed and delicately took it from her hand.

"He's very bold this one. A marvellous specimen," she said.

"What's all the fuss about flesh bags?"

Yin and Yang were lounging around in a new super aquarium surrounded by, *'Ladiiees!'* At one end of their new lavish glass dwelling, a circular opening had been cut into the glass just above the water line. Yin and Yang swam towards it and then leapt through it, like performing dolphins would do a ring, landing comfortably on a strategically placed soft brown velvet cushion next to the table.

"That's really quite impressive, sirs," said Jill.

"Yes, well. I and I is not being caught out by some sort of SPAFF dribbling human again! Now, what's the coup Dim Sum? And what is that raven doing on the table tucking into I and I's Kalamatas?"

"No idea, sirs, it just landed on the table from the skies," John replied.

"And you both don't think it strange, or even a little coincidental that, after all that we have been through, a raven, I and I repeat a raven, lands on this very table?"

John and Jill just shrugged and looked pretty gormless.

"I and I would pull one's hair out if I and I had any!"

The elevator gave a ping.

John and Jill jumped to their feet. John armed himself with his chair and Jill grabbed and brandished a cracker!

"Of course, why wouldn't a villainous secret hideout with *the only entrance being an elevator from a concealed cavern have a visitor?"* Yin and Yang said sarcastically. *"Okay so what* are we expecting and why?"

The elevator doors slid open with the sound of cushioned hydraulics. There was a brief moment of stunned silence.

"What the ugly crawly *is that?"*

There was something a little strange in the lift!

"It looks like some kind of sea spider, maybe Ammothella Symbias, but it's unusually large and spiky and it's bald and crustacean like. However, they don't usually have legs like that, not arced in that way like a normal spider. They're normally flat and sprawling, allowing them to attach themselves to rocks and coral on the seabed so they can pull themselves along. I wouldn't say they were usually crimson, either," said Jill.

"Well, well and who made you *Jacque Cousteau?"*

"Sea creatures are her passion, sirs," John said proudly.

The visitor fired out a shot of webbing across the room which flew straight though Hopi's glossy plumage and body and into the sky beyond.

The bird just squawked and ruffled its feathers.

John and Jill's expression said it all.

"Right, two things! That's not a normal raven and that's definitely not a normal whatever it is."

"Sea spiders don't usually have the ability to do that!" said Jill nervously.

"I'm a sea spider?" said a familiar voice.

"Wait, wait, don't say another word. We're *going to open up the airwaves to the Tittytufts. This is going to be* hilarious. I and I are so excited! OK, done. You can speak."

"What is happening?" said the visitor.

Jill suddenly piddled herself!

"Oh Yeah baby, the diobolical dream team *are back! Hahahha!"*

***

Vincent rang the circular brass doorbell to the townhouse in Sebastian Street, Islington. The brass plaque underneath it that read, 'Blanc, Aspro and Abyadh Solicitors,' and underneath that, attached to the wall, was a steel box some 10 inches by 10 inches or so square and deep that had a speaker grid.

"Hello who is it?" said a voice with a Mediterranean accent from the speaker.

"It's Vincent Russell, I've come to see..."

"First door on the left," said the voice.

The large white door buzzed and clicked open. The hallway was clean and tastefully furnished, white walls, high ceilings, gilded mirrors and a black and white decorative ceramic tiled floor. Everything seemed normal, which itself was a little weird, as this was supposed to be the office to a firm of solicitors and not a lovely neat and tidy family home. Vincent was a little taken aback. His one and only prior visit down to the family solicitors resulted in him not getting past the front door! Last time, the steel box merely popped open and there were his father's notes just sitting there in an envelope inside and he was just told to take them and leave!

Vincent did as he was told and walked through the first door on the left, where, to his surprise, he encountered a man wearing a casual blue tracksuit and bright white training shoes sitting behind an old wooden desk.

"Hello, Mr Russell," said the stocky Mediterranean man who was somewhere in his 40's.

"Sorry to disturb you sir, but…"

"Yes, I know, isn't it wonderful, Mr McCool has already contacted me. Mr White is finally going to be reunited with his loved ones!"

The man gleefully clapped his hands together.

"I'm sorry?" Vincent replied completely confused. "You know Mr McCool?"

"Yes, of course I do, wonderful chap. We often meet in the Garden of an evening for a snack. He does love his grilled Halloumi cheese!"

Vincent was lost for words.

"Now, I've got a few things for you Mr Russell and please could you tell Miss Faith not to worry when you get back. Mr White has made provisions for everyone. It's all so thrilling!"

"I'm sorry to say sorry again, but you do know Mr White is dead, right?" asked Vincent.

"Yes," said the man grinning from ear to ear. "As is Mr Bedivere!"

"Sorry again, but you catch me at a disadvantage, sir. What is your name? Are you Mr Blanc, Aspro or Abyadh?"

"Yes!" the strange man answered. There was a pause. "I am all of them."

Vincent was now completely lost.

This man, that has three names and speaks to giants in his garden, likes the fact that his clients are dead and is happy wearing a bright blue tracksuit! He thought to himself.

"Now I could sit here forever and go through Mr White's will with you page by page, but that could take a very long time. So shall we just skip the formalities and take the 'being of sound mind' thingamajig, as read, yes?"

Vincent just nodded.

"So what do I call you sir?" Vincent asked.

"Just call me Zachery or Zach, after all you're the boss, please sit down."

Zach gestured for Vincent to take a seat on the opposite side of the desk.

"I'm the boss?" asked Vincent!

Oh Vincent, for heavens sake, will you just shut up and let Zach get on with it. It was all most amusing to begin with, but now you're really boring me!

"Peuja?" said Vincent jumping out of his chair looking for a speaker.

Yes, yes, Zach's laptop.

Zachery leant over the desk, raised his eyebrows and rolled his eyes.

OK Zach, get on with it, and don't you roll your eyes at me!

"Yes Peuja, of course, sorry." Zach replied slightly embarrassed.

So, Vincent, you are very rich, a billionaire in fact, about 10 times over and so is Miss Faith. Mr Jonas is very wealthy, too, although he really doesn't know what to do with money! I'll leave you to give Faith the good news. Now, nitty-gritty! Alcatraz Island was bequeathed to the Costa Rican Government under the proviso that it remains a wildlife sanctuary. The Manor House now belongs to Miss Faith, as do the surrounding lands, however, Mr White gave explicit instruction that, should he pass away before his friends and companions, Mr Bedivere and, or, Mr Jonas, that they, would be given residence in the Manor Penthouse Apartment and also remain under the employment and serve, both Miss Faith, and yourself in your various enterprises."

"Enterprises, and there's a Penthouse?" Vincent repeated.

"Didn't Miss Faith tell you there was a Penthouse? Anyway, you own things, stuff and companies, that sort of thing."

"I do? And they are what stuff exactly?" asked Vincent.

"Right, well, this will take a very long time if you continue to ask questions as often as you are, so please, just shut up and listen!"

Vincent was a little taken aback, but Zach seemed to carry off being obnoxious with the charm of a well-heeled politician.

"You have a finger in many pies. Mainly pies that are environmental, such as, wind farm technology or hydroelectric power plants or tree planting, things like that. You also provide charitable funds for research projects and survival schemes regarding endangered wildlife. Now making the money? Many technological advances over the centuries have also been the result of Mr White's endeavours, and thus you own a respectable amount of shares in the world's greatest businesses and corporations, in fact, thousands of them, businesses' not shares I mean. The amount of shares goes into millions. So to cut a long 'Will and Testament' short, anything you want you got it, sonny, and that goes for Miss Faith too!"

Zach opened a drawer in his desk and pulled out a saucer of tantalising bite sized pastries and then poured himself a sip of water from a jug in front of him. Popping a pastry, whole, into his mouth he offered the plate forward to Vincent.

"Baklava? I find them irresistible, and yet I despair at the vice that owns me. Would you care for one? Peuja, Turkish coffee please, medium."

On it!

Vincent was once again sent off kilter. The strange little man was getting weirder by the minute. Vincent leant forward, took a pastry and had a bite.

"Aren't they wonderful?" Zach asked delightedly, "I have them sent here daily from my favourite Patisserie in Palmers Green. It's called Aroma. The lady there who looks after me, Nitsa, is a fantastic woman, completely mad, I love her. She also sends me fresh Koubes and Shamishi and sometimes if I'm feeling really filthy, Boureki. Oh, but her Lokouma, oh my god, heavenly!"

Vincent didn't have a clue what Zach was on about, but watched as he drifted dreamily off into his own little pastry paradise. Zach was only brought back to the present, by two leather bound books parting on the nearby bookshelf. From the divide a mechanical arm brought out a small cup of steaming Turkish coffee.

"Ah, thank you Peuja, oh sorry, Vincent would you like one?"

Before Vincent could answer…

"Peuja another one of your wonderful coffees for our new boss, please."

Not a problem, darling. Coming right up.

"Now, that's the second time you've called me the boss," said Vincent.

"Well, you are young man. You own this solicitors' practice too, and the building. Well, the street really, under all kinds of different guises that is. This, however, is also my home as well as my place of work."

"Oh right, so how many clients do we represent?"

"Well, something very exciting has recently happened to the business! Our client base has just doubled!"

"Really," Vincent replied.

"Yes, we now represent you and Miss Faith!" Zach was again grinning from ear to ear.

"So, Mr White was your only client?"

Another cup of coffee slid out from the bookcase. Zach took it and handed it to Vincent.

"Thank you Peuja," he said. "Sip it slowly it is very hot!" Zach warned.

Always a pleasure and never a chore!

"Vincent," he continued whilst hopping up onto his desk, "looking after the interests of one of the world's most powerful and most invisible men, i.e. Mr White, was much more than a full time job. Legitimacy can be a messy business!" Zach raised a knowing eyebrow. "If you get my drift! Now, there are some other titbits you should know. Mr White and Mr Bedivere died tragically in an aeroplane crash over the Pacific. Their bodies and the plane were never recovered. Which is a shame because dumping that lovely little jet was a sin."

"We dumped a jet?" asked Vincent.

"Yes I know, don't look at me like that, it couldn't be done any other way. They had to be lost and never found."

There was a little pause for thought and then Vincent changed the subject.

"So, how do you come to know Mr White and be trusted with all of this?"

"Ah well, Peuja runs everything with me and if I ever let any thing slip that I shouldn't, then she detonates the explosive microchip I have in my head and that makes sure I don't do it again, which, of course, hasn't happened yet!"

"What?" said Vincent, somewhat horrified.

Vincent looked at Zach with real concern.

Zach fell into a fit of laughter.

"Only joking my friend, you should have seen your face. No, no, no, I have been around for a long time! I was made an orphan in the Greek Revolt against the Ottoman Empire in 1831. Mr White both rescued and saved me, and had me brought up by nuns in Austria. The rest is history. I am paid very handsomely for my service and I have a wonderful long life!"

"Is there a Mrs Zach?"

"Do I look like I sailed down the Thames on a doughnut? No, just many that would like to be, hey?" Zach gave Vincent a knowing wink! "So, we are about done, do you want a lift home?"

"No, that's ok Zach, it's quite a distance. I'd be taking up your entire night. I'll just grab a late night train.'

"Don't be silly, I am your humble employee. It would be my pleasure."

Vincent, finding it difficult to refuse, stood up and smiled nervously.

"Good, follow me then," said Zach.

Zach walked out of his office and straight up the stairs in the hallway. Vincent, of course, found this a little strange because he thought the way out, would be through the front door, but he followed Zach anyway. They walked up three flights and then stopped at a loft hatch, which Zach opened with a wooden pole that was to hand.

"Come on my boy," he said clambering up.

Vincent, not sure what to think, did what he was told and followed Zach up the ladder into the darkness. There was the sound of the flicking on of a light switch and then, 'Zap', a room crammed with futuristic technology. A huge, lit engraved glass, map of the world speckled with little red, green and yellow dots, obviously locations of some importance, took up an entire wall. Everywhere else was chock-a-block with desks that were loaded with servers, computers, monitors and other communicative gadgetry, except the centre of the room that is, where a small rotor-less helicopter with a mirrored outer surface, reflected everything around it!

"Zach this is amazing, how…?"

Zach interrupted.

"You are not the only one with many toys! How is the Commando by the way and that sidecar? The Egg was my idea you know? Anyway, back to business, the roof of the building opens up and is lined with lead, makes all of this invisible. The 'Heli,' that flying machine, has many modes and the British government, well, they adore me!"

"What? The government know about all of this?"

"No, just some of this! I work for them also, from time to time that is, periodically, to keep an entente cordiale. 'Call me Bondigis, Zach Bondigis!'" Zach laughed at his own joke! He then returned to being very serious, immediately. "Now, don't ask any more questions, or I will have to kill you! Oh, and remember, this is all just between you and me, not even Miss Faith must know what I do. We must remain discreet and secretive, everything hush hush, or I will have to kill you, okay? Now, you may think that I cannot kill you after killing you, but believe me, if I want to, I can kill you twice!"

Zach smiled and opened the door to the Heli.

"Are you coming?" he said.

Vincent, once again looking a little concerned, did what he was told and climbed in. Zach flicked a few switches and put on a set of headphones.

"I don't need these because there is no noise. I just like wearing them. I look good, yes?"

Vincent smiled.

"Peuja, are we clear for off-taking?"

Yes, Zach, all clear, no cameras pointing this way, I've dealt with them all, stealth mode is activated, as is whisper mode. Commencing roof opening.

The roof silently opened like a flowering bud and exposed the London night sky.

"Now Vincent, do not be alarmed, you see, the Heli is no ordinary helicopter."

"Yes, well that's pretty obvious!" Vincent answered.

Zach took mild offence!

"Listen carefully smarty-pants and you may learn something! The Heli reacts in conjunction with the earth's magnetic core for take-off and landing. So, when I press this button here," Zach pointed out a large red ignition button that had the word, 'start' blazed across it, "we will shoot vertically into the air at great velocity and then, I will dispel air at an even greater velocity! It always makes me do that! When we reach 300 feet the turbine system atop the Heli will spin at great speed and suck in the air around it, which, in turn, will travel through the rotating head and then be expelled from several little horizontal slots. These compressed jets of air will act akin to traditional rotor blades, but of course be invisible! Got that?"

Vincent nodded, utterly confused.

"So don't scream, like a member of the cast of Priscilla Queen of the Desert, the musical, having just been told you've won a trip to Disneyland, okay?"

Vincent nodded again and Zach reached down and pushed the start button. There was a brief moment of nothing and than, 'whoosh,' the Heli shot into the air like a bullet from a gun. Vincent, as if he was riding the world's scariest roller coaster, couldn't help himself and screamed at the top of his lungs. Zach turned to him with an imperious look of highfaluting disgust.

"Mickey Mouse here we come!" he muttered with disdain, and then, he broke wind!

***

A mysterious, milky vapour formed at the mouth of the cavern entrance belonging to the Pool at Shangri-la. It twisted, shifted and then united with the gasses surrounding it to form the body of a creature not seen upon this earth for an eternity. In a flash of light, the beast crashed onto the dirt, landing face down as if thrown by, 'Hate.' Battered and bruised, it opened its fist to reveal, that within its grasp, it held something that shone a heavenly glow. Pained and distressed, it dragged itself into the glistening fountain pool. A sense of euphoria washed through its bones, it sighed and groaned with relief and then it disappeared beneath the mirrored sheen.

***

"Now fill us all in, will you."

Yin and Yang were looking impatiently at the visitor!

"White is dead, as is his bearded flunky," said the spidery thingy!

"Hooray, than we shall celebrate."

"There is nothing to celebrate, I am dead too!"

"*No, you're not dead ba*by, you're just a little different *that's all. You're smaller and your molecular make up is* different, but you're alive. *Hahaha!*"

"I saw myself crushed by the jaws of a giant lizard; I saw, and remember fire, and a monkey thrusting a spear into me, and then, nothing, just darkness, until today that is, when I suddenly found myself in the sea. Then I crawled out of the water and saw the elevator doors, pressed the button and now, I am here with you guys, and you say I look different?"

"*Tittytufts, fetch I* and I a mirror. No, forget *that, would you mind placing a laptop before I's guest!*"

John jumped up and grabbed a Laptop from a nearby shelf, opened it up, and placed it on the floor. The spider thingy crawled over to it and shot a strand of silk at the casing. The screen came to life and the computer's web cam programme sprang into action, revealing all!

"What kind of thing am I?" asked the upset spider thingy.

"*Well love, you tell* I and *I. What was the first* thing you remember seeing *when you, err, let's say, woke up.*"

"I told you, the water."

"*Are you* positive? Think, search *your mind.*"

The spider thingy searched the corners of its memory and found its thoughts to be surprisingly clear.

"I saw feathers first! Glossy feathers!"

"*Just like the ones* on this *cracker crunching bird perhaps?*"

The raven gave a caw.

"Yes!"

"*Ah ha! Now, tell I's about that date you had* with that Sea Spider *a while back, I's have seen some curious footage.*"

"Well, I remember it started off pretty well, a bit of ... anyway, but then, if I remember correctly, it didn't end so well for him!"

"*So you remember.* Which can only mean one *thing. You have the microchip within you!*"

The raven cawed, leapt off the table and flew off into the distance.

"*The Tittytufts and I discovered footage* of you wrestling with an egg sack and throwing it into the ocean. We found it whilst watching a rerun *of the torching* of Arcadia. *Thus I and I conclude that you,*

183

our wonderful arachnid friend, are the offspring of I and I's dearest Freak and have been implanted with her microchip, which means, SPAFF has once again worked its magic! Hahahaha! You are a one off. Half Tarantula, half Sea Spider and some God, too!"

"Is that possible?" asked Jill.

"There are *examples of* interbreeding between species. Tigers and lions have produced Tiglons and Ligers, there are Mules, so why not? We all know that *SPAFF is miraculous and it is definitely* within I's friend here! *You are Freak's brain and memories within* Freak's child. *You are your mother's* daughter. *You are…"*

There was a pause.

"Freak the merciless, and I want revenge!" said the spider angrily.

"And you *shall have it, baby. Oh* yes, you shall. Haha*haha*!" Yin and Yang changed the subject cautiously. "So, err, where are your brothers and sisters, an *egg sack usually carries* hundreds of little ones?"

"I got peckish! Oh, and one more thing, and you won't like this boys!" said Freak.

"Yes, Freaky dearest."

"Clipboard Girl is a Titan!"

"What? Really? That gawky irreverent sapling a Titan! *Now* I and I *are truly peeved!"*

***

A mysterious, milky vapour formed at the mouth of the cavern entrance belonging to the Pool at Shangri-la. It twisted, shifted and then united with the gasses surrounding it to form the body of a creature not seen upon this earth for an eternity. In a flash of light, the beast landed on the cavern floor, crouched and secure as if gently ushered in by angels. Slowly it rose to its feet. Strong and upright, it strode around the hollow, dragging its sparking bronze claws along the surface of the mineral encrusted wall. Cutting itself to leave a trail of blood that would allow it to find its way back, it slipped into the glistening fountain pool and disappeared from sight beneath the mirrored sheen!

***

"Prepare yourself for landing, and no screaming!"

The Heli's engines cut out. There was a moment of complete silence, a hiatus in time, in which Zach turned to Vincent, gave him a wink and broke wind, and then the Heli plummeted towards the earth out of control. Vincent screamed at the top of his lungs.

"Do something! We're gonna die!" he yelled.

As the earth drew nearer at breakneck speed, Zach again turned to Vincent but this time, fell into maniacal laughter! Then, like an elevator in a sky rise approaching the requested floor, the Heli slowed and gently touched down on the Manor House drive as if cushioned by a pile of marshmallows. Jonas, who was sat in his dressing gown having a Cognac on the Penthouse balcony and reading a copy of The Times, leapt, startled to his feet.

"Out you get then lad and remember, shh!" said Zach raising a finger to his lips.

"Thanks for the lift," Vincent replied gibbering and climbing hastily out.

"See you soon boss!" said Zach, blowing Vincent a kiss.

Vincent, unnerved by the gesture, mustered a wave in return and then inquisitively asked a question.

"Zach," he said, "how did you test this, err, flying machine?"

"With many pairs of trousers," Zach answered smiling insanely and then, "whoosh.' he shot up into the air! Jonas jumped down from the balcony, landing safely, on the gravel drive, like a cat, and ran up to Vincent to greet him.

"Hello Jonas, is everything alright? Where is everyone?" Vincent asked.

Jonas grinned and led Vincent into the Manor. It hadn't changed much; it was just as Vincent remembered it, sort of. They took an elevator that was hidden behind some oak panelling and zipped down to the fourth underground level where the doors slid open into a corridor that had seen a recent bit of excavation work done! A large hole had been dug out in the middle of the floor and a rudimentary staircase fitted! Jonas again led the way, and down into the dark they walked. There was a sudden burst of light.

"Surprise!" everyone called.

As Vincent opened his squinting eyes, he discovered he was

standing in Level 5, with the entire team sitting around Avalon's round table in front of him. It was piled high with food and drink and Chief and the rabbits were sat around it on the floor, knee deep in hay, vegetables, nuts and shallow trays of water. Faith stood up;

"Come on we've been waiting. The solicitors sent us a message letting us know you were on your way, so we thought it would be nice to have a surprise family dinner."

Vincent noticed that Arthur and Bedivere's seats were left empty, but both had a full glass of juice set for them.

"How did the table get here?" Vincent asked, astonished.

"Well, we don't quite know," Seth answered, "but believe me, I'll ask Finn as soon as he arrives."

And sure enough, through a crack in Level 5's floor, just as Vincent walked around the table to take his seat, the huge kilted figure of Finn rose from the ground and shook himself free of dirt.

"Welcome, Finn," said Seth, "how are you? Have a seat my friend."

Finn looked troubled he wasn't his usual chirpy self.

"Finn, are you alright?" Vincent asked.

Finn pursed his lips.

"I've got to be honest with all of you. I took a quick trip to Madagascar, you know to take in a few sights after you guys had left, just to fill the day after dropping off the table and chairs, I thought they would be a nice touch," Finn was rambling, "but, when I got back, I found Triope going absolutely nuts, bouncing off the walls, making all kinds of racket! The hatch to her hollow was banging and clattering, but I, of course, couldn't get to her side as I can't weave my way through the spikes of the shield, as I'm not a descendant of Kronos. I did, however, eventually manage to understand something of the ranting, through old-fashioned Morse code. She kept repeating a clattered out message. We've been communicating like that for years."

"Oh really, that's very interesting," said Albert not really very interested. "Can we have some more popcorn over here, Sinatra, please?"

Sinatra whizzed round with a bowl.

"What did she say?" asked Bandi duly concerned.

"Yez, come on Finn, out with it." Maurice was getting impatient.

Finn looked around the table at the expectation surrounding him, and then, with a certain amount of trepidation replied.

"Gorgon!"

Albert choked on his popcorn, and the room fell silent! The group's exploits had taught them that there were forces out in the world and beyond, and even within themselves, with immense power.

"Did she elaborate any further?" asked Garston trying to add a little light-hearted humour to proceedings.

Finn shook his head,

"No, she just tapped out the word over and over."

"Oh, heavens it's a bad horror movie script!" said Albert. Bandi jabbed him in the ribs with a sharp elbow.

Vincent turned to Faith and then to Seth, who returned him a look that spoke a thousand words, before smiling a gentle smile and taking Faith by the hand. He glanced around and saw the rest of the group waiting anxiously for his response.

"Then today," he said raising a glass, "we begin a new adventure. We are the Knights of Camelot and we can do anything!"

"Yes we are and yes we can!" said Steve.

"Yes we can," repeated Spike.

"Si Baroni's," said Escobar.

"Shiver me timbers, ye olde sea dogs!" Albert replied.

The gang stopped what they were doing and gave Albert a stare.

"Only joking, luvs!" he said smiling at the group.

And with a cackle of laughter, the partying began, with all and sundry tucking into the sumptuous feast. All that is, but Seth! He was consumed by contemplation and unable to summon any real feeling of optimism. How much did Mr White leave within him? He asked himself. His own, distorted reflection stared at him from the back of a spoon. He fell under its spell. 'Two legs good, four legs bad', he remembered the pigs from George Orwell's Animal Farm.

"Seth, Seth. Are you okay?" asked Hannibal shaking him from his daze.

"Yes, yes. Sorry, just wandered off there for a moment. I'm fine," he said, returning Hannibal a forced smile. "I just need to pop out and water the plants. I'll be back in a mo!"

"OK, mate!" Hannibal replied, not truly believing his friend.

"You sure you're alright," asked Bandi, having overheard.

Seth nodded as he left the table and set off down the tunnels. However, he didn't head for the exit but instead snuck into his Lab where he climbed up on his tabletop and had a lay down. He asked Peuja to turn off the lights and he closed his eyes. The warmth of solitude filled him with peace and his thoughts meandered.

Dear diary,

It seems to me, that for centuries, man has tried to understand his dreams, fathom their meaning and comprehend how they relate to a personal existence. He appears to have lived through epic moments of darkness and often scavenged for a mere glimpse of light. With the weight of gravity upon his shoulders he has habitually been led to believe in the, 'rivers of plenty' where he imagines that one day he will be able to glide blissfully beside angels of self-preservation and disregard a speculated life.

It is evident that historians, archaeologists, theologians and geologists have for so long hunted for the answers to man's future by reading scripts from the past, a past that was once made so simple by self-imposed or natural borders. In doing so, this has helped him learn everything he has, regarding the floating, rotating sphere that he survives upon. However, findings have and are, frequently interpreted differently and so now, with a mind twisted and poisoned by contradictory beliefs, man's lonesome search for sustainability regularly leads him to self-destruction. What he considers to be correct is often, without a doubt, incorrect and increasingly harmful to life on this beautiful benevolent world. It occurs to me that the continued threat from his own marauding kind has left him with few options! Today those who are considered to be the saviours of mankind, like Vincent, are frequently locked away! They are condemned to live a life not meant for anyone, anyone at all. From desks and laboratories they are made to watch in misery, as the world becomes a graveyard for a myriad of the globes inhabitant species. People like Vincent recognise that most of mankind is blissfully unaware of the devastation it's creating and they, all alone, seem to be struggling with the guilt. But no more! No more will they stand unaided behind their many pairs of entrenched bespectacled eyes and gaze on with hope as man and Mother Nature battle for life. Why? Because we the few who were originally given the honour and responsibility of watching over this amazing planet have returned and we have had enough. With our friends and companions, we will stand up, and we will fight for her.

Regards
Seth.
Rabbit King of England, Knight of Camelot and Lord of Pangea.

Seth's ears twitched! He sat, bolt upright for a moment before jumping down from the tabletop and poking his head out of the Lab door. He peered left, and then right along the long narrow tunnels; they were bare, empty of security! Sliding out, he slinked towards the exit that lay at the base of the old tree in the woods. He sniffed at the starry night, as he entered the crisp moonlit chill and allowed himself the luxury of a self-indulgent grin. Boldly, he made his way to the patchy clearing, where he was previously reunited with the subjects of his kingdom and then, a little oddly, he sat down on his haunches at its centre. The bright moon illuminated his soul and cast his shadow across the grassy landscape. He remained still, as if waiting for something and then, all of a sudden, from nowhere, and as if from everywhere, a large, well-fed, rusty red fox with flashing teeth, pounced at him. Within the beat of a pounding heart, the fox, confused and shrieking, was flat on its back, pinned and squirming, struggling to free itself from the grasp of a powerful, gnarly-clawed monster. Seth had transformed into Tecciztecatl and was peering down at the yelping, helpless fox. He ran a claw gently down its silky exposed belly.

"Do not fear Mr Fox," he said in a calming tone, the fox remained distressed. "We are both creatures of a worshipped moonlight, we live in shadows and we hide in time. We are both loved, and yet both revered, we are, in many ways, very much alike.

The fox kicked and scratched, but to no avail. Tecci, completely composed, bowed his head and muttered a few words in a forgotten tongue and then raised his head and placed a forearm to the fox's throat. It squealed and gasped for air, but soon an eternal sleep began to seize the beautiful predator. Tecci, flicked out a sharpened, disfigured claw and, like a butcher skilfully yielding a blade, carved open the fox from collar to hind, effortlessly slicing though his victims breastplate. With salacious glee, he pulled the ribcage apart, exposing the fox's still, beating heart. He appeared void of any emotion, but his mouth foamed and dripped with spicy saliva as a warm pungent, stench rose from the open torso and tantalised his senses.

"Tecci, what have you done?" said a voice.

Tecci, knowing all along that he was being watched, didn't turn around, but instead, plucked the fox's heart from its sinewy vessels and tossed it whole into his mouth. Chewing it slowly and pleasurably, he savoured every moment before feverishly gorging upon the rest of the fox's pulsating organs!

"Oh, that's truly disgusting! For heaven's sake Tecci!" said the voice.

"Then turn away, Sullivan," Tecci replied, his face covered in blood. "You don't have to watch me. In fact, your days of watching and supervising ceased with the end of the 'Grid' and our incarceration.

"Is that what you believe?' Sullivan replied. "That you were all imprisoned. Well let me tell you…"

Tecci tore at a piece of liver, which liberally splattered blood all around.

"Careful!" Sullivan called. "Mind the suit!"

"Ah, yes," Tecci replied, "the grey, neatly pressed suit. The cloak of a scarred, tortured mind."

"There is no need for that sort of thing," said Sullivan.

Tecci was becoming agitated.

"What do you want? Why are you here? Your master is gone. You should be living out a bored, lengthy life in a Dry Cleaners somewhere," he said, chuckling to himself.

"I'm going to rise above all the sledging, and finish what I started saying. So, as I was saying, you were not imprisoned! All of that was merely a precursor to your, err, resurrection!

Oh, and by the way, I'm here for a reason, and now, so are you!"

"Of course you're here for a reason, or you wouldn't be here!"

Sullivan closed his eyes and shook his head in exasperation.

"But, what am I here for?" Tecci asked. "We were all just

exploited by an old loving couple so they could dupe the big man in charge and get to Paradise. And now, that's over and all we have got to look forward to is an eternity hiding from the human race.

"You always this cheery?" Sullivan asked sarcastically.

"Get on with it Sullivan, enough of the chit chat." Tecci replied curtly.

There was a brief pause as Sullivan thought about how to impart his next sentence, which eventually he did, be it, slightly embarrassed!

"I've received a message!" He said.

"From who?" Tecci asked.

"I don't know! It was in a vision!" Sullivan replied.

Tecci laughed out loud.

"Oh, Sullivan, you truly are a hoot! What happened in this vision? Is there to be a great flood?" Tecci chuckled.

Sullivan paced over to the beast and looked him in the eye.

"Yes," he replied, "a flood of blood!" Tecci fell silent as he pondered the statement. "You know me and where I have come from. You and I both know that this is not just any old, look into the future," he said. "There's another thing too!"

"And what's that?" asked Tecci.

"Someone's here, on Earth." Sullivan replied.

"Yes I know. Finn has already warned us that a, 'Gorgon' is here!"

"Oh, that's not who I'm worried about!"

Tecci swiftly dug a pit and buried the fox's remains.

"Thank you Mr Fox," he said graciously, before turning to Sullivan. "I don't know who you're talking about, but, to my mind, it's the human race you ought to concern yourself with. They are, because of ridiculous religious and political beliefs, needlessly and indiscriminately slaying each other all over the world!"

Sullivan sighed deeply.

"You're absolutely right," he replied. "We are standing on the edge of an apocalyptic precipice, and a resolution isn't remotely close."

"Unless, of course, the resolution is the apocalypse!" Tecci rebuffed.

Both mused a while over the bold statement before Tecci began to amble away.

"Are you coming back to the house then?" He asked. "It's about time you were properly, brought into the fold."

"You don't mean properly, properly introduced, do you?" Sullivan replied, with a cheeky and yet somewhat nervous smirk, as he briskly followed behind.

"No! Introducing you as Longinus, the centurion that speared the side of Jesus Christ, would only cause a stir! Let's just keep it to the adopted Sullivan for now, shall we?" Tecci replied sarcastically, before transforming from beast to 'Seth!'

"Why did you slaughter and then eat the fox?" Sullivan asked in a general chitchat kind of way.

"I didn't eat all of the fox, only the necessary bits," Seth replied, "and it wasn't slaughtered, it was sacrificed."

"Why?" Sullivan pried.

"It needed to die, so that I may live," said Seth.

Sullivan seemed to accept Seth's answer with little recourse.

"Right!" He answered.

An uncomfortable silence then engulfed the pair.

"What's on your mind Sullivan? Just ask me? I'm not an idiot, far from it. Come on, I can feel your puzzlement."

"So, Seth!" Sullivan tentatively said," I've been bouncing this thought around in my mind for a while now and the only way I feel I can get a definitive answer is from the rabbit's mouth!"

"Then ask what you will, Suit," Seth's patience was running thin.

Sullivan looked down to his hands and then raised a finger to his chin!

"Why are you the beast you are when you transform? I mean, in your tale of mythology, you are not a rabbit beast but a more human like god, and in fact, due to a, and please excuse my insolence if I'm wrong, 'cowardly act,' you had a rabbit thrown at you which left its mark upon you! A kind of rabbit shaped birthmark! The myth also states that you are the Moon, which you are obviously not! Plus, you're North American, so how on Earth did you come to be Lord of South America?"

Seth again fell into laughter, and with tears running down his cheeks eventually got himself to a calmer place so that he could deliver his measured response.

"Wikipedia has much to answer for. I mean who writes this stuff? Were they there?"

Seth then erupted into his Tecciztecatl form, which frightened the living daylights out of Sullivan.

"Sullivan, I have always been this beast. And as for a 'cowardly act,' well, that is not true either. Those stories were probably perpetuated by those among the Aztec deities who were not chosen for my station of office. I am also, as you said, obviously not the Moon, but I am responsible for one of its features, its luminescence! Where I dig, the sunken surface darkens, where I pile, the raised surface becomes brighter. It's all to do with sunlight and reflection! As for being Lord of South America, well that one is down to being in the right place at the right time. Keys have many teeth and I'm a tooth that is deliberately difficult to find!"

Sullivan said nothing, but responded with a strange nodding twitch, which by all accounts said, 'I don't quite understand but I'll go with it!

Tecci continued. "Now, I have a question. How does a Roman centurion come to have a lance made from the bones of a dead gorgon and, how does he happen to then be gifted with visions that enable him to see future events?"

Sullivan stuttered, his eyelids began nervously fluttering as he recalled his past from memory.

"There is a long winded answer, which is basically the same as the shorter version however, it doesn't involve an odd fellow with a familiar glint in his eye who just happened to be my commanding tribune! Therefore, the long and the short answer is a laconic one, and it is; I have no idea!" Sullivan replied.

"Then we must begin." Said Seth.

"Begin what?" Sullivan asked.

Seth reflected for a moment.

"Life is like walking through an orchard of apples! At times you may come across sour apples, at times you may come upon apples that are sickly sweet and at times, you may stumble upon rotten apples! When this happens, there is only one thing to do." He said.

"What's that?" Sullivan asked.

"Dig a hole, plant a seed and grow a pear!" Said Seth.

TO A NEW ADVENTURE!